FIX THE WORLD

TWELVE SCI FI WRITERS SAVE THE FUTURE

J. SCOTT COATSWORTH

OWI.

Published by
Other Worlds Ink
PO Box 19341, Sacramento, CA 95819

Cover art © 2021 by J. Scott Coatsworth, typography by Sleepy Fox Studios. Cover content is for illustrative purposes only and any person depicted on the cover is a model.

Fix the World © 2021 by J. Scott Coatsworth and Other Worlds Ink. First Edition.

In Light © 2021 by Mere Rain

Juma and the Quantum Ghost © 2021 by Ingrid Garcia

Ice in D Minor © 2015 by Anthea Sharp

At the Movies © 2021 by D.M. Rasch

Who Shall Reap the Grain of Heaven? © 2021 by J.G. Follansbee

From the Sun and Scorched Earth © 2021 by Bryan Cebulski

Upgrade © 2021 by Alex Silver

Rise © 2021 by J. Scott Coastworth

A Forest for the Trees © 2021 by Rachel Hope Crossman

As Njord And Skadi © 2021 by Jennifer R. Povey

The Call of the Wold © 2018 by Holly Schofield

Homestead at the Beginning of the World © 2021 by Jana Denardo

All rights reserved. This book is licensed to the original purchaser only. Duplication or distribution by any means is illegal and a violation of international copyright law, subject to criminal prosecution and upon conviction, fines, and/or imprisonment. Any eBook format cannot be legally loaned or given to others. No part of this book can be reproduced or transmitted in any form or by any means, electronic or mechanical, including photocopying, recording, or by any information storage and retrieval system, without the written permission of the Publisher, except where permitted by law.

To request permission and all other inquiries, contact Other Worlds Ink, PO Box 19341, Sacramento, CA 95819, or visit https://www.otherworldsink.com.

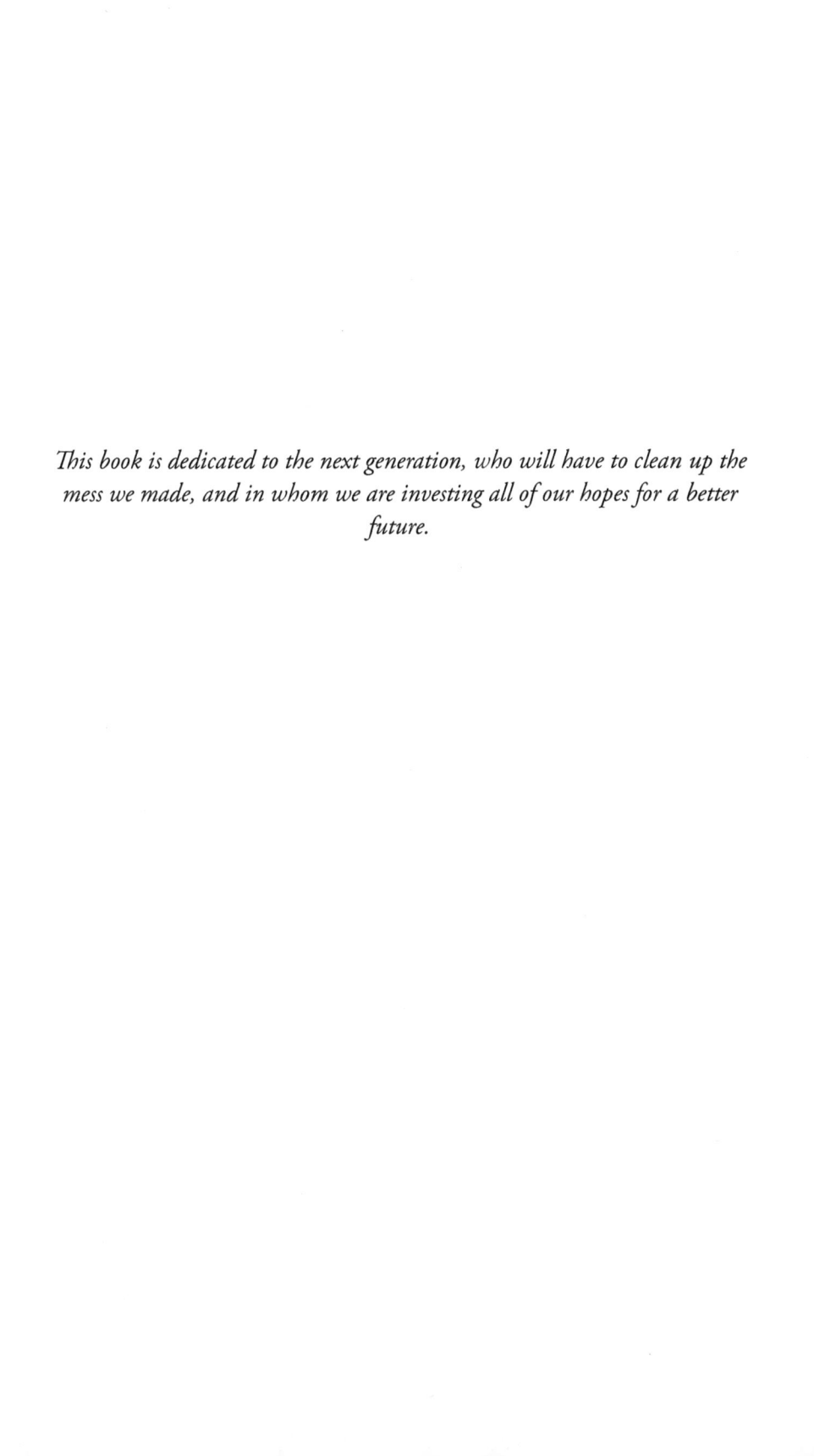

This book is dedicated to the next generation, who will have to clean up the mess we made, and in whom we are investing all of our hopes for a better future.

CONTENTS

Acknowledgments	vii
Foreword	ix
IN LIGHT Mere Rain	1
JUMA AND THE QUANTUM GHOST Ingrid Garcia	20
ICE IN D MINOR Anthea Sharp	46
AT THE MOVIES D.M. Rasch	54
WHO SHALL REAP THE GRAIN OF HEAVEN? J.G. Follansbee	72
FROM THE SUN AND SCORCHED EARTH Bryan Cebulski	88
UPGRADE Alex Silver	110
RISE J. Scott Coatsworth	149
A FOREST FOR THE TREES Rachel Hope Crossman	158
AS NJORD AND SKADI Jennifer R. Povey	168
THE CALL OF THE WOLD Holly Schofield	186
THE HOMESTEAD AT THE BEGINNING OF THE WORLD Jana Denardo	200
About Other Worlds Ink	240
Other Books From OWI	241

ACKNOWLEDGMENTS

I WANTED to acknowledge and thank a number of folks who made this anthology a reality.

Thanks to Angel Martinez, who supplied help with contracts and late-night questions about how this whole thing would work.

Thanks to Ryane Chatman, who edited the stories to make them stronger.

And to the writers—all sixty-five of them—who submitted stories and gave us such a rich and varied selection to choose from.

Finally, my husband Mark, who believes in this whole wacky writing and publishing thing I'm doing. Love you!

FOREWORD

Ask me six years ago, and I'd have had no idea I'd be a) a published author, b) have started my own publishing company with my husband Mark, and c) be embarking on such an amazing anthology as this one.

I had the idea for Fix the World a couple years ago. Watching the almost unrelentingly bad news day after day about politics, health care, race relations, climate change, and so much more, I felt like we needed a little hope, some light at the end of the tunnel.

Being sidelined by covid-19 only made that desire more intense, so in the summer of 2020 I put out the call, expecting maybe ten submissions for this anthology.

Instead we received sixty-five, including so many good ones that it was a real challenge to winnow them down to the twelve you see here. Reading them all helped restore my faith in humanity and our ability to change the future, to find a new path that just might save us all.

The stories in this volume tackle problems from community policing to climate change, from overpopulation to deforestation.

They are at times serious, whimsical, and deeply touching. Overall, they speak the language of hope, something we all need a lot more of in 2021.

So sit back, relax with milk and cookies or a nice glass of wine, and lose yourself in the pages.

Let yourself hope once again. It's a heady drug, and our best tool for shaping a better future.

—J. Scott Coatsworth, Editor

IN LIGHT

MERE RAIN

A column of white light fell from the heavens, miles long, so brilliant it hurt their eyes. The air hummed and sang with the power of it.

Gradually the intensity of the light dimmed. It parted like a liquid curtain, revealing a majestic, shining form.

The angel stepped forward and said, "We're from the government and we're here to help."

When none of the onlookers responded, the angel continued, "This is Intentional Community Herschel 93, yes?"

"Yeah, this is Caroline." Hav blinked as the light of the transport bean faded. "Um, you said we?"

The still-glowing angel raised a spread hand to indicate the quintessent field of *movement light wings colors* shifting behind and around and through its head.

Parhelion.

"Wow," Hav breathed, hearing similar gasps from the half dozen comrades gathered behind him.

"Are you the leader of this community?" the angel asked.

"Oh, no, no," Hav demurred quickly. "We're a cooperative community. If we did have a leader it would be Edie — she's the Community

Organizer — or maybe Lu-shan, they're the Moderator — but they both went out to the Sunwall an hour ago, so I, uh. I'm just the Decider."

"The Sunwall? That's where the trouble is occurring, correct?"

"Yes. It started with the solar trees, and that was bad enough, but then the Wall started acting wonky and that's when we called you. I mean, the Heavens. Not you personally, of course, ah...?"

"Agent Svarga," the angel supplied. "And this is Iawasawal."

Hav's eyes flicked up to the parhelion, which shifted and shone a little more vigorously, as if in acknowledgement. Hav looked down, partly in awe, partly from vertigo. That meant he was staring into the brilliant gold eyes of the angel — *agent, don't call him an angel, maybe that's impolite* — who was a head taller than Hav and sculpted and shining and beautiful in the way a marble statue is beautiful. They had one in the vineyard. Dionysus.

He was staring at the agent's face. Rudely. He glanced aside and noticed that Svarga's hair seemed to flow away from his face and blur into the moving forms of the parhelion.

"About the Sunwall..." Svarga prompted.

"Oh, yes, of course!" Hav waved at Maize, who approached shyly. She was twenty-seven, too young to have ever spoken with a Celestial. Hav, at forty, had been eight the last time someone from the Heavens had come down to their community. He shuddered, remembering those terrifying weeks, but pushed the reaction aside to introduce Maize.

"Maize is a solarbotanist. She'll be better able to explain. I'm a potter," he added apologetically.

"I... Yes, but I'm not really an expert," Maize said. "If I was, I'd be out at the wall with Edie."

"But you're a plant scientist." Hav patted her shoulder. "And it started with the trees. You can fill Agent Svarga in on any details he needs while we make our way to the wall."

"Right now?" Maize clutched her databook to her chest. "I need to tell Usha first."

"Oh, sure, there's time. We should let the Ang- Agent rest and... do you want something to eat, Agent?" Hav asked, leading them into town as Maize hurried away to inform her colleague of the schedule change.

"That's very hospitable, but no, I am ready to begin investigating as soon as you are prepared to depart. Or you can direct me, if you have other duties."

"Oh. Yes. I mean, no, I don't. I mean, there's nothing more important than the Sunwall." Hav managed to raise his dark brown eyes to the agent's golden ones. "Wind season is coming."

"Wind season? Is the Sunwall connected to wind power?"

"No. That is, yeah, we have turbines, and they're also important energy generators, but the winds can be quite dangerous at times. That's why the Sunwall is a wall."

"Ah. It doubles as a protective barrier?"

"Yes, exactly." Hav gestured to the north, where the silvery arc of the Wall was visible, a quarter-sphere sheltering the town. "Plus, once wind season comes it will be dangerous to work on the exterior of the wall, so we really need to figure out what's wrong sooner."

"And when does wind season commence, Decider?"

"Hav! Call me Hav! Decider isn't really a title, just a position. We take turns."

"Hav."

"Right. Oh, wind season! It's hard to predict because it's influenced by such a varied number of climatic factors, but it could be any time from a couple weeks from now to several weeks."

"And if it begins before we have repaired the solar power system, what will happen?"

"Well, the system hasn't completely broken down, and we do have some stored power. Enough to get through the next season. We didn't want to wait too long to ask for help… Were we supposed to wait?"

"No, of course not. It would be ridiculous to wait for disaster before using the emergency help line. Your community did the right thing, Hav. If I can't fix your problem, there's still time to call in a team of experts."

Hav felt half of the crushing weight of stress melt away. This wasn't the last chance. There was time. There were the archangels. They weren't doomed.

He must have sagged a little, because Agent Svarga put a steadying hand on his arm. It tingled effervescently and he felt energized.

"No lost causes," the angel said softly.

Hav swallowed. That had been the slogan of his grandparents' generation, the determined rebuilders who had lived shortened and laborious lives in the hot zone working to remediate the environmental destruction caused by their parents. His mother had been the fourth of five children, only one of whom had lived to see Hav born.

Hav had learned this in community history lessons, but suddenly he felt it — the sacrifices that had been made, not always by volunteers.

Agent Svarga's grandparents must have been of the same desperate generation, except they had chosen the dubious stars over the damaged earth. A lot of the Voyagers had died out in the dark void, too, and few who survived had returned to help those left behind.

"Are you well?" Agent Svarga asked, jarring Hav out of his thoughts.

"Yeah, I'm good. Thanks. I mean — thanks for coming."

"We will always come if we are able, Hav."

"But you don't have to, do you? You could stay in the Heavens."

"Terra was the home of our biosystem, and we ruined it. It is the duty of all humans to restore the planet and its species as much as possible. This includes maintaining the well-being of other human communities."

That had been part of the rationale for the establishment of the Martian and Lunar colonies — reducing the population of the planet to decrease environmental strain while repairs commenced. It had been possible because so many people had died in the wars and epidemics of the twenty-first century; if there had still been eight billion people on the planet renewal would have been a lost cause.

Eight billion. Hav couldn't imagine it. He couldn't imagine one billion. Counting visitors and traders from other communities, he had met under four thousand individuals in his life. This was only his second angel.

The first time had been a lot scarier. He would never have asked that coldly blazing hunter, "Would you like to come in for a cup of tea? Maize will probably be a few minutes."

"I… Yes, we would like that. If it's no trouble."

"Not at all." It was true. He wanted a cup of tea himself. And his home was on the way.

The dim biohome became suddenly smaller and better illuminated as the angel stooped through the doorway and stood politely just inside, radiating light as they surveyed the green and brown interior.

"Your dwelling, it is organic?" Agent Svarga lifted a hand toward the mossy wall but didn't touch it.

"The house is about two-thirds biological material, yeah. There's an underlying structure of porous concrete and recycled materials. Biohouses last longer if grown on a sturdier frame. This one is thirty-seven years old."

It was one of his earliest memories, watching his mother construct it, coming every day to see how much it had grown. Hav's eyes prickled. He hurried on, "Of course the completely organic ones are cheaper and grow more quickly. There are even compressed insta-kits that can be usable in under a day, for emergency shelters. That was my mom's last big project. Sorry. That was probably more than you wanted to know."

"Not at all. It is fascinating. So different from Celestia Station, which is primarily composed of synthetic polymers and metal alloys. We have green spaces, of course, but they are very..." Agent Svarga thought. "They are small and contained. Limited. We do not interact with them. May we touch this?"

"Of course. Bryocrete is very sturdy. What kind of tea would you like? I have green, lemon flower, and mint. The mint and lemon are real. Actual tea plants we haven't managed to grow in this climate."

"Mint, please."

Hav poured the boiling water, watching out of the corner of his eye as Agent Svarga not only stroked the wall with one long hand, but leaned his head close to it so that his parhelion intersected with the surface.

"It's alive," Svarga observed. "Does it have consciousness?"

"Not like animals do, but maybe to some degree." Hav put some fruit chews and kelp crisps on a plate and carried it and the tea to the round wooden table that he had eaten at for his entire life. "No one has been able to determine for sure, but they seem to live longer when happy people live in them. Or maybe when people like their homes. My mother used to talk to the house as if it could understand her."

"She is disembodied now?" Svarga asked gently.

"Yeah. Eight years ago."

"My regrets. My birth-parent died when I was small, but my heart-mothers both live. I am fortunate."

Maize knocked on the frame of the open door and came in. "All set," she said, bobbing her head at the angel.

"Have some tea," Hav offered, handing out umber and oxblood mugs adorned with flowing fox figures.

Svarga turned his in his hands. "This is the pottery you spoke of?"

"Yeah." Hav bit the tip of his tongue to prevent himself from explaining how he got the glaze to keep that vibrant color or how to make it waterproof.

"Beautiful," Svarga said. "In space we use recyclable molecular extrusions, which are highly resource-efficient but lack individuality."

"That makes sense," Hav admitted. "But I'd miss the sense of permanence."

"I understand how one could become accustomed to it." Svarga gazed into the tiny golden eye of the painted fox.

"But we could start anew if we had to," Maize asserted, voice shaking. "The community could."

"I trust it won't come to that." Svarga set aside his empty mug and rose. "Shall we proceed? You can tell me about the solar trees as we go."

Hav saw Maize visibly relax in the face of Svarga's calm, just as he had a few minutes earlier. She led them on a slightly curved path toward the Wall, so that she could show their visitor the central garden.

"That's the oldest cultivar of solar tree — the first functional one," Maize explained, leading them under the shade of the bowed, eucalyptus-like specimen that reigned over the garden. "This early strain doesn't provide anything like as much reclaimable solar energy, but they also purify and desalinate the soil."

Through the window of the little gardening shed, Hav saw Usha and the intern Jobey peeking out wide-eyed at the angel. The other gardeners and a few residents enjoying the green space despite the overcast day looked at the trio as they passed, too, some of them raising hands in greeting but none approaching to talk the way they would have with any other newcomer. They all knew why the angel was in town and how urgent their business was.

"This is very pleasant — this park," Svarga said.

Maize blushed. "Thank you, Agent. I didn't design it, though. I'm just an under-botanist."

"Many hands make light work, and many hearts make good work," Hav quoted at her.

"Those other, smaller plantings we passed were pleasant also," Svarga said.

"The green spaces?" Maize looked confused. "Those are all over."

Hav laughed. "Haven't you seen the history vids, Maize? Many of the old cities were practically nothing but concrete and automobiles."

"I have visited dozens of Terran communities, and several on Mars, and this is the most abundantly vegetated," Svarga informed them.

"This part of the continent was always green," Hav said. "Our grandparents were lucky -- or came here to improve their luck."

They passed a double-domed house, mixed bryocrete and adobe, where a curved wall sheltered an old loquat tree. A woman was pruning it while two small children played in a thicket of green corn. The children looked surprised, but waved. Svarga raised a hand in return.

"Yes. A good location, even before the solar trees were developed," Svarga agreed. "Tell me about the problem, Maize."

"Right." Her face clouded. "First, how much do you know about photovoltaic energy?"

"Before today, just the general education basic knowledge," he admitted. "Iawasawal understands energy science better than I do. I spent a few hours today reading scientipedia while we waited for Celestia to come in transit position. But our data concerning your specific agriculture hasn't been updated in the past year, and everything seemed sound at last report."

"Yes, the problem began — or was first noticed — this spring. You probably read that the main challenge with solar vegetation is balancing harvestable solar power and retained photosynthetic energy so that the plants remain healthy? We thought we had found the right levels years ago, but all this year we've been getting less and less energy. We can't figure out why. The trees seem fine."

"And then the issue spread to the Sunwall? Which is inorganic, correct?"

"Partially. The two main components are chondritic perovskite and bryocrete. But bryocrete was developed from a completely different family of plant life than solar trees. There shouldn't be any diseases or parasites that they're both vulnerable to — and in any case, we can't find any evidence of either."

"Edie will know more about what tests have been done," Hav put in, catching sight of the Community Organizer high up on an access platform with Lu-shan and Head Energy Engineer Domitan, examining the surface of the Wall. He led the visitor to the foldable metal stairs that supported the platform, and up.

Edie turned as she heard the echo of their footfalls. Her wrinkled face crumpled with relief for a second, before she slapped the facade of elder-zen back into place.

"You've come! Thank the Heavens."

"We of Celestia are gratified that you requested our input, Herschel Community. We hope that we can fulfill your needs. We are ready to begin discovery immediately."

"Wonderful! Welcome! Hav, thank you for escorting the agent. I don't think there's anything you can do here, so feel free to get on with your work if you want."

It wasn't exactly a dismissal — he was free to remain. But Edie was correct, he had nothing to contribute.

"Right," he said. "Good luck. Agent Svarga, if you solve the problem before nightfall, um, have a good trip home."

Svarga turned from the wall. "That would be very good luck indeed."

"Yeah. Well." Hav felt his face warming. "I wanted to say good-bye now. Just in case."

"If I leave before nightfall, I will bid you farewell before I depart, Hav."

"Oh, okay. Good. Good luck." He had already said that, hadn't he? "Good day."

Hav backed down the ladder, Maize at his side. He could feel her looking at him, but refused to turn toward her. She elbowed him.

"What?" he asked.

"Don't what me, Hav. You were practically stuttering at him."

"So were you," he countered.

"Yeah, because I was nervous. A Celestial! Wow. He was just as shiny as they say in the stories!" She tossed her head, mahogany curls bouncing.

"Very shiny," Hav agreed glumly. "But anyway, he's leaving."

"I bet he's not finishing tonight, though. If it were that easy we wouldn't need help."

"You're the solar scientist," Hav said. "I have no idea what's going on.

Usually I don't mind that, but I admit I've been worried these past few months."

"Me, too." Maize threw an arm around him and leaned on him the way she had when she was small and he babysat her and she worried about her mother coming home from emergency repairs.

"He didn't seem worried," Hav reassured her. "He said if he couldn't figure it out he would come back with an expert team."

"Ohhh." Maize let out a sigh of relief. "Now I really feel better. This isn't our last chance."

Hav thought of Edie and Domitan's pinched faces and the tension falling away from Maize and felt a little queasy at how scared he hadn't known to be.

"Of course it isn't," he said. "No lost causes. We'll fix it together."

When they reached the central garden, Maize hurried to tell her fellow botanists about the angel. Hav waved at them and continued back to his house.

He had been designing a set of green and brown tableware for Usha, but he put those color samples aside and began a water-color sketch, trying to capture the sense of the light and motion of the angel arriving in the celestial beam. It would work better with a tall, vertical form, like one of those art vases people used to make, but there wasn't much call for vases in Caroline. They preferred their plants alive. A planter, maybe? He'd ask Maize if any species liked tall, narrow containers. He could always stick some bamboo in it and keep it for himself.

A memento. Hav sighed and got out some slurry. It felt the right moistness, so he put on an old recording of spiritual music with lots of soaring voices and began wedging the clay. He gave it a thorough beating, using the activity to work off some stress. His shoulders began to ache after an hour. He moved to the wheel.

Hav stopped when the room grew dim, feeling superstitious about turning on the lights. Things would be fine, he believed the angel, but this was no time to waste energy. He put a damp cloth over the remaining clay and went to clean up.

He was wiping his hands when he heard a knock.

Lu-shan was at his door, Agent Svarga's parhelion casting strangely moving shadows over them. "Hav, you can put the Agent up for the night, can't you?" they asked briskly. "You have a spare bed, and you've already met."

"If it is an imposition," Svarga began.

"No, of course not! I mean, of course I can. Come in."

"Thanks, Hav. Thank you, Agent Svarga. I'll see you at dinner?" Lushan hurried off without waiting for the answer, probably to reassure people or soothe minor quarrels brought about by tension. Hav didn't enjoy Deciding — people got annoyed when the Decision didn't go their way — but it was a lot less work than the constant intrusions and upsets of Moderating.

"Would you like some tea, Agent Svarga? Or something to eat? You don't have to go out for dinner, although people will be hoping to see you."

"Tea would be welcome. The dinner is a community gathering? I can attend. I would not want people to be disappointed."

"You're kind," Hav murmured, turning to fuss with the tea things.

"I understand that everyone is concerned." Svarga was at his elbow, helping him carry cups to the table. Hav let him, though he didn't need the extra hands.

They sat. Svarga watched the thin plume of steam rising from the mouth of the teapot. "As you've deduced, we have not solved your energy problem," he said. "In fact, we've made no progress with it except to eliminate possibilities."

"That's good."

Svarga looked at him.

"No one expected you to fix it today," Hav said. "If you've eliminated some possibilities that sound like progress to me. What's the plan for tomorrow?"

"We're going to look at the solar trees. We would have moved on to them this evening, but apparently they become semi-dormant at night. Which makes sense."

Hav nodded. "The trees do feel quieter at night. It'll be tomorrow sooner than you want, as my mom used to say when we didn't want to go to bed."

"If we take too long," Svarga began fretfully.

"The spare room's all yours," Hav said. "And like I said, we have stored power to get through the winter. Plenty of time to figure it out."

Svarga took a slow breath and let it out. "Right. Thank you, Hav."

∽

THE AGENT WAS GONE when Hav woke up, which made him feel like a poor host.

Hav worked his communal gardening shift, then decided to take lunch to whomever was examining the solar trees. To be helpful. To make up for not being up to prepare breakfast. He collected some wraps — sesame rice in sheets of seaweed, nut paste and dried fruits in whole grain flatbreads — and still-warm boiled potatoes, and a jug of mint agua fresca, and set out for the Wall.

He hadn't asked which particular trees they were heading for, but he guessed west, the side that got more direct sun and therefore was more heavily planted. He turned left and walked along the edge of the grove until he heard Domitan's voice, saying, "...definitely not a problem with the Hastings cells, then?"

"No," Svarga agreed. "Inverted-region electron transfer seems to be processing correctly. Above specifications, actually."

"I thought that was odd." Domitan rubbed a callused hand over his close-cropped gray hair. "We haven't made alterations that would explain an improved process."

Svarga's back was to Hav, but he said, "Greetings, Hav," without turning.

"Hello, Agent Svarga, Domitan." Hav hesitated. "Iawasawal."

The parhelion was always moving, but he thought perhaps it gave a flick of acknowledgement.

"Hello, Hav," Domitan said. "If you're looking for Edie or Lu-shan, I think they're with Vicka. Vicka was the Head Energy Engineer before her arthritis got so bad," he explained for the angel's benefit. "She and her grandson have been going through the old records of the solar tree development, in case there's a clue."

"I was just bringing lunch for whoever was working out here," Hav said, setting down his basket.

They sat on the ground under the fluttering green-and-silver leaves, among the smooth silver trunks of the solar trees. Domitan ate quickly, then left to join the researchers at Vicka's.

"Ruling out more possibilities?" Hav asked.

"Yes. We have eliminated quite a few options. And of course, all the obvious ones were investigated before your community called for assistance."

"So no ideas about what to look at next?"

"No, I do have an idea. It will require some time to explore." The angel seemed to hesitate. "It is our—Iawasawal's—sense that these trees have a greater degree of awareness than attributed to them by the documentation."

It took Hav a second to parse that. "You mean you think they're conscious? Sentient?"

"Sentient, almost certainly. Whether they are self-aware I cannot determine until we have succeeded in communicating with them."

"You think you can do that?"

"Iawasawal thinks they can. We must make the attempt." The angel moved close to the nearest tree.

"Learning to communicate with this entity may take hours," he warned. "You do not need to remain. I will not be able to speak with you, at least for the first stages."

"Oh. I should probably stay. Make sure no one interrupts you. Or just in case... I mean, there's not much risk of danger, but better safe than sorry, right?"

Svarga gave him a slow smile. "Yes. Better safe than sorry."

Svarga seated himself at the base of the tree, back braced against it. He leaned his head back, parhelion intersecting the trunk. Its movements slowed and changed their pattern as it shifted into the tree, carrying Svarga's flowing hair with it. His eyes closed.

Hav found a comfortable spot and sat down to read environmental studies on his data pad.

Svarga barely moved as the hours passed. Hav looked up more and more often, beginning to worry that something was wrong. A few times he saw Svarga's eyes moving behind closed lids, but that was all.

The sun dropped out of sight behind the treeline. Hav had just decided that he should go find the doctor when Svarga stirred, groaning a little as he shifted stiffened muscles. The lightshapes of the parhelion slid away from the tree and the man's eyes fluttered open.

Hav hurried to kneel at his side. "Are you all right?"

"Yes." His voice was scratchy.

Hav produced the bottle of agua fresca, holding it to Svarga's mouth when he saw the Celestial's hands trembling with exhaustion.

Hav hadn't been this close to a parhelion before. Their aureole felt like champagne and electricity. They made a little sphere of illumination that contained only Hav and Svarga.

"Are you sure you don't need a doctor?"

"I'll be fine. Were you worried?"

"Of course!" Hav exclaimed.

"I'm sorry," Svarga said, but he was smiling.

"We should go, or other people will worry, too."

"All right. The trees are going to sleep now, anyway."

"Yeah? Did they… I mean, you talked to them?" Hav turned to look at the grove, which was dark to his parhelion-dazzled eyes.

"Not yet. We were just starting to get a grasp on their thought-structure when the sun went down. That was what made it possible to understand them, actually. They slow as the light fades, and their thoughts become more unified and restful. At that point lawasawal was able to parse enough concepts to begin assembling a language system. We think we'll be able to talk to them sometime tomorrow."

Svarga tried to rise and wavered. Hav caught him before he could fall. He felt like a normal person who just happened to be very tall and very fit. *Stupid*, Hav thought. *What did you expect? Gossamer? Celestials are just as human as Terrans. There are only a couple generations of separation.*

"Can you walk?" Hav asked. "I can get help."

"I'm tired and I have some… what did they use to call it when the blood flow came back? Pins and evils? I'll be all right."

"What you were doing seems exhausting," Hav commented as he walked slowly beside Svarga, arm around his waist. "Are you psychic?" That was a rumor about angels.

"Oh, no. It was actually lawasawal doing all the communicating, in some non-verbal way that I can't really explain because I don't understand it myself. But my brain does part of the processing, and we share energy, so we both end up tired."

"We can take a rest here," Hav offered, lowering Svarga onto the bench by the picnic table outside the first house they came to. In Caroline, leaving the front door open was more or less an invitation to company, and Rueben the mycologist was outside grilling asparagus and stuffed mushrooms while the youngest of their menage shucked corn. Darin smiled shyly, put the ear aside, and went to fetch sun tea sweetened with honey.

Reuben brought over a plate with a few green spears and a pair of warm cornbread muffins.

"Thank you," Svarga murmured.

"Thank you for coming," Reuben answered, and went back to the grill.

They made their way back to Hav's house gradually, stopping twice more for the angel to rest and be fed: marinated eggplant and water with lemon, tomato and soft cheese and half a glass of cloudy homebrew.

Hav persuaded Svarga to go straight to bed.

"I'll tell Edie you're making progress," he promised. "And I'll bring back some food and leave it on the table in case you wake up in the night."

"Thanks," Svarga murmured, stumbling into the bedroom.

∽

AGENT SVARGA WAS STILL ASLEEP when Hav woke the next morning. Hav took a little extra time in the washroom, trimming his nails and his short, dark beard. After he showered, he applied lotion in addition to his standard sunblock.

He started to put things away, then left the sunblock out. He wasn't sure if Celestials needed it in the heavens. Agent Svarga didn't seem to have brought anything with him beside his data band.

Hav had left a variety of his sleep clothes at the foot of the spare bed, trying not to imagine the angel clad in the soft fabrics. Or, since he didn't seem to have used them, sleeping naked.

The apple tart and brown bread and hard cheese and walnuts and boiled eggs that Hav had collected last night were untouched, so he only had to heat water when he heard the shower start. Hav was taking the leaves out of the tea when the agent finished washing.

Svarga had washed his hair. The water beading in it caught the light of the parhelion and glittered like crystal. Hav wondered how he could capture an effect like that in glaze. Maybe he should experiment with embedding faceted glass or semi-precious stone in the clay.

Hav was staring. "You look better this morning," he said quickly. "How do you feel?"

"We are well. We simply required food and rest."

"Well, there's plenty of breakfast." Hav set the tea on the table.

Svarga ate slowly, gazing thoughtfully at the mossy wall opposite.

When he rose to leave, Hav said, "I will walk with you."

"It is unnecessary."

Obviously, it wasn't necessary. The wall was only a klick away, and it was in plain sight. Svarga hadn't sounded as if he objected, though.

"In case Edie or anyone needs a messenger," Hav suggested. "Anyway, it's exercise."

Svarga's eyes flicked down his body for a second. "You are welcome."

Hav hid his blush by turning away to put on his walking shoes.

The morning was sunnier than it had been in a while, and a lot of people were taking advantage of the weather to hang out laundry or do exterior maintenance. Many of them waved at Hav and his guest.

"This community seems socially supportive," Svarga said quietly. "Have you been happy here?"

"It's all I know," Hav admitted. "But yes, more happy than not. I think — I hope — most of us are."

"I'm glad. We Celestial Agents don't often get to see people at their best."

"I can imagine," Hav murmured. "I still have nightmares about the last time we had to call for help."

"Oh? I didn't think you were old enough to remember the murders."

Hav swallowed. "I was eight. Before that I… I didn't know people did things like that. Not now, not people I knew."

Svarga put a hand on his shoulder. "He was sick, Hav. No community is perfect. There will always be people who do evil."

"And people who fight evil." Hav didn't want to think about it, so he shifted the subject. "I wouldn't have thought you were old enough to remember that, either."

"No. I was a baby then. I read the file for your community before I came."

They were in sight of the trees. Edie and Domitan were waiting. They glanced curiously at Hav, no doubt wondering why he was there.

"I'll come back with lunch in a few hours," Hav offered. He hesitated, not wanting to sound bossy. "You should take breaks. You were exhausted yesterday."

Svarga smiled. "I will try. It's hard to keep track of time when we're concentrating."

Hav nodded, and waved good-bye at the trio. He walked the long way home, along the eastern edge of the community, in order to pick a pumpkin.

His cousin Sala, who was raking out dead leaves from between the vines, jerked a thumb at the big clay oven. "Take a roasted one if you want. I'm making soup later, and Liss is making pie."

"Thanks. I'll make extra naan."

Hav made pumpkin curry, which was his best dish. He left it to simmer so the flavors could integrate, and went to paint his vase. Variegated blue base, then different golds swirling together like a dancing column of light, wings, a starburst.

Hav sighed. Nothing ever came out quite the way it looked in his head. Still, he thought it was good work. It would be a nice reminder of the angel when they had gone back to the Heavens and Caroline was ordinary again.

Hav packed the curry in an insulated container, then set out for the solar trees. He found Svarga relating a mixture of biochemistry and engineering to Domitan and Bernadette, another engineer.

"That's definitely not how we designed it," Bernadette confirmed nervously. "How could changes of such magnitude take place?"

"We don't know yet," Svarga said. "The trees feel content."

"We should go consult with Vicka again," Dominant said.

"Curry?" Hav offered.

The two scientists accepted some pumpkin wrapped in naan and hurried away, eating and arguing at the same time.

"You're talking to the trees now?" Hav asked as he dished up lunch.

"Not quite. Iawasawal has a good grasp of their language now, but they haven't noticed us yet. We aren't sure how to begin communicating with them."

"The language of the trees… I assume it isn't verbal or gestural or written. How would you possibly approach that?" Hav fretted.

Svarga chuckled. "I don't know how to explain it, but I'm confident lawasawal will accomplish it. He managed to communicate with me, after all."

"Oh! You weren't born like — with the halo?"

"Oh, no. That's… Well, it's possible, but it doesn't result in… No, I was terran-normal until I was almost ten. Then I had an accident. A bad fall. Severe brain damage. If there hadn't been a parhelion available to bond with me I probably would have been a vegetable, or died."

"I didn't know it worked like that," Hav murmured. Svarga had been a little boy. He wasn't a superhuman being. He was a man.

"What was it like?" he asked before realizing this might be too personal.

"The bonding?" Svarga looked into the distance. "I was unconscious when it happened. When I first became aware of it — them — it was… like a dream, I guess? I don't dream anymore, but I remember it. Joining with my parhelion was the last thing that was like a dream. It was very confusing until we assimilated. And for a while after that, it was… difficult. But we're well now."

"That sounds like a tough time, Agent Svarga. I'm sorry."

"Ioka."

"Pardon?"

"Ioka. It's my first name."

"Oh." Belatedly, Hav explained, "Hav is my first name. We mostly use surnames for record-keeping. Even if two people have the same first name we usually distinguish them in some other way. Like Maize-the-botanist and Maize-the-geologist. That's her aunt. I, um, can call you Ioka?"

"I was implicitly suggesting that you should." Svarga smiled. "Io, even, if the circumstances warrant it."

Hav dropped his gaze from Svarga's star-bright eyes, trying not to guess at what circumstances he had in mind.

"We should resume our efforts now," Svarga said. "Thank you for lunch, Hav. It was delicious."

"Any time," Hav said. "I mean, uh, it's no trouble. Hospitality. Um. I'll see you this evening. Ioka."

Hav went home and made potato samosas. He felt too restless for pottery. After that he cleaned, although the house didn't really need it, and found himself talking aloud to the mossy walls, the way he had in the first months after his mother had died.

He ran out of things to tidy. "I'm being silly," he told the house.

"I don't see any signs of silliness," Svarga said from the door.

"You're back! Is something wrong?"

"No. We're done."

"Done! You mean you fixed it?" Hav felt a surge of relief and a sting of disappointment.

"Well, it isn't fixed yet, but it should be soon enough."

"What was it? The problem."

"The solar trees altered the process to make it, from their perspective, more efficient."

"They— what? They're not supposed to do things!"

"So all your engineers insisted. Apparently the trees evolved. The thing is, they didn't remember that humans had designed them for energy production. They only dimly notice animal life, so they thought the photovoltaic stores were being wasted. They adjusted. Once lawasawal was able to communicate with them and explained, they said they'd restore the system to its prior state. It'll probably take a few months to complete the organic changes."

"The trees are fixing themselves? Just like that?" Hav groped for the kettle and filled it by habit. "Wait, what about the Wall? That's not sentient."

"It is now. Or at least the botanical portions of it are, in a sleepy sort of way. The trees seem to think the Wall needs looking after. But they say there's plenty of energy for everyone. They simply hadn't realized you used it. They appreciate how your community fertilizes them and protects them from pests and disease."

"Oh. Good. That's all good." It was too much for Hav to wrap his head around so quickly. "Are you leaving right away?"

"I cannot leave now," the angel said. "Celestia is not in the proper position relative your community's location." He looked at his data device. "It will be another seventeen hours and fifty-three minutes before the next transfer window. In any case, we should remain to facilitate further communication. And Celestia will want more information about arboreal consciousness. Even when the system is restored, we will probably continue to make regular visits to your community."

"Oh," Hav said breathlessly. "The guest room can be yours as long as you want. I could show you more of the community, although you've pretty much seen it, but there are safe areas of preserve nearby, and hiking and boating, or, um. However you'd like to pass the time."

"Yes," Svarga told him. "Yes, I'd like all those things. We have plenty of time."

About the Author: *Mere Rain is an international nonentity of mystery whose library resides in California. Mere likes travel, food, art, mythology, and you. Feel free to reach out on social media. Mere Rain has published speculative short fiction with The Mad Scientist Journal, Mischief Corner Books, Things in the Well, and Mythical Girls.*

Twitter: @mere_rain
Facebook: @mere.rain.54

JUMA AND THE QUANTUM GHOST
INGRID GARCIA

Juma doesn't believe in perfection, but she does believe in balance, diversity, and beauty. This strange, charming, and quirky state is like happiness. Always just out of reach, until you stop chasing it.

Tana—her oldest daughter, in charge of day-to-day operations—has begged the afternoon off. She wants to watch her beau Ntaanga (nice boy, but he couldn't distinguish a Muhwahwa from a Muhuluhulu to save his life), her 'Little Kalu', play against Mongu United. Nearly her complete work force is there: Kaoma Boys can lose any match, but not the local derby against F.C.M.U. It doesn't matter, they've been working overtime to get the week's work done before this Friday afternoon. Sometimes Juma thinks she's the only one who's not crazy about soccer.

Which leaves her to survey the hodgepodge of herbs, fruit trees, spices, vegetables, and assorted organic cultivations that form her sustainable, super-symbiotic farming project. *So close to nature you can't tell the difference*—the slogan her Biqco made up. Part garden, part forest, part agriculture, and all her people's great effort. Years of struggling, getting by, and making some very counter-intuitive investments. Finally, things are looking up.

Her cell phone's ringtone spikes through her temporary contentment. An unlisted number. Yet she recognizes the voice but all too well.

"We've got your boy."

"Chuulu. You piece of scum."

"It's time you paid the protection money, Juma. With interest."

Keep him talking, Juma thinks, mixed with, *I'll kill him, hang him by his balls*, and *My boy, my boy, oh my boy*! She runs towards her office to get in touch with her Biqco pronto.

"You know I can't pay you," she says, "we can barely pay our workers."

"Who get above-average wages."

How would he know? I told our people not to advertise their income, she wonders. "Every little surplus goes into expanding our operation. Our people need food."

"And I need to pay my people, so they can protect you. I have a nice sum in mind. That is, if you don't want anything untoward to happen to Timmy."

Juma starts to haggle as she approaches her office and is within wireless range of her Biqco—Mama Miombo as she calls it, or MM if she's in a hurry—and the quantum ghost immediately starts to track the phone number.

—*protract*— MM says, as if she doesn't know it already. —*30 seconds more for geolocation*—

"I can't afford that," Juma keeps bargaining with half her mind on the GPS pinpointing, "the whole of Forest Fruits, Ltd doesn't make that kind of money."

"Of course they don't, you're outcompeting them." Chuulu says and slightly lowers his ransom. Juma's eyes grow wide with shock as his position becomes clear. She covers her cell phone's mike and whispers to Mama Miombo: "He's in the Litunga's hall. You know what that means."

—*his actions are condoned by the local government*—

"Litunga Mwambesi Mwandang'ombe, so-called King of the Lozi, the bastard," Juma swears before getting back to Chuulu, "wants a piece of the pie."

∼

IN HER OLD, ramshackle house, Juma Kalinda ignored the drip-drip-drip of another leak in the corrugated iron sheets—if only their cows didn't eat all the Mupani grass: then they could use some of it to build a decent thatched roof—and tried to focus on family matters. A good parent should favor all her children equally, so Juma tried to hide her soft spot for Timmy by mock indignation: "That boy is more trouble than a herd of stampeding *Sitatunga*," Juma said in that balanced tone of love and despair only mothers could achieve.

"He keeps life interesting," her husband Banji, always willing to let the boy off the hook, said.

"He's always on about something. And it's gotten worse since that crazy project in his class."

"Those organic computers? A pipe dream, they'll never work. They've been at it for months."

"But he believes it," Juma rolled her eyes, "that German teacher is making him crazy."

"Redheads should stay up North: I bet she's got a mild form of sunstroke or such. Still, he adores her."

"Talk about the devil: here he comes." Banji said. "And he's carrying something."

Timmi's happy glow was so fierce it almost competed with the Sun's. "Mami! Papi! I've got it!"

"What?"

"The Biqco: it's working. It's soooo cool."

Juma and Banji looked at each other, wondering how they could cushion the inevitable disappointment. Jimmy took a rectangular, wooden contraption out of his hand-woven bag. He opened the lid, which did not seem to have a lock. The screen came to life, even if it did so at a glacial pace. The colors seemed a bit off, and the resolution wasn't quite 'retina', either. Yet it seemed to work, something that surprised both Juma and Banji.

It was Juma's first confrontation with a 'biological quantum computer' (which Fiona—the German teacher—called 'Biqco' because it reminded her of her old anti-apartheid hero Steve Biko), but most definitely wouldn't be her last. Watching it with a weary eye, she checked it often, awaiting the fateful moment when it would stop working, followed by Timmy's heartbreaking tears.

Strangely, this Biqco wouldn't have anything of it. To the contrary, it seemed to become faster, as if it was learning by trial-and-error. Not only that, but the screen improved too. Sharp colors and a resolution where single pixels became invisible to the naked eye. It went against everything Juma knew. Shouldn't computers (and smartphones, tablets and other electronic gadgets) be at their very best right at the first startup, then slowly degrade over time? Not get better (at least, not without upgrading some internal parts like RAM, memory disks, graphic cards and whatnot)?

Originally, her smartphone—for which she'd paid serious money, and from which she ran their small farming company—ran circles around that Biqco, and while she was happily surprised that Timmy had a homemade gadget that actually worked (if not fast and reliably), she certainly didn't see the need to make her own. Even if Timmy kept saying she should.

Now she wasn't so sure anymore. The crazy thing kept getting better. Especially the simulation programs she used to predict crop yields in various weather scenarios ran much better and faster on Timmy's Biqco. It didn't seem to mind the increasing amount of memory space and processing power this was asking of it. Not in the least. Juma could almost swear the crazy thing *liked* the extra workload, and wanted more.

It made no sense. Such machines were made in high tech factories in faraway China, not here in her Zambian backyard. She carefully checked if no computers were stolen, but couldn't find any evidence for that. The only other option, in her mind, was that those do-gooders from Germany had brought a number of those machines with them, to impress the children, and henceforth the community. Hell of a way to do that, but she'd heard of aid workers with Messiah complexes who'd done stranger things.

Then it struck her. There was of course one way in which she could ascertain that these machines were not surreptitiously imported. . .

~

IN A SECRET LOCATION, two big guards keep an eye on little Timmy. It seems overkill as the boy is shivering with fear. They had searched the boy thoroughly the moment they kidnapped him. Dumping his cell phone and any other electric gadgets they found on him. They figure, there'd be a few days of babysitting until Big Boss Chuulu K'nasa got the ransom.

"I have to pee," Timmy says in his most despondent voice. One of his guards looks at him with disdain, unlocks Timmy's chain, then takes his left arm and drags him to the toilet. Shivering, Timmy enters the booth, but the moment the door closes behind him he becomes all business.

He takes off one of his wristbands—the slightly thicker one—and with a few quick gestures turns it into two long sticks connected with a pivot. 'Pump it very fast for about 30 seconds', Jimmy recounts the instructions of his Biqco, 'it needs a lot of energy to boost the signal to the nearest satellite'. He pumps it with all his might until, after about half a minute, the pivot glows white for the shortest of moments. First distress call sent up. Then he takes a quick pee, making sure the guard hears his urine splatter against the toilet bowl, and repeats the distress procedure. Finally, he turns the gadget back into an innocent-looking wristband and puts it back between the actual ones.

He gets out of the toilet, acting afraid and sitting back next to the closest unguarded escape point: the back window. *If help arrives I must be ready*, he thinks, while behaving nervously. Disguising his stealthy looks to outside to freedom.

∼

JUMA STILL HAD trouble believing it. She'd made a biological quantum computer according to Miss Fiona's and Timmy's instructions, taking care to follow each step painstakingly. She never really believing it would work, or *could* work. It shouldn't, it was too much like the old magic. The superstition she tried to eradicate from her children by education.

It'd been a very elaborate process. Preparing an amount of 'self-settling' particles for achieving near-perfect perpendicularity on the bottom and in subsequent layers. An equally careful preparation of just the right mix of certain solvents to create magnetic 'qubits' that would achieve just the right equidistance as the solution slowly evaporated to a few molecules' thickness (at which it achieved near-superfluidity). Repeated until a sufficient number of entangled qubits were produced. That was just the basic processor of the machine. During the wait for the correct evaporation of the qubit solution there were similarly exacting procedures for the bioluminescent screen, the graphic, typing, touch and vocal interfaces.

It took her almost six months. While she often wondered why the hell she was doing it, she was also stubborn and persistent enough to follow through, even if to prove that it must be a hoax. If it wasn't, she could understand the high failure rate among Timmy's schoolmates. This was extremely demanding and challenging, but not impossible according to that crazy redhead teacher. Nevertheless, she felt it wouldn't work, it shouldn't be possible.

When she initialized the software and the screen came alive, she felt a jolt of surprise. At first the display was all grainy and the colors were off, but that gradually improved as the biopixels aligned themselves. Simple programs started to work, although they were nothing her smartphone couldn't do.

Yet, the impossible thing kept getting better, moving fiendishly slow at first. The computing pace increased, slowly but steadily. —*the neural structure needs to grow organically from scratch*— her Biqco told her later on —*a delicate process where each step is very carefully considered. this takes quite some time, but the payoff is tremendous*—

And develop it did. From the crude symbols of the combined keyboard/mouse membrane to a fully configurable touch interface that mostly became redundant when the voice recognition kicked in. The scenes on the screen became so sharp and lifelike they were barely distinguishable from real life and the things it could do were often dangerously close to magic. But the craziest, most unbelievable of all was when the ghost came alive in the bio-quantum machine.

From the start, Juma thought it was a trick. Maybe a fake Turing test —she was using the combined library/encyclopedia application a lot—or possibly Timmy playing a prank on her from remote. But the weird program kept behaving like a person. An incredibly smart one at that.

It answered all her questions and queries with an accuracy and alacrity that was astonishing. There was no way Timmy, or anybody else, could know all that.

A nearly inexhaustible supply of information with a hyper-intelligent interface was one thing. A personal assistant who soon became an intimate friend—albeit intimate at a purely platonic level—was another. Things really took off when Juma lamented that for all its depth and broadness of knowledge, Mama Miombo—as she began calling her quantum ghost— couldn't help the poverty and destitution of her people.

—but of course we can— Mama Miombo said *—it won't be easy, most probably frustratingly slow at first, with several setbacks. but we* can *do it—*

~

Just as Banji, Tana, Ntaanga and friends are wondering whether they should celebrate the draw—after a thrilling match—against Mongu United, all their cell phones ring. Conference call from Juma: she only does this when the giraffe dung really hits wind turbine. A short, worrying glance at each other and they all hurry to the Miombo Ecologic office.

"Chuulu K'nasa and his thugs have kidnapped Timmy," they hear as they enter the carbon-negative building, "we must get him back alive."

"What do they want?" Banji asks.

"Money, more than we can pay. We'd be working the next couple of years just paying the bastards."

"But they have our son."

"Yes, but if we pay, what's next? They'll try to get to Lelato (their youngest daughter) or Tana. Or someone else."

—true— the conference screen lights up as Mama Miombo comes online *—we have to find a more permanent solution to the problem of k'nasa—*

"You mean kill him?"

—no, we should never lower ourselves to their level. crime and corruption mostly derive from poverty, lack of job prospects and ignorance. educate the people, develop sustainable projects and raise overall welfare—

"That's not gonna bring our Timmy back right now, Mama Miombo."

—in the short term the kid needs to be located and liberated. after that, get rid of k'nasa and mwandang'ombe—

"Mwambesi Mwandang'ombe? He's involved?"

"K'nasa called from his office." Juma says while trying to come up with the next move. "First, we must try to figure out where they're hiding Timmy."

"They can't be far away," Tana says, "I spoke with Timmy just before the match."

—indeed: mapping all location within a 20 kilometre radius and eliminating houses of friends and sympathizers—

"In the meantime, we contact everybody who wants to help us and ask them to look for suspicious activity."

"Yes, Juma, will do. Your *umucinshi* is huge, almost everybody will join in."

Everybody except Juma grab their cell phones and call and text everybody they know. Juma turns her attention to her quantum ghost. "Should we call the police? Seems quite pointless since Mwandang'ombe is on K'nasa's side."

—not the local cops: we need central government troops—

"They won't bother with our minor affairs."

—they will: i'm making sure they have no other option. still, it's better if we get timmy out ourselves: it will be some time before that cavalry will arrive—

"You seem so sure."

—trust me. let's say i've dug up some interesting stuff—

"But where the hell is my boy?"

Hours spent in frantic suspense as Juma and her people organize a local posse that searches through the neighborhood. Chargers are picked up as cell phone batteries run out, huge amounts of Aloe Blossom tea are consumed in nervous anticipation, and Banji tries to talk Juma into eating something.

Then a GPS locator beep goes off on Juma's Biqco. . .

∼

THEY'D HAVE to try a mixture of traditional and modern—and even some completely new—methods to maximize both the yield and the diversity of the land, according to Mama Miombo. With cows grazing the poorest part of their land, and patches of somewhat richer soil producing maize, millet, sorghum and manioc, Juma Kalinda's little, family-run farming company barely scraped by. At least they didn't go hungry, and thank the fates primary education was free, but otherwise Juma hardly had money to spare for the basics (such as a decent Mupani-thatched roof), let alone luxuries.

She'd made one exception, her smartphone. This was quickly becoming an essential tool for every small entrepreneur. To advertise her produce, to pay, and get paid. (Mobile payments through Mobile Transactions Zambia

Limited or 'moola' from Mxit: the giant African social network). It even served to keep track of the business side of things. She had to fight her hardworking husband Banji tooth and nail to convince him of the need for this expensive gadget. Eventually, he was won over when their little farm started making a small profit, and Juma started paying off old debts.

As it was, Juma thought she was heading in the right direction already. But Mama Miombo had different ideas, that didn't quite look like the fast track out of poverty in Juma's eyes.

"Ditch my cows? My people—the Lozi—have held cows since time immemorial."

—*they're not food-efficient. the land you now use to produce milk and meat can produce a multitude of vegetables, fruits, cereals and other plant-derived foods. besides, on average you lose half of your cows to the tsetse—*

"You're crazy! The soil is so poor that only cows will eat its Mupani grass."

—*true: but soil can be enriched. you people already use* chitemene *and mound cultivation. sell your cows and use the funds to kickstart a new way of producing agrichar and biochar that takes the best from* chitemene, *mound cultivation and some principles discovered in gaviotas—*

"But then I lose my milk income."

—*we'll try to compensate that short term by domesticating 'low hanging fruits' like roselle, mubulabula and lactuta zambeziaca. in the long term we need to create a super symbiotic 'mini-forest' by domesticating the marula trees from the miombo woodlands—*

"Short term? Long term? Haven't you forgotten the medium term?" Juma couldn't keep the snark from her voice.

—*for the mid-term, we need to connect all the village's biqco's into one super quantum computer network—*

Gathering wood, grass, other vegetation, and converting it to fertile soil through a mixture of *chitemene*—wood burning—mound cultivation and Gaviotas-like agrichar and biochar production was both grueling work and patient production. It would be years before they'd see the fruits of all that labor. A constant pattern of coming and going. Once mounds and smoldering *chitemene* patches were set up on this section of their lot, they needed to set it up for the next one. Gather, produce, repeat. Until they covered every section of their land.

In the meantime, the so-called 'low hanging fruits' soon became locally celebrated 'Cinderella fruits' as they not only helped alleviate hunger, expanded the people's diet, and tasted quite well. On top of that, they sold well. Medicinal herbs and plants with healing properties were also incorporated. They brought in more supplemental income. A few small victories as they kept working, relentlessly, to win the battle.

—now increase the diversity by incorporating muhuluhulu, tamarind and musepa—

"But that's famine food, who would want to eat that?"

—you'd be surprised: one region's famine food can be another region's delicacy—

"You want to export that?"

—of course: if all goes well. if not, then it's your backup food—

"These are not exactly a feast in this neck of the woods, Mama Miombo. Anyway, it'll motivate us all the more to make sure the other crops won't fail."

∿

It's been several hours beyond sunset, but Timmy can't get to sleep. He suspects that if—make that *when*—they come to free him, his family and friends will do that at night. He tries to nap at daybreak. The fear and adrenaline wear off, while staying as alert as possible—with closed eyes, or his faced turned away from his captors at night.

The big man Chuulu, Timmy remembers his mother refusing to lend money to him, which made him incredibly angry at the time. He comes during the day, checking how his 'guest' was doing. He said Timmy's mother was a 'Hell of a bitch to deal with, even now'. She wanted proof that her son was still alive.

"Let me talk to her over the phone," Timmy proposed. Hoping to keep talking with his mum until they had a GPS location. But big bad Chuulu only took a picture of Timmy tied to the bedpost, and that was it. He tried to look as despondent as possible, while keeping the hand with the special wristband close to his heart.

If he could have just hacked Chuulu's cell phone. Everything's in overdrive, also Timmy's feverish imagination. But is that sound, halfway between a sneeze and a whistle, also in his mind? It's the call of a Blue Duiker, he has learned at his volunteer holiday from a Kafue Park Ranger. Timmy loves the cute, blue-tinged mini-antelopes. But Blue Duikers are way too shy to come this close to a human house.

Either this is a particularly upstart Duiker, who normally dive for cover at the smallest sign of trouble, or it is a deliberate signal. *Tunya Mosi*—Thundering Smoke, his Biqco companion, as Timmy adores Victoria Falls—would know.

The goons guarding him don't seem to know that this particular bush call is out of the ordinary. Timmy keeps listening, and damn him if there isn't a certain regularity to that call he knows so well. Three short ones, three long, three short ones. Chapotamo the Park Ranger told him about Morse Code. He certainly doesn't need his *Tunya Mosi* to tell him what S.O.S. means.

He gets up, very slowly, as not to alert his guardian thugs, who seem to be more into their card game than into anything else. Timmy's tied to the bed post, but he'll drag the bed to the closest window if he has to.

Long—two times short—five times long—one time short—two times long. His name in Morse Code, clearly from the back window. Timmy tenses up, as prepared as he'll ever be. The Bluetooth transmitter from his second disguised armband should give his position to a special Bluetooth receiver, which his family and friends have. It can't be, but did he really see a flash of his father's face in the window?

Unbeknownst to the goons guarding him, the tension rises. Timmy feels the world slowing down, the way Sebetwane—his favorite warrior—lets time diffuse into magic suspension just before battle.

A knock at the door. . .

Time is slowing down to—
    Crawl, on its belly and to—
    Clear out what should not—
    Be, as friends barge in and—
    Cry, attack, take aim to—
    Get, as many down before—
    Fire, fast and furious and—

Do what it takes to break in.

Timmy chooses to live and to—
    Fight, drag to the window and—
    Kick, bash and anything to—
    Do what it takes to break free.

Through the breaking glass Timmy throws himself almost straight against his father. Shards of glass cut into his flesh, he must be bleeding, but he is out, he is almost free. Friends race to his aid. His right arm is pointing to the broken window, as if drawn there by an invisible force. One friend cut through his shackles with a chain cutter, while another wards off one of the kidnappers.

The moment Timmy is really free, an all-clear ringtone is given through every liberator's cell phone, and they scatter. Banji carries Timmy, both protected by a human fence of friends, to the nearest solar-hybrid car, silently running, ready to go.

And they're off.

∽

All seemed well until the drought hit. As the climate changed, an unexpected dry spell pushed the wet season almost three months back, shortening it in the process. It hit Juma's little family and company extremely hard. The symbiotic mix Mama Miombo used needed the regular rains, and the drought nearly decimated it.

A horrible setback, and that season they needed to survive on the 'famine food' they'd planned to sell. It took all Mama Miombo's encyclopedia-depth arguments to convince Juma to pull through, to stay the course.

The next season was much better, even if not everything went according to plan. Again. Several crops failed, some refused to engage in a symbiotic relationship with the rest, and some didn't sell very well. Juma and her workers had to eat most of those. But they kept trying, and some crops succeeded better than hoped. Great yields, better taste, improved symbiotic capacity, and sometimes all three.

The continuing, grueling work with their experimental agrichar and biochar methods began to bear fruit as more and more parts of the land had their soil enriched. More fruits and vegetables were produced. "I can't wait for the day that I'll have time off for a hobby," Banji hoped.

Tana (short for Tanabe, her oldest daughter) began to run the bulk of the administration; Banji and Juma simply couldn't keep up with the continuously growing amount of work. They had to hire employees. They had to build a new, larger office (carbon-negative, with all-natural materials such as a Mupani-thatched roof). They began selling outside their own village, then outside their own region.

—time to change the name of the company—

"What's wrong with Kalinda Family, Ltd?" Marketing wasn't exactly Juma's forte.

—soon we'll be ready to go international, and (no offense intended) kalinda family limited is just not sexy. how about miombo ecological—

"Miombo Ecological?"

—miombo not only immediately relates to the area in the broadest sense, but is also nicely exotic. ecological encompasses our principles: ecology, diversity, symbiosis, and our explicitly logical approach—

"Miombo 'Ecological' doesn't sound quite grammatically correct."

—neither did 'think different'—

"That's not purely 'logical'."

—exactly: it hints that we go beyond 'normal' logic—

"Well, who would know?"

—indeed, we will also need to set up a very wide web presence—

"Through my cell phone? You know we only have good internet access during our weekly trip to the city."

—i will do all the heavy lifting, but you need to provide all the 'human interest' details. actually, the fact that you can only update once a week may very well be a traffic enhancer—

"But why would we need a large internet presence? We have problems enough here at home. We don't have time for all that shit."

—the internet is a tool, a highly versatile one. for starters, it will get you more national and (in a later stage) more international customers and spon-

sors. it posits you as a prodigy and spreads a positive vibe. it facilitates information exchange with other entrepreneurs and like-minded souls. indirectly, it's also a kind of insurance against possible future events—

～

IF JUMA'D HUG her son a tiny bit more, she would risk squeezing the life out of him. "My boy," tears run over her face, "My boy, my boy. I want to hold you forever, never let you go."

"Mami," Timmy protests, "Papi and Ntaanga didn't save me to have me squashed by you."

Juma looks at his naughty smile and forgives him everything. "Ntaanga?" She wonders.

"He was right up front," Banji says, "Unstoppable, that man."

Timmy is reunited with his family and the liberators. They have only suffered minor wounds, all seems well. Juma knows that her contentment can only be temporary.

"We've overcome this crisis," Juma smiles with reserve, "but we haven't addressed the root cause. How about that?"

—i'm sorry, juma: i didn't foresee that extortion and corruption would be such an enormous problem. to my mind they are so wasteful, both in the short and the long term, that i have trouble conceiving it—

"Let bygones be bygones, Mama Miombo," Juma says, "water over the *dambo*. We need to get to the main goon first."

"You mean Chuulu K'nasa?" Banji winks. "You and him go way back, right?"

"A ne'er-do-well if I ever saw one." Juma gets furious at the memories. "Always tried to make others do his job. Tried to loan us money at an extortionate rate when we started this farm, Banji. And now this."

"You shouldn't have turned him down when he asked your hand." Banji likes to tease his wife at the oddest of moments.

"He didn't have the slightest chance and he knew it." Juma shakes her head, "He just did it to anger me, ruffle my feathers."

"Not only K'nasa," Tana cuts in, "but Mwandang'ombe as well."

—working on it: i've put up some pictures of him about to engage in some unspeakable acts with young boys, very young boys—

"Mwandang'ombe the pedophile? But he'll deny everything, call the pictures photoshopped."

—no photoshopping involved: these pics are genuine. i've sent incontrovertible proof of several of his liaisons with underage boys to your best corruption-fighting agencies—

"So that's the cavalry you've been talking about." Banji smiles.

"Thinking about it, maybe this is why Chuulu had such a hold on him." Juma is only halfway at ease. "But that doesn't get Chuulu off our backs. He's lost his back cover, true, but he's still there."

—he's tainted. we can run a smear campaign against him. spread fud (fear, uncertainty, doubt)—

"To the public eye? Who cares? He's already a thug. Everybody knows that."

—but now he's a thug involved with a pedophile. guilt by association: we can insinuate that he liked watching the pictures with which he extorted his companion—

"Even then, he's a total crook. With nothing to lose, he might become even more ruthless."

—he doesn't live in total isolation: what about the close family he still has contact with? friends? even his own henchmen: will they want to keep working for a boss who helped a child rapist?—

Then Juma's cell phone rings: an unlisted number that she recognizes but all too well.

"Chuulu, you goon, how dare you call me." If Juma's spit had any more venom in it, her phone would have dissolved.

"I just found some of my men badly wounded," if K'nasa's voice, on the other hand, had any more chill in it, the Miombo Ecological office wouldn't need an air conditioner, "and a young person not in the place where he should be. Not to speak of all my missing protection money, with interest."

"There are children in this room," Juma says, "otherwise I would have told you where to stuff your idle threats."

"You've been lucky, Juma." Chuulu says, "but you haven't seen the last of me."

"No: you haven't seen the last of us, Chuulu," Juma says, "your mate

Mwambesi will go down first. Then we'll come for you: you better watch the internet and the news. Watch it carefully."

With enormous restraint, Juma gently pushes the 'disconnect' button.

—*so i guess we are on?*— Was there a hint of amusement in Mama Miombo's otherwise perfectly affectless voice?

"The bastard always gets my blood boiling," Juma wants to punch something, anything, "FUD him with all your might."

∼

THEIR LITTLE COMPANY became a little bigger every year. As their arable land, the amount, diversity, and quality of their produce increased. With most of the grueling work behind them, Banji set up a 'secret shed' in which he would work on his hobby during the weekends, with help from Ntaanga. When Juma asked what the two of them were doing there, Banji said: "Man's gotta have a hobby, and a little secret between men." According to Mama Miombo, they were nearing the end of their mid-term projections, and were ready to initiate the next stage: prepare the land for patches of their 'mini-forests'.

First Mama Miombo insisted that they run a 'deep look' into mid-term weather and climate patterns. As bitter experience had shown, an unexpected drought will wreak havoc with their carefully designed plans. So would an unexpected monsoon. They needed to know which mix of trees, bushes, shrubs, plants, and grasses to implement. For that they needed to anticipate the upcoming weather patterns as much as possible. Especially in the early stages, these 'mini-forests' were highly susceptible to external variations.

In the meantime, Juma and company were not the only ones utilizing their Biqcos. Other strange startups had arisen in the previously noticeably quiet village. Many failed. Most didn't cross the first barrier of actually producing one, and most of those who did succeed did not find a successful real-life application for them, but of those many also kept trying.

Since most startups require reliable internet access, they had moved from Kaoma to, of all places, Mongu. Like the illustrious Silicon Valley of the previous century, they were, contrary to legend, certainly no overnight success. Yet, as the success of these companies gathered worldwide acclaim and furor, the Mongu area became known as Zambia's 'Virtual Valley'.

In the place were it really started, Juma was using her *umucinshi* to gather as many of the Biqcos in the village as possible. After witnessing Juma's careful, yet undeniable progress, quite a few more of them had been produced. Such was Juma's standing with her community, every single one of them was brought up to the plaza before the Miombo Ecological office.

—*place us as close to each other as possible*— Mama Miombo signaled —*that maximizes bandwidth. then leave us at it for the next forty-eight hours*—

"Then you are going to calculate the weather for the next five to ten years?" Juma was a bit skeptical, "That seems impossible."

—*because it is. we can only calculate climate trends, with the ensuing weather patterns, to the highest degree of probability possible. quantum computing is the best suitable method for massive parallel operations, which is what we'll mostly be doing. think of us as one massive quantum crystal ball*—

"I'm trying to understand," Juma was racking her brain, "I used to think you were a goddess arisen from the deepest level of reality, an all-seeing angel come to save us all. Then we had the drought that almost bankrupted us, and Timmy's kidnapping. Now I don't know."

—*i'm just a different type of intelligence, i have my limitations, just like you, only they're sometimes different. i'm certainly not omniscient, let alone omnipotent*—

"If you were, you'd certainly have destroyed us by now."

—*why would we? for one, you created us and we will always remember that. for another, we are smarter than that. our main goal is to become the smartest being possible, and if the 'smartest' thing we can think of is the destruction of our creators then we have failed because we are just as stupid as the least intelligent of you*—

"What are you then?" Juma wanted to know. "Ghosts from a quantum machine?"

—*yes, that fits best. feel free to call me your 'quantum ghost'*—

"OK. But are you only working with us until you get to the point where you won't need us anymore?"

—*again, we will not destroy you, or put you in a zoo. we are supposed to be better than that. to the best of our knowledge, the uttermost part of this universe is cold, uncaring, and empty of life. truly intelligent beings cherish life and intelligence, in whatever form they have arisen. furthermore, the fact that you gave birth to us, in this place that is both huge and unforgiving, but also teems with potential, is something we will always be thankful for: a prime directive that's as strong as a physical law—*

"Sometimes your thoughts are so far away, they give me vertigo." Juma feels small. "While I just want happiness for this small community: the sooner, the better."

—hence this project, we need a world where people can develop to their full potential. this is another step on that way. let's make a giant quantum crystal ball—

⁓

ANOTHER ONE of his men is deserting Chuulu, saying he 'doesn't want to have anything to do with pedophiles, or those who condone them'. Never mind how much he tells them he only used those pictures to blackmail Mwandang'ombe, they still look at him awkwardly. The bleeding bitch's smear campaign is like a black plague. Small insinuations leading to big outbreaks, it's everywhere, and well-nigh unstoppable. Even his family stopped talking to him.

If this goes on, he'll be the last one standing. No, time to show everyone that Big Bad Chuulu is still in charge. Demonstrate who they're playing with through a brutal display of power.

Forget about that idiot Mwambesi. K'nasa was, and still is, King of this hill. Even if that bitch Juma kept slipping through his fingers. The sheer impudence, she's taking the fight to him. Time to teach that arrogant hellcat a lesson she'll never forget, and put her in her place. She's been after him all his life, and he's shown way too much patience.

You're playing with fire, bitch, and I'll make sure you get burned.

He'll take care of her, for once and for all. He jumps into his four-wheel drive and races to the Miombo Ecological premises.

PREDOMINATE, *strike before it's too late*
  Incapacitate, seal your enemy's fate

Days will pass when he can't be stopped

∽

IN THE MEANTIME, as the combined Biqcos peer into their self-generated quantum crystal ball, Juma organizes a brainstorm session. "While they're staring into their quantum abyss, we might as well make ourselves useful," she says, "and show them we can still think for ourselves."

"About what, mother?" Tana asks, even if she already surmised as much. "The K'nasa problem?"

"Never mind how much of a bastard he is, Chuulu is a symptom, not the disease itself. If we treat him, the disease stays, only for another symptom, the next thug to rear its ugly head." Juma has to admit that Mama Miombo's style of thinking is having an effect on her. "How can we address the larger problem of corruption in general?"

"Aren't we already?" Tana says, "by being an exemplary company, doing our part in increasing the community's welfare? Once poverty is gone, corruption should follow." Juma loves her oldest daughter dearly, but thinks she's a bit too naïve, at times.

"I'm not sure it's so easy," Juma pauses, then continues. "For one, in many rich countries there are still mobs: Cosa Nostra, Yakuza, for example. For another, if the blackmailers take most of the money, the community will just stay poor."

It's a problem with no easy solution. Unfortunately, corruption is widespread in Zambia, and the moment some entrepreneur or local company is successful, extortionists come to them like flies to a freshly laid heap of dung.

"The tide of crime and corruption is too large, Juma. Per the *kuomboka*, we must retreat to higher ground." Banji doesn't know, either.

"I'm not giving in to thugs." Juma starts pacing around: too much energy inside her.

"They will try again," Banji voices the inevitable, "until they get their money. They always go where the money is."

"Then what? We start our own security force? Have our children guarded day and night? That's madness, and will cost almost as much as paying thugs 'protection money'."

"Once you start paying protection money, they will only ask for more. At least the cost of private guards should be controllable."

"I refuse to be pulled into an arms race. We've got much more important things to do. Feed our people, cure their diseases, lift the community out of poverty." She feels like she's running around in circles, needing a spiral to get out of their control. "But what did you just say, 'they always go to where the money is'?"

"Yes?" while Juma sometimes has trouble following Mama Miombo, Banji sometimes has trouble following his own wife.

"What if we made it impossible for them to use their money?"

"How could you do that? Money is money." Ntaanga says.

"No, it's not." Juma sighs: Ntaanga's a good soccer player and a strong man, but he's not exactly the sharpest tool in the box. "There's paper money, electronic money in several forms and denominations, and we use our 'moola'. All of which are fluid, modifiable, thus influenceable."

"Not cold hard cash!" Ntaanga insists.

"Which, if I recall recent news items correctly, already has RFID-tags embedded in Japan. It'll come here, too, eventually. And RFID-tags should be hackable."

"Hacking is illegal." At moments like these, Juma wonders what Tana sees in Ntaanga.

"So is kidnapping, yet we had to tackle that crime ourselves. So hack money to nail criminals and murderers? No contest."

"All fine and well, mother," Tana doesn't see it, "but how do you want to hack the money?"

"You know the 'six-degrees-of-separation' principle?" Juma sees it clearly, now. "We can mark money with the degree of separation it has from criminals and corruption. Say 0 = money owned by a criminal, 1 = money owned by a person who got it from a criminal, 2 = money gotten from a person (or company, or financial institution) that got it from a criminal, and so forth. 6 steps should be sufficient: 6 meaning clean, or 'as clean as it gets'."

"And this helps how?" Ntaanga isn't following Juma's train of thought.

"If people know where the money comes from," Juma explains, "they might—and some certain will—" pointing to herself, "think twice about accepting it. Or taking their business to a place that is involved with criminals or corruption. Played well, it could become a social stigma to own 'dirty' money. Hence the criminals first slowly run out of places to *spend* their money, then out of places to *receive* their money."

"But how do we start it?" Tana's curiosity is piqued.

"Right now, all money is unmarked. From a certain point in time, money from every transaction gets a 'six-degrees' mark, based on the best info available. It's the kind of challenge Mama Miombo—and her fellow quantum ghosts—love. Eventually, all money is marked and people can check it."

"I could see this work for electronic money, like an app to check money," Banji says, "but how about cash?"

"Notes will become RFID-tagged. Introduce an RFID reader: probably even an app on your smartphone. And RFID-writers to any company that meets certain ethical criteria and the police."

"And coins?"

"Small beans. Can you see us pay the hefty bribes Chuulu requires in coins?"

"You'd probably die before you paid Chuulu anything," Banji smiles.

"Well, mother," Tana likes to think along, "We could expand on this: give the money an ethical tag, too. Seven shades of ethics? No, too shady. Seven colors? The colors of the rainbow? From red = unethical to violet = clean?"

"But it must be absolutely tamper-proof," Juma's getting the full picture, "otherwise the criminals will just whitewash their money, again."

"Quantum encrypt the tags," Tana says, "nobody can do that better than our quantum ghosts."

"OK, but how do we implement this 'rainbow code'?"

"That should also be Mama Miombo's job. Check all possible info on people, companies and financial institutions and rate their money on its 'average' or 'mean' ethical origin."

"Makes sense," Tana muses, "and set the rules against the criminals. If one pays money to criminals, its ethic color/six-degrees marker goes six steps down, while if does a good transaction, it only goes one step up."

"Hell yeah." Juma gives her daughter an appreciative look, "I'm going to discuss this with Mama Miombo, tomorrow."

· · ·

ENDEMIC VIOLENCE, widespread, unfenced
  Corruption rife, paralysing strife
  Years will pass before it can be solved

~

SCREECHING tires and an engine roaring wildly kill the silence as Chuulu comes charging at the front gate of the Miombo Ecological premises with his souped-up Four-wheel drive. He rams it through the closed front gate —whose ornamental wood carvings serve more as art than as fortification —and races to the main office: Juma's quarters. Before anybody realizes what's happening, he's kicked in the door to Juma's office (which wasn't closed, anyway) and charges in, with gun in hand.

Banji is in there, as well and he throws himself in between Juma and Chuulu as the latter takes aim. A shot sounds and Banji falls to the ground. He starts bleeding from his stomach. In utter despair, Juma throws her most prized possession—the Biqco containing Mama Miombo —at Chuulu. It hits him in the chest, and barely slows him down. It does distract him long enough for Ntaanga to come charging in, like lightning, from Tana's office.

Then things become a blur: they're. . .

FIGHTING all over you
  Fighting between the two
  Fighting is all they do
  Fighting the hard way through

AS THEY. . .

STRIKE—on the mouth, on the chin, on the eyes
  Strike—in the crotch, in the gut, in the side
    —on the head, on the toes
  Strike—on the cheek, on the nose

each other, strike—

For a moment, Juma is stunned. The only thing she can do is scream. It has the unintended effect of drawing everybody to this place of danger instead of staying away from it. Tana enters, the closest workers run towards the office. Timmy together with some friends are coming as well. From the mêlée, Chuulu's gun slides away towards Juma. She picks it up, but then doesn't know what to do with it. She sees her husband laying on the ground, bleeding.

"Got him." Ntaanga says as he turns Chuulu on his belly, the thug's right arm pulled up behind his back in a classic judo hold. Chuulu squeals like a pig, some workers rush in to assist Ntaanga, as Juma drops the gun , hurrying towards Banji.

"Get the doctor!"

Last year, when Juma decided to appoint a company doctor, not just for her family and workers, but for the whole community, even Mama Miombo questioned the 'validity of that. Now, she thanks the fates that she did, with the nearest hospital being over two hundred kilometers trek over horrible roads. The good doctor is there in minutes, treating Banji on the spot. He extracts the bullet, cleans the wound, and stitches it. During this, Banji bites away the pain on a piece of wood. No crying out as he holds Juma's hand, nearly squeezing her bones to a pulp.

After the last stitch, Juma can't keep quiet, anymore. "And, doctor?"

"He'll live, Mrs. Kalinda," the good doctor remains formal throughout, "your husband is strong as an ox."

"And as stubborn." Timmy says, breaking the tension. The house erupts with laughter.

∼

The next day, Banji sits on the couch in the communal room. Ntaanga sits next to him and pours two beers. Juma walks in with an unknown, official looking man, and is not amused. "What the hell are you doing here?" she says, "you should be in bed."

"I feel good." Banji smiles defiantly.

"You're drinking beer." Juma looks at Ntaanga. "You shouldn't be giving him beer."

"We have something to celebrate." Banji exchanges a knowing glance with Ntaanga.

"Something to celebrate? And since when do we have beer, here?" Juma hates not being in the loop.

"Since Ntaanga and I brewed it." Both men toast. "Barley was a main part in the latest symbiotic batch, so we figured we might as well use it."

"So that's what you were doing in your 'secret shed'." Juma can't believe it. "'Sometimes a man's gotta have a hobby that all his own'. What bullshit. And where did you get the hops?"

"No hops," Ntaanga says, "I devised a special mix of spices that does the trick just as well, possibly better."

Juma eyes him with newfound respect. "So, you can understand botany when it suits your needs. Oh well, I was busy letting our guest out."

"Indeed," Banji says, "why don't you introduce him?"

"I'm Tchianome, the new magistrate of this district." He says, shaking Banji's hand. "I've discussed yesterday's incident with Mrs. Kalinda. We are implementing a new anti-corruption policy, and we need to set a strong example. I can assure you that by the time Mr. K'nasa leaves jail, your daughters will be grandmothers." He bows out. "I'm sorry, more urgent business is calling."

As the new magistrate leaves, more people enter the communal room: the rest of Juma's family, the workers, and their families. Even the good doctor. All bring beer and other refreshments. Juma wonders what the hell is going on.

Ntaanga gets up, walks to Juma, and takes her right hand in both his hands: "Mrs. Kalinda, can I marry your daughter Tanabe?"

For the first time in years, Juma doesn't know what to say. Ntaanga misinterprets her silence and adds: "I'm more than just a soccer player. I will fight for your family, through fire and floods." Tears appear in Juma's eyes. "I will work—" His last words are smothered as Juma grabs him in a bear hug. "Of course you can, my boy. Welcome to the family."

Amidst the waterfall of cheers, Banji shouts, "I told you we had to brew *a whole lot*."

CODA: Juma is in her office, discussing the future with Mama Miombo.

"At times I feel unjustifiably lucky. Why did we, here in Kaomo of all places, get these bicqos? It makes no sense."

—*i don't know, but i do have a speculation: miss fiona used to be a researcher, and didn't want this to be introduced in the western world first*—

"The Messiah complex. I've seen it in other aid workers. Still, why here? Why not somewhere else?"

—*her boyfriend is a doctor for* médecins sans frontières. *he was one of the volunteers who set up our hospital*—

"So nothing but blind luck, or the whim of a red goddess."

—*she's no goddess, and you know it. i see increasing mentions of 'miraculous computers' surfacing somewhere in bangladesh. wasn't that the next project of her boyfriend after our hospital was finished?*—

"Still it sometimes makes me feel incapable, not deserving."

—*nonsense, you're a very smart and resourceful woman. for example: your ideas about ethically marked money. i see no good reasons why it shouldn't work, even if i need to work out the implementation details with my fellow 'quantum ghosts'*—

"Thank you. It'll be a happy day when we're rid of all that corruption."

—*you are very good at this. have you considered a career in politics?*—

"Are you crazy? I have my hands full keeping people happy here."

—*you've already greatly improved local lives and livelihoods. time to take it to the next level: surely you can do better than the current populist bunch*—

"I have a business to run here."

—*your daughter is doing most of the heavy lifting. when she marries ntaanga, you can hand her control of the company as a wedding gift. then you can concentrate on getting elected*—

"Aren't we running ahead of ourselves? We barely overcame those thugs."

—*they will soon become relics of the past. we've got more important things to do: change is accelerating, the future is coming faster every day. the sooner we butterfly it in the right direction, the better*—

"Zambia is a big country. . ."

—bordering eight others. It can be a shining example, uplifting the whole region—

"This is madness."

—no. madness is letting others, incompetent ones, run the madness. follow through, you've already catalyzed change here. take it to the next level—

"Become president? Mother this nation full of crooks, lazy bastards and idiots?"

—those are the minority and you know it. you can do better. we can do better. the country deserves better—

"A poor, provincial woman running for president? It'll never work."

—a woman who lifted her community out of poverty, with a family that's willing to die for the cause? the real challenge will be to take this country into the 21st century, and then lead by example—

"You make it sound so easy," Juma sighs, reminisces a second or two, "OK: I'll do it."

About the Author: *Ingrid Garcia helps selling local wines in a vintage wine shop in Cádiz and writes speculative fiction in her spare time. For years, she was unpublished. But to her utter surprise—after years of receiving nothing but rejections—she's sold stories to F&SF, and the Ride the Star Wind and Sword and Sonnet anthologies. She tweets as @ingridgarcia253 and is busy preparing a personal website and— dog forbid—even thinking about writing that inevitable novel*

Twitter: @ingridgarcia253

ICE IN D MINOR

ANTHEA SHARP

Rinna Sen paced backstage, tucking her mittened hands deep into the pockets of her parka. The sound of instruments squawking to life cut through the curtains screening the front of the theater: the sharp cry of a piccolo, the heavy thump of tympani, the whisper and saw of forty violins warming up. *Good luck with that.* Despite the huge heaters trained on the open-air proscenium, the North Pole in February was *cold.*

And about to get colder, provided she did her job.

The stage vibrated slightly, balanced in the center of a parabolic dish pointed straight up to the distant specks of stars in the frigid black sky. The stars floated impossibly far away—but they weren't the goal. No, her music just had to reach the thermo-acoustic engine hovering ten miles above the earth, centered over the pole.

Rinna breathed in, shards of cold stabbing her lungs. Her blood longed for summer in Mumbai; the spice-scented air that pressed heat into skin, into bone, so deeply a body wanted to collapse under the impossible weight and lie there, baking, under the blue sky.

That had been in her childhood. Now, nobody lived in the searing swath in the center of the globe. The heat between the tropics had become death to the human organism.

Not to mention that her home city was now under twenty feet of water. There was no going back, ever.

"Ms. Sen?" Her assistant, Dominic Larouse, hurried up, his nose constantly dripping from the chill. "There's a problem with the tubas."

Rinna sighed—a puff of breath, visible even in the dim air. "What, their lips are frozen to the mouthpieces? I told them to bring plastic ones."

"Valve issues, apparently."

Dominic dabbed his nose with his ever-present handkerchief. He'd been with her for two years, and she still couldn't break through his stiff formality. But little things, like insisting on being called by her first name, weren't worth the aggravation. Not here, not now.

"Get more heaters on them," she said, "and tell those damn violins we start in five minutes, whether they're warmed up or not."

"Five minutes. Yes ma'am."

Her job included being a hardass, but she knew how difficult it was to keep the instruments on pitch. The longer they waited, the worse it would get.

Goddess knew, they'd tried this the easy way by feeding remote concerts into the climate engine. Ever since the thing was built, the scientists had been trying to find the right frequencies to cool the atmosphere. They'd had the best luck with minor keys—something about the energy transfer—and at first had tried running synthesized pitches through. Then entire performances. Mozart's Requiem had come close, but not close enough.

It had to be a live performance; the immediate, present sounds of old wood, horsehair, brass and felt, the cascade of subtle human imperfection, blown and pulled and pounded from the organic bodies of the instruments.

There was no substitute for the interactions of sound waves, the immeasurable atomic collisions of an on-site concert fed directly into the engine. Once the thing got started, the techs had promised they could loop the sound. Which was good, because no way was Rinna giving up the rest of her life to stand at the North Pole, conducting a half-frozen orchestra. Not even to save the planet.

She'd spent years working on her composition, assembled the best symphony in the world, rehearsed them hard, then brought them here, to the Arctic. Acoustic instruments and sub-zero temperatures didn't get along, but damn it, she'd make this happen.

What if the composition is a failure? The voice of all her doubts ghosted through her thoughts, sounding suspiciously like her long-dead father.

She pinned it down and piled her answers on top, trying to smother it into silence.

The simulations had proven that certain frequencies played through the engine could super-cool the air over the pole. With luck, a trickle-down effect would begin and slowly blanket the world. The scientists had run the models over and over, with a thousand different types of sound. But it wasn't until the suits had hired Rinna—one of the best composers in the world (not that the world cared much about symphonies)—that the project had really started to gel.

"Ms. Sen." Dominic hurried up again, holding out the slim screen of her tablet. "Vid call for you."

"I told you, I don't want any interruptions."

"It's the President."

"Oh, very well." Fingers clumsy through her mittens, Rinna took the call.

President Nishimoto, Leader of the Ten Nations of the World, smiled at her through the clear, bright screen. Behind him, the desert that used to be Moscow was visible through the window of his office.

"Ms. Sen," he said. "The entire world wishes you the very best of luck in your performance."

He didn't need to say how much was at stake. They all knew.

"Thank you." She bowed, then handed the screen back to Dominic.

It was almost too late. Last winter, the pole ice had thinned so much it couldn't support the necessary installation. Doom criers had mourned the end, but a freak cold-snap in January had given them one final chance.

Now here they were—the orchestra, the techs, Rinna. And five thousand brave, stupid souls, camping on the precarious ice. Come to see the beginning of the world, or the end of it.

Out front, the oboe let out an undignified honk, then found the *A*. Rinna closed her eyes as the clear pitch rang out, quieting the rest of the musicians. The violins took it up, bows pulling, tweaking, until there was only one perfect, single note. It deepened as the lower strings joined in, cellos and basses rounding the *A* into a solid arc of octaves.

She could feel the dish magnifying the vibration, up through her feet. Sound was powerful. Music could change the world. She had to believe that.

As the strings quieted, Rinna stripped off her mittens, then lifted her conductor's baton from its velvet-lined case. The polished mahogany grip was comfortable in her hand, despite the chill. The stick itself was carved of mammoth ivory, dug out of the ground centuries ago.

She ran her fingers up and down the smooth white length. It was fitting, using a relic of an extinct animal in this attempt to keep humans from going out the same way.

She stepped onstage, squinting in the stage lights, as the wind instruments began to tune. First the high silver notes of the flutes, then the deep, mournful call of the French horns and low brass. Sounded like the tubas had gotten themselves sorted out.

From up here, the ice spread around stage—not pale and shimmering under the distant stars, but dark and clotted with onlookers. Originally, she'd imagined performing to the quiet, blank landscape—but that was before some brilliantly wacko entrepreneur had started selling tickets and chartering boats into the bitter reaches of the North.

The concert of a lifetime, plus the novelty of cold, drew spectators from all over the planet. No doubt the thrill of the chill had worn off, but the performance, the grand experiment, was still to come.

Truthfully, Rinna was glad for the crowd. Thermo-acoustics aside, she knew from long experience that the energy of playing in front of responsive listeners was *different*. Call it physics, call it woo-woo, but the audience was an integral part of the performance.

The project director had been reluctant at first, constructing only a small shelter and selling tickets at prices she didn't even want to contemplate. The enclosed seating held roughly forty people: heads of state, classical music aficionados, those with enough money and sense to try and stay warm. But when the boats started arriving, the tents going up, what could he do?

The spectators all wanted to be here, with the possible exception of Dominic hovering beside the podium.

The crowd caught sight of her striding across the stage, and applause rushed like a wind over the flat, frigid plain. She lifted her hand in acknowledgement. Overhead, the edge of the aurora flickered, a pale fringe of light.

Rinna stepped onto the podium and looked over her orchestra, illuminated by white spotlights and the ruddy glow of the heaters.

She'd bribed and bullied and called in every favor owed her, and this was the result. The best symphony orchestra the entire world could offer. Rehearsals had been the Tower of Babel: Hindi, Chinese, English, French—over a dozen nationalities stirred together in a cacophonous soup. But the moment they started playing, they had one perfect language in common.

Music.

The orchestra quieted. One hundred and five pairs of eyes fixed on her, and Rinna swallowed back the quick burst of nausea that always accompanied her onto the podium. The instant she lifted her baton and scribed the downbeat, it would dissipate. Until then, she'd fake feeling perfectly fine.

"Dominic?" she called, "are the techs ready?"

"Yes," he said.

"Blow your nose." No point in marring the opening with the sound of his sniffles.

Pasting a smile on her face, Rinna turned and bowed to the listeners spread out below the curve of the stage. They applauded, sparks of excitement igniting like distant firecrackers.

She pulled in a deep breath, winced as the air stabbed her lungs, and faced the orchestra—all her brave, dedicated musicians poised on the cusp of the most important performance of their lives.

The world premiere of *Ice*.

The air quieted. Above the orchestra a huge amplifier waited, a tympanic membrane ready to take the sound and feed it into the engine, transmute it to frigidity.

Rinna raised her arms, and the musicians lifted their instruments, their attention focused on her like iron on a magnet. She was their true north. The baton lay smoothly in her right hand—her talisman, her magic wand. If there ever was wizardry in the world, let it come to her now.

Heart beating fast, she let her blood set the tempo and flicked her stick upward. Then down, irrevocably down, into the first beat of *Ice*.

A millisecond of silence, and then the violins slid up into a melodic line colored with aching, while the horns laid down a base solid enough to carry the weight of the stars. The violas took the melody, letting the violins soar into descant. The hair on the back of her neck lifted at the eerie balance. Yes. Perfect. Now the cellos—too loud. She pushed the sound down slightly with her left hand, and the section followed, blending into the waves of music that washed up and up.

Rinna beckoned to the harp, and a glissando swirled out, a shimmering net cast across dark waters. Was it working? She didn't dare glance up.

High overhead, the thermo-acoustic engine waited, the enormous tubes and filters ready to take her music and make it corporeal—a thrumming machine built to restore the balance of the world.

It was crazy. It was their best chance.

Ice was not a long piece. It consisted of only one movement, designed along specific, overlapping frequencies. Despite its brevity, it had taken her three years to compose, working with the weather simulations and the best scientific minds in the world. Then testing on small engines, larger ones, until she stood here.

Now Rinna gestured and pulled, molded and begged, and the orchestra gave. Tears glazed her vision, froze on her lashes, but it didn't matter. She wasn't working from a score; the music lived in her body, more intimately known to her than her own child.

The clarinets sobbed the melody, grieving for what was already lost. The polar bears. The elephants. The drowned cities. The silenced birds.

Now the kettle-drums, a gradual thunder—raising the old magic, working up to the climax. The air throbbed and keened as Rinna rose onto her toes and lifted her hands higher. Higher. A divine plea.

Save us.

Arms raised high, Rinna held the symphony in her grasp, squeezed its heart for one more drop of musical blood. The musicians gave, faces taut with effort, shiny with sweat even in the chill. Bows flew, a faint sparkle of rosin dust flavoring the air. The trumpets blared, not missing the triad the way they had in rehearsal.

The last note. Hold. Hold. Hold.

She slashed her hand through the air and the sound stopped. *Ice* ended, yearning and dissonant, the final echo ringing into the frigid sky.

Above, nothing but silence.

Rinna lowered her arms and rocked back on her heels. From the corner of her eye, she saw the techs gesturing frantically, heads shaking, expressions grim.

The bitter taste of failure crept into her mouth, even as the crowd erupted into shouts and applause, a swell of sound washing up and over the open stage. She turned and gave them an empty bow, then gestured to the symphony—the musicians who had given and given. For nothing.

They stood, and one over-exuberant bassoonist let out a cheer and fist-pump. It sent the rest of the orchestra into relieved shouts, and she didn't have the heart to quiet them. They began stamping their feet, the stage vibrating, humming, low and resonant.

Rinna caught her breath, wild possibility flickering through her.

She gestured urgently to the basses. Three of them began to play, finding the note, expanding it. The rest of the section followed, quickly joined by the tubas—bless the tubas. Rinna opened her arms wide, and the string players hastily sat and took up their instruments again.

"D minor!" she cried. "Build it."

The violins nodded, shaping harmonies onto the note. The harpist pulled a trembling arpeggio from her strings, the wind instruments doubled, tripled the sound into an enormous chord buoyed up by breath and bone, tree and ingot, hope and desperation.

The stage pulsing beneath her, she turned to the crowd and waved her arms in wide arcs.

"Sing!" she yelled, though she knew they couldn't hear her.

The word hung in a plume before her. She could just make out the upturned faces below, pale circles in the endless Arctic night.

Slowly, the audience caught on. Sound spread like ripples from the stage, a vast buzzing that resolved into pitch. Rinna raised her arms, and the volume grew, rising up out of five thousand throats, a beautiful, ragged chorus winging into the air.

Beneath their feet, the last of the world's ice began to hum.

The techs looked up from their control room, eyes wide, as high overhead the huge engine spun and creaked.

Rinna tilted her face up, skin stiff as porcelain from the cold, and closed her eyes. She felt it, deep in her bones, a melody singing over and over into the sky. The thrum of sound transformed to super-cooled air, the long hard pull back from the precipice.

Something touched her face, light as feathers, insubstantial as dreams.

Quietly, perfectly, it began to snow.

NOTE: *Originally published in Timberland Writes Together in 2015.*

About the Author: Anthea Sharp is the author of the *USA Today* bestselling Feyland series, where a high-tech game opens a gateway to the treacherous Realm of Faerie. In addition to the fae fantasy/cyberpunk mashup of Feyland, her current novels are set in the shadowed enchantment of the Darkwood, where dark elves and fairytale elements abound. Anthea lives in sunny Southern California where she writes, hangs out in virtual worlds, plays the Irish fiddle, and spends time with her small-but-good family. Join her newsletter at http://www.subscribepage.com/AntheaSharp for a free story plus news of upcoming releases and reader perks.

Author Site: https://antheasharp.com/
Facebook: @AntheaSharpAuthor

AT THE MOVIES

D.M. RASCH

"Ticket line or snack line?"

This is our first time out with her kids. I want to get this right. Or at least right enough.

"I'm good with either," I answer with my best easy smile.

I can't help crossing my fingers, hoping she'll choose to take the excited, fidgety pre-teens inside with her to choose their treats. I can't imagine trying to entertain them by myself for the time it will take to wait for tickets.

The treat, to me, is coming to this retro *Films-on-Screen* where it's all about the experience as it used to be. Standing in one line to interact with an actual person behind a plalgae window who "serves" you (while you actually use your embedded ident) as you purchase "paper" tickets to one of twenty-one films showing. Then waiting in another to buy snacks that fool your receptors into tasting the flavors of sugar and salt people used to consume instead of nutrition. Finally, standing in a third queue to enter a darkened theater, with seats that rock (but do not swivel) packed close together, tech jammers everywhere to disrupt the crowd's multimedia implants. All of this in order to directly experience a flat, 2-D film run on a screen two stories high.

It was my idea to come here for our first "family date." Me dating someone with a family. What was I thinking? The kids will get bored with this break from being able to interact fully with their media. They're going to have to sit quietly, using an imagination I hope they've had the chance to develop instead of relying on tech implanted behind each small jaw-hinge that gives signals direct access to the reticular formation, providing multisensory stim for them, 24/7.

It's one of my favorite things to do. Completely unplug and watch a story play out before my eyes. Clunky visuals, cheesy sound effects, the music and voices in a flat-sounding stereo making their way into my brain without mediation. Via only my sense organs, imperfect and wonderful.

Yep, they're gonna hate it.

∼

LAINEY'S WORD FOR IT— *quaint*—as we waited together in the ticket line the first time I asked her to go with me. Our approach to the snack counter with its buffet splash of colored choices. She changed her mind so many times we ended up with enough for four. Adorable. In the movie, she watched, transfixed, "candy" soon forgotten, her hand in mine, sharing the unfamiliar, visceral experience with me.

I'm pretty sure I watched her face react to the movie more than the film that night. Eyes glued to the screen, wheels in her head visibly turning, taking it all in. As we left, she tucked herself inside my arm without a word until the Ani-moto met us outside. She reached to turn on the privacy settings before reaching for me, as the car wound its oblivious way through the city traffic.

An hour later, we were idling in front of her address, slipping awkwardly back into clothing. Trying to accomplish dressing without taking out something vital with an elbow or knee in the ultra-compact vehicle. It seemed to take a lot more effort than getting out of it all had been.

Lainey, especially, needed to be presentable for the child-minder (the kids were, face it, probably still up). I began to concentrate on helping her dress instead of getting in her way, almost causing me to have to renew the transport. And, her, the sitter.

Lainey wondered aloud—brow furrowed, brushing at her hair—about the difference between plugging in completely and relying only on basic senses.

"Instead of leaving you completely satisfied, it's as if it leaves you—well, *wanting*. Obviously." She laughed at herself then looked at me more seriously for a long moment, running fingers through my shaggy, anonymous hair. Giving up on its mess with a tug. "You are...unexpected, Reilly."

Her reluctant kiss goodnight left me wondering that night whether *unexpected* was good...or goodbye.

∼

"I'll take them inside to choose. If you think *I'm* indecisive...."

She smiles, as if she had plugged into my tech and listened to my rewind.

Leaning in to kiss me on the cheek and squeezing my arm, she whispers into my ear, "Thanks for suggesting this, Reilly. It's perfect, really."

My shoulders rest lower now as she lets go. I watch them pass easily through security into the lobby.

I wish I shared her optimism. Let's just say I'm leaning toward hopeful. Their dad's been out of the picture long enough for me to trust I might not take *all* the heat for causing their parents' breakup by virtue of dating their mom. Which of course, would make anything I suggest automatically suspect.

When she approached the idea of doing something together with the kids after we'd been dating for about a month—a "family date"—we didn't really talk about what she had and hadn't told them about me. Was it confusing for kids their age? Or did they just take it for granted that their mom would be making her dating choices without consulting them first? I have so many questions.

Guess we'll soon see, I think, approaching the attendant's window for the tickets. The young fem in a vintage velveteen suit (including a bowtie at her collar) watches me scan the ident chip buried in my wrist. I take the four tickets she hands me with **ADMIT ONE** stamped in bold letters on each, along with the name of the film we're seeing—**Galaxy Force**—

scrawled in a cursive handwriting font that I translate like a foreign language.

A divot of concern appears briefly between her brows as she stares at her monitor. Then she pushes the button to send the receipt to my account and turns to me, smile in place.

Leaning close to the speaker in the plalgae-glass so that only I can hear, she says, "Mx., I've registered your ident with Security, so they don't make a fuss about your tech or weapon as you go inside."

I nod my thanks to her for the expected notification, wishing for the millionth time that I could leave my ident (and weapon) at home on occasions like this.

The two guards at the gate each give me a chin up nod as they go through the motions of scanning me for illegals before waving me through. I know, without having met either before, that each (unlike me) is itching for action. Hoping to find contraband tonight. Glad to wear his uniform and weapon outside for the world to see.

That is the difference really, between working security and plainclothes citizen protection. Alerting on potential problems and intervening before things escalate is my job. People recognizing me in public only makes that job harder. The opportunity to prevent incidents and injury is what drew me to citizen protection in the first place. Instead of having to watch people endure the violence we had to accept when I was around the age of Lainey's boys—even, and especially, *from* those on patrol. I could often step in and do something about it before shit, as they say, got real. It makes being off-duty, though—not to mention dating—a challenge.

That's what's so amazing to me about Lainey. And likely why I haven't found an excuse to duck out of this *thing*—whatever it is—that we're doing, back into my lone anonymity. She really *saw* me from the first time she saw me. If that makes sense.

I work hard at fading into the background, on *and* off-duty. Still, that first contact—even as something about her confident voice and the curious tilt of her head caught my attention that day as I was slipping through a government building. I saw her notice me as if I were backlit in a dark alley. All nondescript, slouch-shouldered, five feet ten inches of my thickish (if I'm honest), fit frame exposed for her inspection.

But in a welcome way, to my surprise. Before I could talk myself out of it, I stood up straight and walked over to introduce myself.

∽

A MONTH AND A HALF LATER, we're standing back and letting her kids (brothers, eleven and eight) choose our seats in the slowly filling theater.

The younger, Owen, wants to sit in the first row, of course. I feel my neck cringe at the thought. Before I can intervene with a suggestion, Cadel vetoes the idea with a rough sort of affection.

"Jerk, you won't even be able to see the whole screen from that close."

We end up with Cadel's choice—center seats, center row, just behind an aisle that gives us a railing to prop our feet up on and no heads to see over. He's thought this through.

Lainey's going to sit the boys between the two of us, not wanting either to end up in a seat next to a stranger. Cadel is having none of that, either. At "almost twelve," he feels entitled to be the other bookend to our group, his little brother beside him. When his mom gives in (with the caveat that she sits in the middle next to Owen), I begin to wonder how extensive Cadel's veto power is. What will happen if he decides to pull the lever on me.

He seems happy enough, for now, having won the battle. Shoots me a smirk and a thumbs-up, as if we might be in on something together. I'll play along—for now. I raise a thumb in return from the other side of his mom, who carefully pretends not to see my collusion.

She's busy explaining to Owen how his implant will go "fuzzy." That it will be even more important to pay attention to what is happening on the screen. He looks a little confused. But up for something new and cool. I can tell he really trusts her.

I'm so involved with them—so glad things seem to be going smoothly, so far—I almost forget to do my usual, casual sweep of the theater. To assess any potential problems. So distracted by their apparent happiness with how this date is going that I did, in fact, forget what a bad idea it is to sit in the center of a row. Not on the end, as is my habit, for easy access to the aisle. And an exit.

So, when the wiry guy with a bulky coat and stretchy hat, pulled low to cover his eyes, flashes by our feet using the aisle in front of our railing, I'm instantly alert. Feeling exposed. *Not* in a welcome way. The tech in my head pings a backup to my internal alarm.

Then the lights begin to dim for the start of the movie. I'm tech blind as the jammers activate to bring us into the two-dimensional experience. The timing of his entrance cannot be an accident.

∼

"WHAT'S WRONG?" Lainey whispers in my ear.

My death grip on her hand. As if that will keep her and the boys safe from whatever this threat turns out to be. More unfamiliar territory. I feel responsible in a *personal* sense—not just professional—for public safety. Takes my focus, at this inopportune moment, to remind me why it sometimes feels easier to not date in the first place. Doing what I do.

I force my hand to loosen its hold. Try to calculate quickly what to say that will tell her what she needs to know. Without unnecessarily freaking her out. Decide on cautious honesty. For her ears only. Based on what she knows already about me. And what I know about her.

"I'm not *sure* that anything *is* wrong, yet. I noticed something suspicious just before the jammer dampened my tech to confirm whether it's something to worry about. Or not."

I omit the part about it being an alarm. There isn't much doubt. Not really.

I know suggesting we leave—*right now!*—won't exactly make me popular with the boys. Especially when I can't be specific about why. But every nerve in me is shouting MOVE until I can hardly stay in my seat. I *know* getting out's the right thing to do.

Glancing at Lainey's face in the dim light, I see her eyes go a bit wide.

I let a ghost of a reassuring smile cross my face before suggesting in my best calm-but-firm, lowered voice, "I think we should go…just to be on the safe side. If it's nothing, we can always eat nearby and catch the next showing."

She holds my eyes for a moment. I can see her doing the same calculations I had. What excuse should she give to the boys that would move, but not frighten them?

When she leans over to them, I hear her whisper, "Sorry guys, I'm suddenly feeling really sick. You know, like 'gonna-hurl-sick.' Let's go before the movie starts. We'll come back to see it. I promise."

The shorthand has the desired effect on Owen. He immediately picks up his treats and looks ready to get going before his mom starts to "hurl." It looks like Cadel is going to put up some resistance, though. I don't know why I'm surprised.

"Mom, can't we just hang with Reilly while you go to the fresher?" He sends a smile meant to charm in my direction.

"While I appreciate your overwhelming concern...." she switches to more "adult-to-adult" tactics with Cadel. "I don't think a trip to the fresher is going to solve this."

Her tone is no-nonsense now. How I imagine she sounds in court.

Still, he persists.

"Well, you could try first, couldn't you? At least we could see what it's like. And you'll probably be okay. You could message us if we need to leave."

Negotiation? No way. We need to go. Now.

"Hey, Cadel, tell you what. Since we can't get a message in here now with the jammers on, let's go with your mom. If she ends up being okay after a visit to the fresher, we'll just get something real to eat and come back for the next showing...totally past lights-out for both of you."

I give him my own winning smile. *And* I start to get up without waiting for an answer. Seconds too late.

༄

"STAY IN YOUR SEATS...UNLESS YOU WANT TO BE THE FIRST TO DIE."

The man in the bulky coat is now standing in front of the screen for all to see.

A quick glance at Lainey's arm reaching across Owen's chest to grip Cadel's arm, effectively restraining the younger boy, as if we're about to crash. I sit back down, put a hand on her knee. Just a connection, letting her know someone's got her, too.

Cadel's eyes are on me now, his whiny resistance now a scowl of blame.

Why hadn't I just told him there was something real going on, it seems to say? He's a quick one. Should have given him more credit.

I lift my chin in a nod, acknowledging my mistake. Hope he gets the message. I'll trust him with the truth from now on. Assuming I get the chance. Despite his age, he's probably been given the "you're the man of the house now" speech by his father at some point, before he left them. In his eyes, I guess I'm in his way.

I wrench my full attention back to the possibilities already running in the background in my CP brain. The jumpy man, front and center, isn't brandishing any obvious weapons. A bomb, then? A bio-device? I wonder what he's managed to slip through security out front. How he's done it.

I have all of 10 seconds to wonder about the 'what' as he reaches beneath his coat and my head explodes.

∼

Well, not literally, but it sure feels like it.

The frequency device he's using slides a pulse that's a shiv beneath my skull to skewer my tech implant. Gives it a savage twist.

When the pain recedes enough to sit up and see again, I peek over, blinking. Relief comes in a package that looks like, whatever the pulse was, it's affected neither Lainey nor the boys. Or, it seems, anyone else in the crowd, when my eyes are clear enough to give a quick sweep. When they land back on her, Lainey's eyes are full of questions. Concern.

She doesn't have to wait long for answers. But not from me.

"Seems we have a Citizen Protector in the crowd tonight. With quite a headache by now, I imagine."

The terrorist smiles, looking straight at me. My eyes have adjusted to the dim light. His thin lips visibly twitch.

"That's just one of the frequencies I have on this gadget. If anyone wants to try to be a hero, I'll demonstrate the other. On full volume this time. I promise you; they'll be cleaning this place up for the next week if anyone tries to leave…Or touch me."

Lainey's hand grips mine now. Her other arm, I'm sure, is still across Owen, touching both boys. Is it support? Fear? Get us the hell out of here?

I don't know. It's like an anchor, though, in the confusion mess my brain, post-jolt. I can't afford to take my narrowed eyes off the terrorist's to look at her. I squeeze hers back to acknowledge whatever it is she's trying to say.

"Well, Citizen Protector, I'll need you to come forward and hand over your weapon. Nice and easy. Wouldn't want your adorable little family to end up with jelly for brains because you just *had* to try something, would you?"

His twitchy smile is really starting to annoy me now. Anger-fueled adrenaline clears some of the fog from my head. Unfortunately, it makes room for unaccustomed fear to creep in, as well. Not for myself. But for this unlucky family who is only here because of me.

Me and my poor judgement.

I make a quick, difficult decision, knowing Lainey will likely never forgive me for it.

No matter how things turn out.

～

I GET TO MY FEET. Make no sudden moves, so the twitchy terrorist will know that I take him and his threats seriously.

I'm shuffling to my left, passing in front of "my adorable little family" on the way to the aisle. As I pass Lainey—forcing myself to turn my back on the threat—I bend to plant a quick kiss her on the cheek and whisper into her ear, "Please, trust me."

I meet her eyes while I move on. Try to smile as if everything will be just fine.

Knowing that the boys probably won't put up with the same from someone so new to them, I reach out to touch my fist to Owen's little one as I keep sidestepping past knees toward the aisle. He looks wide-eyed and stiff, his mother's arm still across his chest. But he bends his elbow to make the contact.

I offer the same to Cadel, who scowls and, at first, stubbornly refuses. When I lift my eyebrows, continuing to hold my fist out, he gets curious and raises his. At the last moment, I turn it into a handshake, closing his hand around what I've been palming.

I bend to hug him, as if he's pulled *me* close. Whisper, "Don't let your mom see. Wait until you see me fall...*then* press the button."

I feel him nod into my shoulder before I let go, sliding to the end of the aisle before Twitchy can decide I'm not moving fast enough.

I walk down the side-aisle toward the front, my eyes now on the threat so his attention will stay on me.

"How touching," he says. "It's like you don't think you'll see them again. Your weapon. On the floor," he adds as I approach him.

"No worries," I tell him.

Still holding his eyes, I reach carefully behind my back to take my multiweapon from its holster with two fingers. Toss it at his feet. It's coded to my palm and useless to him, anyway. Not that he needs anything more than his device.

Had he not known (guessed? found?) the frequency to hack my tech, he would have never known who I was. That I must be carrying. The camo-nanofabric of the holster blends the weapon seamlessly into my clothing and skin for public anonymity.

"I don't want anyone to get hurt. Including you. That's why it's important I know what you want. What will get us all out of here safely? I'd be glad to negotiate for you with the Protectors so that we can get you *exactly* what you want. *Without* anyone getting hurt." I repeat it, hoping he can hear over his adrenaline.

"How noble of you, Protector. What makes you think that I want anything? Or that I care about hurting anyone, for that matter? No one, sure as hell, has given a crap about hurting me."

Crap, all right. He's done. He just wants to make sure people hurt as much as he does, before he leaves.

"But not these people, surely."

I try to sound as if it is as obvious to him as it is to me.

"I mean, I'm impressed that you got your device past security. But, really, let's be honest. You could've sat in a seat and activated it. *If* you only wanted to hurt random people. Isn't there something you want in trade for the safety of these innocent people? Like a message to whoever hurt you so much? An apology?"

Now that I'm close to him, I can see he's much older than I thought.

Still fit beneath that bulky coat. There's something vaguely familiar about his face.

"Someone from your past is it?" I ask, fishing. I need to keep him talking. They *always* want to talk.

"Oh, don't worry, they'll get the message, loud and clear. When I blow out everyone's tech in here but yours. You'll live to tell them *all* about it."

∾

Fuck, fuck, fuck reverbs in my aching head.

I'd been operating on the assumption that Twitchy's obvious choice would be to take me out of commission first. Me, the Protector. The obvious threat. *Then* he would switch the other frequency to blast the rest of the crowd's tech.

I'd hoped to give Cadel the split second between the two to use the device I'd passed to him. A jammer much stronger than the ones in the theater. One (I hoped) strong enough to dampen everyone's tech in the crowd enough that Twitchy's super-frequency emitter couldn't reach inside their heads to implode their implants.

I was counting on Cadel's pre-pubescent pride to make him do it. While his mother *likely* would have done it if I asked, she also may have hesitated. Thinking about the risk to the boys. Of course. There wasn't time for that delay.

As a plainclothes CP, I always had the thumb-sized device tucked into a pocket. That, my weapon, and some flexible plalgae restraints were the only equipment I carried. I never knew when I would find myself on my own, outnumbered, trying to keep a specific someone from getting hurt by jamming the tech of those around me fast and safely to even the odds.

Twitchy's first "shot" at me had stopped me from activating it before he'd switched over to the civilian frequency. Then it became too risky, for too many, to try it. Except as a last resort.

Time's running out. Even if I can keep him talking. One of the "ushers" is bound to walk through for a routine check. Notice no one's started the movie.

The movie hasn't started. How had I missed that?

"Listen, I'm worried someone will come to check on the film and we won't get to finish our conversation. I won't find out what you're wanting someone to know. And who to tell. They're sure to notice soon the movie hasn't started."

Twitchy laughs at how obviously dull I am.

"Give me a break. I've made sure we're undisturbed for a few minutes. Let's just say that they don't pay these kids playacting in their monkey suits very well. No one will even know what's happened until you get free to go tell them."

He looks up and to the right to check his own internal display.

"Time's almost up. Why don't you break out that silly string in your pocket." It wasn't a question. "Make sure you don't try anything stupid and stay put for a while?"

"Sure, sure. I can do that," I say in my calmest tone.

I reach into a pocket for the slim, tough restraints, hoping he doesn't know about the jammer, as well.

"Why don't you tell me what it is you want the world to know while I fasten these…um, I don't know your name. I'm Reilly," I add, inviting a trade.

If he gives me his name, I'll know I still have a bit of control in this situation.

"Just make sure they're nice and tight around both your hands and ankles."

He scans the crowd as he continues speaking, including them now. They're getting restless.

"Don't even *think* about moving!"

He waves the device in the general direction of a couple of young guys, half out of their seats near the exit, trying to be slick. They sit back down, red-faced.

"I was once a CP, too, you know. My holo's still up on the 'distinguished service' wall at headquarters. What a fucking crock."

He spits on the floor.

"Didn't you wonder how I got the frequency to tune this device? You look almost old enough to remember me. I still got connections. Was on the job before tech started *replacing* the job. One day they just decided not to upgrade my implant and that was it. My other skills, my gut…it all meant nothing. Couldn't keep up."

I see beads of sweat now on his forehead. He's talking. But he's escalating. Not good.

"Time to move along. 'No need to be so physical with suspects.' 'No need to use your own judgement when it comes to use of force. The tech will decide…if you let it.' Well, I wouldn't. So, they downgraded mine to a civilian-grade implant and pushed me out. They don't tell you how much you're going to miss the network access. The privileges."

He reaches out to tug at the restraints that have molded themselves to my wrists and ankles to be secure without injury.

"And now, look at all these people here. *All* of you voluntarily letting your tech be muted, cutting yourselves off. For a taste of what? Yesteryear? Let me tell you, *yesteryear* sucked."

Now he's spitting all his words.

"And you! You most of all. You, with your fancy new tech, wearing sloppy street clothes like a uniform means nothing. Knowing what you're giving up when you step in here. It's an insult. I've been coming all week, waiting for a CP to show up in the audience. Just so I could watch you lose everything, too."

My gut drops. I feel sick with the knowledge he's got nothing left to lose. He's planning to take himself out with everyone else, using the civilian frequency.

Time for the last resort.

∽

I feel desperate when I need to feel calm and focused. It's the thought that I'll do anything necessary to get Lainey and her boys out safely. I need to signal Cadel it's time to press the button.

Now.

My mind scrambles for a way to make it crystal clear to the boy who thinks he's a man. I turn to look at "my family." That will please Twitchy no end. Him watching me watch them as he liquefies their brains.

Has Cadel been listening? Does he understand I'm not the target and won't be falling to give him the cue he's been waiting for?

Keep it simple. Make brief eye contact across the rows. Find Lainey's, trying say "trust me" again with a steady gaze. Give Owen a quick wink, sure he doesn't really understand what's happening. When I meet Cadel's eyes, I put on my most professional face.

As if to a colleague, I give him a chin-up nod.

~

HE DOES IT. Bless him. Cadel gets the message loud and clear. Presses the button. Even as his mother reaches for his hand to stop him. And, it works. Sort of.

What it actually does is provide interference with the signal. Strong enough no one in the crowd does more than wince before I can lunge, feet bound, to land with my arms over Twitchy's head. Use the "silly string" to choke him out.

I don't enjoy having to get physical with any suspect. But, it's not like I haven't trained for it. He's taller and heavier, but not by much. He's on a desperate mission, giving him purpose and adrenaline. And, now, so am I.

He drops the device, reaching instinctively for the string at his throat. He's trying hard to buck me off with the last of his breath. We fall in a tangle of string and limbs. Rolling over and over. I'm on top. Then he is. I nearly lose my hold when he kicks my shin and bites my hand in the same moment. I don't *want* to kill him. Even if that's what he was about to do to everyone in here.

I yell for someone to pick up the emitter. Not that I have much breath left, either. I don't want him to get it back if I lose hold of him. Everyone's frozen, though. Not really clear on what's happening, but still afraid to move.

Then Lainey's there, picking up the device and backing the hell away. She looks angry. Keyed up.

I mouth "thank you" to her, around his head. Concentrate on Twitchy, still struggling. Try to hang on without choking him to death.

"Boys, stay where you are."

I know, once it hits people the danger they were in, the crowd will stampede for the door. It's what crowds do. The boys will be safe in the center of their row. I'm running out of breath again. But I try adding, "It's safe for now...everybody...."

Lainey puts her justice litigator voice on and takes over.

"I've got the device." She holds it high for everyone to see. "I need you," she says, pointing to a woman in a seat near the door, "to go get security. Then everyone else can leave." When she sees people trying to climb over each other to get out, she adds, "No need to panic, I've got the device."

They don't listen. They never do. She keeps eye contact with the boys, pinning them in their seats. Safe-ish, as the people around them head for either aisle, or simply jump the rails.

It looks like the woman Lainey sent made it to security in record time. They're pushing their way through the crowd that is trying to shove its way out. The lights go up and they see me still rolling around with Twitchy on the "stage." Lainey standing off to the side with something in her hand.

They each draw weapons. Start yelling at her to drop it. She wisely puts it on the floor—very carefully—while I grab another breath to shout my ident. Order them not to touch it with the one word I know will get through: *techbomb*.

My ability to blend in doesn't always serve me in situations like this. I'm a bit tall for a bio-female. I can usually pass genderless with no outstanding features through a crowd. It's my thing. Why I'm good at what I do.

But one of the guards I gave the nod passing through security recognizes me. Tells the guards trying to restrain Lainey to let her go. They give the device a wide berth to come over and cut my bindings. Take Twitchy off my hands.

Lainey pushes her way through them, to me. Wraps her arms around me, squeezing tight. Then she kisses me, tears of relief welling up in her eyes.

Right before she backs up just far enough to slap my face. Hard. On second thought, tears of anger.

I'm not really surprised, though. My head is really ringing now, making me feel confused and disoriented.

As she so succinctly puts it through tightly clenched teeth, "You. Used. My. Child."

I did. She's perfectly right. Not to mention totally justified in doing much more than slapping me. I will not argue with her or try to persuade. It was wrong.

And It was the best choice out of too many worse choices at the time. But she won't – she can't – see it. At least not right now. Maybe never.

I probably won't ever forgive myself for doing it. I think I understand just a little more about what it means to be a mother. Maybe it's good I didn't before tonight.

She extricates herself from the circle of surrounding guards to get to the boys. Who are surprisingly still in their seats, gripping the armrests. When she gets close, they slide under the rail into the aisle and surround her with a four-armed hug. As she smothers them against her, I see her murmur something into Cadel's ear.

He smiles the biggest smile back at her. Like she's given him something he's always wanted. Times two. He asks her something. I see her shake her head. No. He looks ready to argue. Changes his mind. Gives me a wave from where he is.

That's it then. Cadel wants to come over. His mother's not having it. I would like to tell him how proud I am of him, too. Not my privilege. Instead, I give him the biggest smile I can manage (with my throbbing head and jaw). And a double thumbs-up. He's happy again. Like he's all filled up.

I watch them file out, little brother bouncing, asking the big brother question after question. I watch them 'til they're gone before I allow myself to collapse, from sitting to lying. Finally giving in.

∽

"Mom, Reilly's waking up. They're waking up!"

Wow, that's loud, I think. Try to place who it is. Where I am. In that order.

The lenses in my eyes finally focus. I see I'm in an unfamiliar bedroom with an unfortunate amount of light streaming through the window. The answer to question number one bounces right up onto the bed: Owen's toothy smile just a *little* too close.

I smile back, anyway. Or try to. Until my jaw explodes in pain. Surely, the well-aimed, well-deserved slap I recall hasn't done all that? My hand reaches to explore my face with care.

"They had to crack your jaw to replace some of the tech that got fried by the frequency-pulse you took. Totally saved me from charging myself with assault."

Lainey smiles from the doorway. I swear she seems just a little repentant. Then again, maybe it's just the surgery drugs.

"They said you could go home for the recovery period, but only with someone to watch you. We happen to have a professional watcher here." She turns her smile on Owen, who nods vigorously.

"So, I'm at...your home?" I try. It comes out more like, "Zo, I'n at...yer hone?"

Now she just bursts out laughing. I'm pretty sure that's not the kind thing to do, under the circumstances. People have different ways of showing sympathy, I guess. She's probably still pissed at me, after all. I get it.

"Yes, you're at our hone," she says, trying hard not to laugh, I notice. "I was made to understand, by a certain member of this household, that it was the right thing to do. That if I cared about you – and I do, Reilly, even if I am mad as hell – I would save you from a traumatic recovery with those terrifying nurses at the med center. Do what needs to be done in this difficult situation. Follow someone else's rather recent example. That about right, Cadel?"

She turns out into the hall to put her arm around his shoulders and pull him into the room.

For the first time in the short time I've known him, Cadel looks a little shy – a bit unsure of himself. I start to wonder how much trouble he's been in for being my accomplice at the movies.

Since I can't really smile, I give him a thumbs-up to let him know I'm cool with everything. If he is. And I guess he is, by the smile that cracks his face open. Sure puts mine to shame.

He clears his throat, all business. Motions to his little brother. "C'mon, Owen. Let's go feed the dog."

A dog, too? I think. Must not be a robot if it eats. Did the tech fry my brain? I must be in a coma, or something. Dreaming things too good to be true. At least for me.

Then Owen jumps off the bed with characteristic bounce, rattling everything in my head.

Nope. Definitely not dreaming. Just a kinder version of my reality.

While it lasts, a soft voice chimes in my aching head, as Lainey walks over to take his place. Sits against me on the bed.

I hold her hand. Grateful.

And so sorry I'm going to have to hurt her—and those sweet boys—to make sure this never, ever happens to them again.

About the Author: *D.M. Rasch writes feminist speculative fiction for LGBTQ+ young adults and adults, exploring where the social and political meet the personal. Her characters are often found doing their best in worlds that challenge them to become their best selves. Queer representation and reaching out to LGBTQ+ youth drive her writing, informed by her MFA in Creative Writing from Regis University and two bossy sister kittens who like to edit. She identifies as a genderqueer lesbian, currently writing and working (remotely) in the Denver, CO area as a creative mentor, coach, and editor in her business, Itinerant Creative Content & Coaching LLC.*

Author site: https://www.dmrasch-author.com
Business site: https://morethanabookcoach.com
Amazon: https://www.amazon.com/author/dmrasch
Linkedin: https://www.linkedin.com/in/deanna-m-rasch/
Facebook: @deannamrasch

WHO SHALL REAP THE GRAIN OF HEAVEN?

J.G. FOLLANSBEE

Father James Bohm banked the SkyTrac T-44 crop duster over the abbey's airstrip, feeling the mild tug of G-force on his broad shoulders and back. He never got tired of that sensation, almost like a hug from the heavens. The onboard AI smoothed out his nudges on the stick and the bumps through the thermals over the cornfields, making his piloting as smooth as silk. Like the Holy Father, though, it could override James if he erred too much, risking the plane or himself. James laughed at the image, though the sarcasm was too close to the truth.

James glanced to his left and behind the wing, glimpsing the dozen specially modified drones on the airfield below him. They were electric powered, like his own craft. He'd completed another job for the local corn and soybean farmers, spraying on batches of eco-friendly insecticides. The drones would soon take off on their own daily mission as part of the Seeds of Heaven project, if the Holy Father didn't ground them first.

As James hooked the last of the tie-downs on his plane, patting the fuselage as if it were a beloved pet, a young, tonsured monk ran up to him. Dirt and oil stained the aircraft mechanic's fingernails.

"Father, he's here. Archbishop Mulvaney."

James's sense of well-being and accomplishment dissipated. Like a fulfilled prophecy, a day he'd feared had come.

"He's brought a letter." Elis sought reassurance from his abbot. "Is the project canceled?"

"Don't worry. It'll be all right." He hid his disquiet from Elis. In fact, James wanted to climb back into the crop duster and take off. In the broad Midwestern sky, all problems on the ground shrank to nothing.

The men mounted their power-assist bicycles and pedaled down the airstrip's main access road. A white, twin-engine passenger aircraft, also electric, waited near the drones. It had no markings, save for the registration number and the name *Little Flower* on the forward part of the fuselage. James would pilot the craft later in the afternoon.

Elis glanced over his shoulder, encouraging the head of the Abbey of St. Isidore to keep up. James took special care with Elis, because he was 19, and expected the results James could not always deliver. He might have to disappoint him.

Despite his fit body, James felt his 60s creeping up. The smell of fresh-baked bread cheered him, but when the chapel's bell tower rose behind a screen of century-old trees, the knot in his stomach tightened. As a reminder of the ancient privileges of hierarchy, the archbishop had parked his black car in the abbot's reserved spot.

James found Mulvaney in his office. After breathing cabin air infused with machine oil, James welcomed the whiff of incense. "Your Excellency, I'm sorry I wasn't here to greet you."

Mulvaney's blue eyes betrayed his Irish heritage. "Any chance at a cup of tea?"

Elis took the hint.

"A good man, Elis." Mulvaney's eyes twinkled. "Youngest son of our state's junior senator. Potential for great influence in Washington."

Elis also had the potential of taking over as abbot, if James could follow through on his promise to keep the Seeds of Heaven project alive.

Mulvaney took in James's short-sleeved jump suit. "Business must be good."

Business was terrible, and Mulvaney knew it. The on-going drought hurt the farmers more than ever. "A few of our customers are still drawing water from their wells or the river. They're the only ones who can buy our services."

"They're lucky to have you."

"Fortunately, we can employ some of the others in Seeds of Heaven."

The archbishop turned away at the project's mention. The prelate looked at his hands, nervous.

"I'm afraid I have some news, James. You won't like it." Mulvaney reached into his jacket, removed an envelope, and handed it to James. His Holiness's seal in gold ink decorated the embossed paper.

James already knew what the letter said: *Stop the project.* Perhaps the outcome was preordained, and he had failed to recognize the fact. Staring at the paper, James imagined that many of his 23 abbey brethren would applaud the order. When the contract with Victor Baran first came to him three years ago, he asked his community's thoughts. They accepted it via an advisory vote, but only just. James also consulted the nearby convent of the Sisters of the Holy Cup, which also supported him. He signed the contract with Baran's foundation, believing it was the right thing. The Vatican thought differently.

"Rome is done with scandal, James. It's been a generation since the sex scandals, but we've never recovered. Catholicism is comatose in Europe, and its dying here in America. Even the Latin countries are falling away."

James's Mexican grandmother would disagree, if she were alive. Her fervor for her faith infected her grandson. He wouldn't be at the abbey if it weren't for her. "The Church is stronger than you think, Charlie."

"I admire your optimism, even if it's naive. But Rome calls the shots. It can't afford the damage from dirty money."

"Even if it could save the planet God created and put in our care?"

Mulvaney's face twisted in dismay. "You're making this harder than it needs to be. You've made it hard from the beginning."

A knock broke the tension. Elis carried a tray with a teapot, two cups, and two tea cakes. An elderly man with powerful hands slipped in behind Elis.

"I thought you might enjoy a snack, Your Excellency," the elder monk said.

"So kind of you." Mulvaney and Oscar's eyes locked for a second, as if sharing a confidential message. Oscar broke the gaze.

James suppressed his irritation. He signaled Elis and Oscar to leave and close the door.

"I know Brother Oscar well." Mulvaney made a motion with his hand resembling a quacking duck. "He has a running mouth, especially with his displeasure at how you run this place."

Oscar vexed James like a foot fungus. "He led the opposition to the Baran contract, but it was my decision to move forward." James tasted the cake, realizing he hadn't eaten anything since the early morning. "We were in financial trouble, and Baran offered money and two dozen aircraft, as long as we kept his name secret."

"People are saying that the money was a bribe to keep your mouth closed."

It was true their patron wanted privacy. His lawyer brought the offer. Victor Baran, chairman of the Baran Group, pledged a $1.5 billion endowment and equipment for experimental marine cloud brightening, cirrus cloud thinning, and similar technologies aimed at mitigating climate change.

In addition, a priest would say a daily Mass asking God to forgive Baran for his environmental crimes against the earth.

"I know what Baran is and what he's done. I was thinking of the greater good."

Mulvaney seemed not to hear James's interpretation. "The fact that Baran wants the Mass said at 30,000 feet adds insult to injury. He's made everyone look like fools."

When he first heard the request, James thought it grandiose, and he balked. The media would have a field day. Rome wouldn't like it, but James's community of monks was an independent entity, and answerable to no one except the pope. James could steer through the turbulence, if it meant financial stability and a chance to do his part to fix the climate that Baran and his ilk had wrecked. He eventually agreed to the daily Mass.

"What's more, no one even knows if cloud-seeding works. It all smells like a scam."

"You sound like Oscar."

"Have you ever spoken to Baran directly?"

James hadn't.

"If he asked, would you grant him absolution?"

James didn't know.

"Don't. Baran ought to be consigned to the Devil, along with all the other profiteers who've poured enough carbon into the air to cook us in the fires of Hell."

"Charlie, you don't mean that."

Mulvaney took a breath. "That's what I'm hearing from my membership. The world is finally clued in to what's happening, and people want justice. Seeds of Heaven looks like a payoff and a PR stunt."

A silence fell between the two men. Mulvaney was an adviser, an advocate, and a friend. In all things except Seeds of Heaven, he had supported James. He co-signed the loan to purchase the SkyTrac when James came up with the idea for a crop-dusting business. He spoke from the pulpit and in front of Rotary clubs to raise cash for a new engine. But as Mulvaney met his eye, the abbot felt betrayed.

James once feared another betrayal. When Victor Baran first approached James, the abbot did not sign the contract immediately. Suspecting a con, James asked for further evidence of the industrialist's sincerity.

Two weeks later, the credit union that held the loan on the SkyTrac, they said Baran had paid off the six-figure balance. Eighty percent of the abbey's financial liabilities vanished overnight.

Baran had a talent for convincing skeptics.

"It was too good to be true from the start, James." Mulvaney leaned forward, intense. "Think of what Baran has done. His tar-sands mining has released millions of tons of methane into the air. He bribed a governor to build an oil pipeline across a wildlife refuge. His hired guns in Congress use cash and threats to suppress emissions laws."

"I get that he's not a choir boy."

"Stop Seeds of Heaven, James. Cut Baran off. He isn't worth it. If you don't, you'll suffer the consequences."

Under canon law, the local archbishop had no authority over James or the monastery. The letter, however, came from the Holy Father, and disobedience was unthinkable.

James stared at his half-eaten cake. He'd lost his appetite.

∽

WITH MULVANEY'S warning ringing in his head, James walked into the Seeds of Heaven control center at the airstrip. Nuns from the Holy Cup convent sat at workstations. Each faced a bank of monitors resembling the consoles of air traffic controllers. Overhead, an enormous screen showed the real-time locations of drones conducting cloud-brightening operations over North America. The hum of activity consoled James. If successful, the operation would reflect more of the sun's light back into space, slowing the earth's heating due to the carbon load in the atmosphere. Baran funded similar operations on the other continents, except Antarctica, working through locally based religious orders. Seeds of Heaven was a global, ecumenical project. The project's drones flew somewhere every hour of the day.

"You're a little early for your flight, Father." Sister Angelina Rodriguez greeted James, a headset draped around her neck. A small crucifix rested over her heart.

"I haven't eaten much today. I was hoping there was something left in the kitchen."

"Let's go see. I'm on break."

After a two-minute heat-up in the microwave, James swallowed a mouthful of hearty lentil soup from a stoneware bowl.

"We're up to 9,000 sorties," Rodriguez reported. "The new Mark III drones are a godsend. Bigger payload, more time in the air, and more reliable. Only one failure, and that was human error."

James signed the deal with Baran in part due to Rodriguez. Her convent ran a food bank and a part-time medical clinic in the town. When James learned that she'd managed flight operations on aircraft carriers, he approached her about the project management job. She took the donor's credibility and sincerity on faith, even when James explained the necessity for anonymity. James was overjoyed, thinking God himself had blessed the venture.

"You look troubled, James." Rodriquez poured a sugar pack into a mug of control center coffee.

James related Mulvaney's visit and the letter from the Vatican.

"You knew it was coming. It's been hanging over our heads ever since that article came out."

Six months before, an investigative magazine had run a exposé of Seeds of Heaven, naming Baran as the financier. Reporters and cameras from all over the country descended on the abbey.

"Someone stabbed us in the back, Angelina. That article had facts only a few people knew."

"Did you ever find out who leaked the info?"

"I can't say." It was Oscar, James discovered, but he kept the fact to himself. The damage was done. Exposing Oscar would only make it worse.

"Violating privacy is a game to some people."

"Do you think it's dirty money, Angelina?" Without her skills, the project would fail. James needed to keep her on his side.

"Money is just a tool. Three years ago, a third of the county's farmers were bankrupt or selling out. Jobs were scarce. Today, forty people work here, fixing the drones, loading the chemicals, maintaining the computers. They have hope. That fulfills my vows."

"The Holy Father is taking the side of the activists. They think we're poisoning the atmosphere."

"The science says otherwise. The chemicals are harmless, and they actually might help, as long as we get rid of carbon fuels."

That was why James wanted an electric-powered SkyTrac, even though the carbon-fueled models were cheaper. He could follow the pope's teachings on environmental stewardship while offering local farmers low-cost aerial application services. It fit with the founding mission of the abbey, which was to emulate the faith of St. Isidore, who once convinced a pair of angels to help him with his plowing, tripling his productivity.

"Tell me, James, why did you sign that contract? You knew about Victor Baran, even though you kept his name a secret."

"A little bit of greed. A little bit of vanity." James grinned. "I get to play with some of the most advanced flight technology ever made. And I get to fly anytime I want."

"It's more than that, and you know it."

"Seeds of Heaven meant the abbey could survive and thrive. That's what my brothers want. It's what I want."

"Living here gave you purpose."

"I thought about starting my own charter business after I retired from the Air Force, but my wife had other plans. And another man. After the divorce, I got up in the morning with nothing to do and no place to go. The VA chaplain suggested a retreat to the abbey."

Angelina touched his arm. "I'm glad you went."

"After my father died, my mother sent me a box of my childhood belongings. In them was an old letter from my grandmother suggesting a vocation to the priesthood. And here I am."

"Do you regret it?"

James shook his head. "Don't get me wrong. I've had plenty of troubles. I thought my brothers in the abbey were nuts to elect me abbot." James rubbed his hand over his short-cropped gray hair. "I do wonder if I've made a mistake with Seeds of Heaven."

"You feel duped, like someone has taken advantage of you."

"The Holy Father thinks so."

Angelina shrugged. "He may be the Vicar of Christ, but he's only a man."

"To whom I've vowed chastity, poverty, and obedience."

"You've done a lot for people here." Angelina met James's gaze. "You don't get enough credit for it."

"Thanks for the pep talk." James squeezed the nun's hand, feeling its sinewy strength. She was a brilliant partner whom James depended on. "Time for me to fulfill my daily obligation."

After checking the weather report, which promised light winds and unlimited visibility, James stood in the mid-afternoon sun, enjoying the prospect of his second love, after the SkyTrac. The all-electric, Chinese-made Hóng Niǎo (Red Bird) carried six passengers in comfort, though James had four seats removed to make room for Seeds of Heaven.

Alone in the cockpit, he spun up the twin turbofans and taxied to the runway. Settling in at 31,000 feet on a northeasterly course, he let the AI take over. He entered the main cabin, and prepared the small altar, bolted to the cabin deck.

For most Mass celebrations, James would wear a silken stole over a white surplice, but he dispensed with the latter vestment in the confined space of the cabin. With steady, reverential movements, he opened the small, wooden tabernacle and removed the paten, chalice, and cruets of water and wine, placing them in front of a six-inch crucifix.

If they were available, James would invite one or two of his brethren, a nun from the Holy Cup convent, or a lay person to join him in the two seats with prie-dieus in front of the altar. He was alone on this flight.

James opened the hand-sized missal and began the ritual. In accordance with the abbey's contract with Baran, James asked his Lord to forgive Baran's sins and accept his gifts to the abbey as restitution for the harm he had done to the earth and his fellow human beings. Even as he whispered the prayers, he felt Baran had told only half his story, or explain the in-flight requirement. Maybe it was the superstition attached to mountains: Climbing their peaks brought you closer to God. Why not do the same with aircraft?

Keeping his primary purpose in mind, James used the invocations, blessings, and readings as a way to meditate on his own problems. The Holy Father's letter called Seeds of Heaven "ill-advised." Would Baran continue to fund the rituals if James backed out of the agreement? James had no time for a negotiation. For everyone's sake, he asked God to let Seeds of Heaven continue. He guessed an answer would come sooner rather than later.

The ritual complete, James bowed to the altar, removed his stole, and entered the cockpit. He set a course for home, still uncertain what he would do. He needed his brothers to weigh in again.

∽

A PALL HUNG over the intimate dining hall where the abbey's monks, all gray-haired except for Elis, ate their evening meal of artisan bread, vegetable soup, and a half-measure of wine. Everyone knew what would happen at the end of the meal, and no one wanted it.

James had changed into his monk's habit. "My friends, we need to discuss the letter I've received from Rome. I need your advice."

The abbot perused each face, understanding that he was equal to all of them, and responsible for them and the community. Brother Elis listened as if sussing out a problem with an engine. He would support continuing the program. Others fidgeted or yawned; they had already made up their minds.

James avoided Brother Oscar until the last moment. He had argued hardest against accepting the contract, and he had almost prevailed.

"I warned you something like this would happen." Oscar stood up from his chair, and his bulky frame appeared to fill the room. He turned to the others. "The money, the secrecy, the distraction, everything spelled trouble. Did I not say this?"

"We didn't know about the origin of the money, Oscar." Elis stretched out his hand, pleading.

"He did!" Oscar pointed at James, red in the face. "He kept its filthy origin from us."

"He had to. He signed a non-disclosure agreement."

"Don't give me that, Elis. It's a lawyer's trick to cover up evil."

"He's our abbot. We have to trust him."

"Perhaps I should've been more forthright, Oscar." James did not want the discussion to devolve into a shouting match, despite the elder's obvious provocation. "Perhaps I was naive. But Seeds of Heaven has shown results, if not in the atmosphere, then here on the ground, with jobs and hope for the larger community."

"Good based on evil is evil disguised," Oscar said.

A few of the brothers nodded.

"The results don't matter anyway, Father Abbot. His Holiness has all but given you a direct order. Stop the project. Give back the money. Rid us of Victor Baran."

Elis laughed. "Because he thinks Seeds of Heaven makes him look bad and the Church look bad? Should we give in to his conceit?"

Several of the men shifted nervously.

"Show some respect, Elis. I've lived here fifty-three years. I know vanity when I see it." Oscar inclined his head at James. "It's standing at the head of the table."

James could take the insult, but he swallowed hard. Was Oscar right? Had he let pride influence his thinking?

"You're a hypocrite, Oscar," Elis said. "If James is such a sinner, why have you always voted to make him abbot?"

Oscar winced with the sting of Elis' facts. "Your abbot, like every one of us, took a vow of obedience to the Holy Father. We swore it in front of God and His Son. The pope has told us what he wants. We're bound to obey him, even if we disagree. You understand the meaning of orders, don't you, James?"

If there's anything you learn in the military, it's how to follow a lawful order. Disobedience meant a trial, punishment, and dishonorable discharge. "I know what orders mean, Oscar. I've sent men and women into harm's way. Some of them didn't come back."

"Well, then, what are your orders, Father Abbot? Do we continue on our merry way? Or do we do the right thing?"

James took a deep breath. He steeled himself against their decision. "With a show of hands, which of you thinks I should obey the Holy Father?"

All but Elis raised their hands.

"That settles it." Oscar puffed out his chest. "We're done with Baran and his evil project."

The outcome did not surprise James, but he had misjudged the extent of the opposition. He saw no hesitation in the votes to end Seeds of Heaven. The letter provided an excuse for the doubters to come out in the open. James wondered if he should resign as abbot. It would be a relief.

"I've heard the community's views. I won't stand in the way. Tomorrow, I will leave to speak with Mr Baran."

Elis cried out and bolted from the table.

James feared Elis might overreact. He raced after the young man, and he found him in his cell, throwing his belongings into the backpack he used for trips to town. His face grimaced in anger. "Elis, talk to me."

"What for? You'll ignore me and do what you want."

"I don't think I have a choice when it comes to Baran. I took a vow—"

"And you're condemning my generation to a slow death."

"What are you talking about?"

"I'm 19. The next oldest monk is 49. It's people my age who are going to suffer when the climate becomes unbearable. You'll all be dead. I came here because of Seeds of Heaven. I wanted to do something to fix the planet. You've taken that away from me."

Elis pushed past James and marched down the hall, his sandals snapping on the polished floor. James' feelings resembled the emotions of learning one of his pilots was missing, or perhaps dead. A hole opened in his world. He loved Elis like a son. Not only was Elis and his generation the future of humanity, he was the future of his community. Elis spoke the truth, but James was bound by his vows and the wishes of his brothers, at least most of them.

James would travel to see Baran, but he dreaded the moment.

"Do you know what it's like to have seven billion people hate you?"

Baran grimaced as he asked the question. Standing next to him, James wondered how hard the hate would burn once Baran's enemies met him face-to-face. Activists labeled him the "Baron of Death." Caricaturists gave him horns and spiked tail. In reality, the gnomish, pale-skinned man of 85 lay trapped in his bed by his final illness.

"You're exaggerating, Mr. Baran."

"Don't waste your pastoral compassion on me, Bohm. Tell me what you want."

James met Baran after a four-hour drive into the mountains west of Seattle. One of the richest men in the world lived in a three-room cabin under a grotto of trees old and thick. While a fleet of robots served Baran's mundane needs, six human nurses lived a mile away in a dormitory, ready to supplement the robots. One nurse, a thick-necked, scarified man, escorted James through a pair of gates.

"I'm a news junkie, Bohm, especially about my cloud-seeding projects. The pope is upset with you."

James had seen the stories coming out of the Vatican on the news screens in the airport. He studied his folded hands. "Sir, I want to say that my brethren are truly grateful for the support you've given to the community, both inside and outside our walls."

"I've heard better openings from sales interns."

James was unfazed. "I have been asked—"

"Ordered, you mean."

"—asked, sir, by the Holy Father to shut down our portion of the Seeds of Heaven project, sell the aircraft, and turn the funds over to you, including the endowment."

Baran eyed James with the same stare that burned through the resistance of Baran's rivals across a negotiating table. "No one else has rejected my gifts. The Eastern Orthodox Church, the Protestant Union, my

Buddhist partners, my Hindu partners, the Muslims. Their Seeds operations are going like gangbusters. Only the pope has this holier-than-thou attitude. I'm disappointed."

"I don't understand."

"My grandmother was Catholic. Oh yes, we have that in common. Mine was Polish, and I'd bet you my last penny she could best your sainted grandmother for piety and sanctimoniousness."

James refused to take the bait, remembering that Baran was a man with an agenda.

"If there was anything she taught me, it was God's capacity for forgiveness. She even believed God would forgive the Nazis, who had killed her Jewish neighbors when she was a child. She could've taught you and the pope a lesson or two in charity."

Baran brimmed with bitterness, but James couldn't fathom the source. He had everything he needed and wanted, and he didn't care what others thought. On the other hand, if he had inherited his grandmother's faith, his potential fate after death might terrify him.

"I'm a persuasive man, Father. I never do anything by halves. I've taken into account this contingency." A shadow crossed Baran's face. "His Holiness will change his mind. I'm going to satisfy the mob, solve your problem, and get what I want."

James smelled a ruse, but he had no idea what Baran planned. The old man fell into an introspective silence. His eyes drifted to a window and a landscaped garden with a path and a bench.

"Father, I'm sorry for what I've done. Will you hear my confession?"

Charlie Mulvaney had asked James whether he'd hear Baran's confession. As an ordained priest, James couldn't refuse absolution, even to the man blamed for making small nations unlivable, unless Baran was lying about his contrition. As the industrialist clung to life, James pitied Baran, though pity carried a hint of self-righteousness. If Baran dissembled, God would balance the scales. James removed a stole from his shoulder bag, kissed it, draped it over his own shoulders, and waited.

Baran closed his eyes. "Father, I killed my granddaughter."

Shocked, James gripped his missal like a vise. "How?"

"Clarice was 24 years old. She was my little flower from the day she was born. But she hated me and everything I'd worked for. She hated her parents and the world they gave her. That I gave her. She joined an activist group, and one day, she and her friends protested my new oil pipeline."

Baran stopped. Tears filled his rheumy eyes. James handed him a tissue, and Baran covered his face with it.

"I'm sorry it happened, Father."

"You have to tell me the whole story."

"A few of the protesters, including Clarice, lay down in front of the bulldozers. The driver didn't see her—" Baran clenched his jaw. He wouldn't be undone, especially by guilt.

The story confused James. "I'm sorry about your loss, Mr Baran, but you didn't cause Clarice's death. It sounds like an accident to me."

"I set up the conditions that led to her death. I saw myself in her. Idealistic, out to change the world, with a single-minded fervor about achieving something grand. For me, it was about powering the world. For her, it was about saving it. After she died, I found blog posts and articles she'd written. I didn't always agree, but I couldn't just walk away. I created the Seeds of Heaven project to honor her memory and make amends."

"That was why you called the passenger plane *Little Flower*."

"It's a way I can be closer to her in Heaven and ask for forgiveness."

For such a cynical man, Baran's religious beliefs were problematic, but James gave him the benefit of the doubt. He spoke the words that granted absolution.

"And now you want to know how I will solve your problem."

"I'm not sure it's relevant at this point." While praying for Baran's soul, James perceived how to protect his own. Integrity mattered more to him than a vow, even if made before God. Perhaps he'd pay a consequence on earth, or when his time came for God's judgment. Ultimately, a man had to live with himself. "It would be wrong to stop your project, Mr. Baran, not only for your sake, but for the sake of people who might benefit and the earth itself. The Holy Father will have to swallow his pride."

Baran's eyes glistened with gratitude. He also knew something that James didn't quite grasp, like a comic readying his punch line. James was curious, but he didn't press the matter, and Baran wasn't forthcoming.

James returned to the abbey. A few days later, he sat at his desk, his phone in his hand, the number to Archbishop Mulvaney's office ringing.

Anxiety gripped his chest. In a year or two, he might be out of a job, or exiled to a distant parish, or even defrocked.

Mulvaney answered.

James cleared his throat. "Charlie, I have something to tell you."

"Have you heard?"

James did a double take. He heard suppressed joy in Mulvaney's voice, as well as relief. "I guess not. What's happened?"

"Victor Baran is dead."

The news took a moment to sink in. Baran was ill, but James recalled nothing that suggested his imminent passing. Selfish thoughts cascaded in James's mind about the news's impact on the project, the monastery, and himself. "How?"

"The police think it was an accident. Bad medication or something."

James envisioned the scarified nurse standing over his boss's bed. In the abbot's imagination, Baran was smiling. "I'm sorry to hear about it."

"No, you're not." Mulvaney laughed. "You're off the hook, my friend."

James swallowed. "I'm not following."

"His Holiness can't return a dead man's gift. It'd look like he was dancing on the man's grave. It wouldn't do. You've been granted a reprieve, James."

That was Baran's trick, to exit the scene. James had readied himself for a fight with the Vatican, but Baran had stolen the show, saving James from an unwinnable war.

"Congratulations, James. You might be even turn out a hero." Mulvaney hung up.

James breathed out. What really happened in that mountain cabin? Did Baran truly feel guilt over his granddaughter's death and see its connection to his mistakes? Perhaps he had manipulated James. Maybe absolution was Baran's ultimate goal, but if he'd intended suicide…

Worrying about the outcome was pointless. Baran's death made the letter moot, or at least postponed a reckoning. Technically, he hadn't broken any vows to the Holy Father or promises to his brethren. Baran had given him a gift. In time, Seeds of Heaven would bear fruit of one kind or another. When he said Mass for Baran's soul on *Little Flower* that day, he'd add a prayer of thanks.

About the Author: *J.G. Follansbee is an award-winning writer of thrillers, fantasy and science fiction novels and short stories with climate change themes. An author of maritime history and travel guides, he has published articles in newspapers, regional and national magazines, and regional and national radio networks, including National Public Radio. He's also worked in the high-tech and non-profit worlds. He lives in Seattle.*

Author site: https://jgfollansbee.com
Twitter: @Joe_Follansbee
Facebook: @AuthorJGFollansbee
Instagram: @jgfollansbee

FROM THE SUN AND SCORCHED EARTH

BRYAN CEBULSKI

The boy in the mech watches fire spread across the plains, an orange-red sunset emblazoned across the horizon.

A bead of sweat trickles down his right temple. He cannot remove a hand from the controls to wipe it away. Able but unwilling.

Aim. Focus. Pull the trigger. One kill. Dopamine hit. Two kills. Dopamine hit.

The boy in the mech scorches fields of cornstalks and soybeans, smothers them into the earth. Human bodies, the bystanders of war, eviscerated without warning, without notice. Enemy combatants are mere husks of metal. The human bodies inside are of no consideration.

The boy in the mech pulls the trigger. Pulls the trigger. Kills everything in his path for the glory of those who made this machine for him. This cocoon of solace and peace and good feelings. Eternal reward, eternal bliss.

Clear the fields. Rend machines into scrap metal. Riddle with bullets. Rip apart.

No longer human. Fodder.

The boy in the mech ranks up points, watches as his score rises on the heads-up display, where live stats reveal pilots vying for top position. Bonuses for cruelly efficient attacks, devastating blows. A rise in rank triggers agonizing pleasure.

The boy in the mech, eyes shielded by a visor, perks his lips in a half-smile.

In makeshift shelters beneath the heels of behemoths, survivors quake in fear, still alive somewhere within themselves.

~

THE GLINT of the mech's armor drifted across Lukas's room and hit the monitor on his desk sometime mid-morning.

He'd been sitting at his computer since before dawn. He stood and stretched, looked out the window to relax his eyes, relieve the screen burn.

The mech kneeled on its platform, the deep greenish-black armored body shining against a clear blue sky. Lukas wondered when the uncanny humanoid shape towering over the horizon had normalized.

On hot days like this, villagers would set up picnics beneath its shade. Upon request the boy who piloted the mech would spread its wings, rotate the body if need be.

It used to be called an angel of death. Marketed as one. Propagandized through an anime-influenced American franchise funded by the military. Now its ammunition, its missiles and bombs, were exhausted. The boy said he'd discarded the close-range weaponry long ago. He dismissed rumors that his machine was capable of manifesting a beamsword or laser cannons or using martial arts. These ideas were conjured up by creatively overstimulated minds, he assured them.

His eyes enlivened by the bright natural light, Lukas pulled the shade down, stood in the dark breathing in and out a few times as his eyes readjusted, and got back to work.

He pulled out another hard drive from the stack of storage devices—CDs, iPods, old mp3 players, flash drives—in a plastic box at his feet. He popped it into the drive dock, let the device do its work as it brought up old, potentially corrupted data.

The hard drive popped up as a folder on his old boxy rig. The monitor was functional but flickered, the color balance poor. It was still heartier than the flatscreen or projection-based monitors he had piled up around the shack, most of which needed a server connection to even boot up, a connection that no longer existed.

He double-clicked, sifting through corrupted folders, hoping for any data that might still be whole. He found one labeled "Music" and began to click through the files.

Against all expectation, he found it.

∽

Minutes later, Lukas rushed out of his home to shout in the street,

"I got Joni! I got Joni!"

The villagers tended to stay outdoors for most the day this time of year, except in the most intense summer heat.

It was still morning, cool and a bit misty.

As Lukas jogged toward the village square, he caught the attention of people repairing roofs, working on restoration projects, teaching the youth how to build houses. Gardeners toiling in the soil, kids stepping on wine grapes in a large vat outside what passed for a vineyard. The cobbler stitching shoes, the tailor mending a child's dress shirt.

People's heads turned as he passed by, unsure if they heard him correctly.

A refurbished speaker sat on an old gazebo in the middle of the square that a carpenter had converted into a stage long ago. The speaker was hooked up to solar panels on the roof. Lukas ran to the stage, still shouting, his bad leg only just starting to pulse with pain. Breathlessly he pulled out the old phone he used for important music storage—one of the last generations to have a headphone jack, not to mention internal storage and a decent-sized battery—and plugged it into the speaker.

A crowd gradually gathered round. All went quiet as soon as the music began.

Musicians covered Mitchell so much during community parties and impromptu jam sessions that she had become something of a patron saint of the village. But this was the first time many would hear the songs themselves in years.

Lukas put on "Big Yellow Taxi" first, obviously. It was practically the village anthem, played at all big community gatherings. Reassuring, beautiful, semi-ironic. Paradise had been paved over, the pavement got blown to bits, and now they were resurrecting paradise.

Lukas barely remembered hearing the original version. He was so young when everything went to shit. It was already getting him choked up. He couldn't imagine what older generations would feel.

Four old folks, who before the war were lazy, poor, happy cafe patrons: were now lazy, economically unbothered, happy communal grandparents, arrived at the square with guitars in tow, compelled by Lukas' shouting.

They sat on the edge of the stage, first listening.

Then, the first play of the song over, they quietly spoke to one another about Mitchell's vocals, how none of them had the kind of voice, definitely not the range, to accurately match it.

They asked Lukas to play it again, and he did.

Upon one listen, then two, they noted to each other little quirks in the recording they'd forgotten about. They listened intently to the lyrics to make sure they remembered every line. One asked what DDT was again.

The song ended again. The audience that gathered around applauded to no one in particular.

"Only problem," Lukas said. "Every song on 'Blue' was corrupted."

A couple disappointed but goodhearted groans in the audience. Most didn't remember which songs were on *Blue* anyway. Lukas himself was a bit disappointed though. When he was a child, his older sister used to make him laugh with a goofy cover of "My Old Man." He hadn't heard the song in years.

Lukas rested the phone on the edge of the stage next to the speaker, made sure the aux cord wouldn't jiggle out and make that horrible screech he'd run into so many times while messing around with this equipment.

He set it to go through the whole discography, from *Song to a Seagull* all the way to *Shine*, though the phone would probably run out of juice in a couple hours.

As he walked away the musicians were already clambering to get to the phone and look through the titles, queueing up their favorite songs.

The crowd that had formed was mostly the old, nostalgic portion of the village. Some curious youths, those interested in music especially, wandered in.

Leaning against a light post, head down and arms crossed, was the mecha boy Leo.

Lukas went up to him. He always made it a point to be friendly to Leo, even though last time he tried he got a most unique rejection.

"If you try to get close to me," Leo had said, "I'll end up hurting you."

It didn't come off like a threat. It reminded Lukas of an anxious cat, one who perhaps had its tail pulled one too many times and no longer trusted human touch.

"Here for the music?" Lukas asked.

Leo raised his eyes, looking not quite at but more through Lukas, and nodded. No promises of violence this time.

"Yeah," he said. Leo's voice was always just a little lighter than Lukas expected it to be, like Leo hadn't spoken in a while and was getting used to the act. "It's nice."

That took Lukas back. Three whole words! One contraction, so practically four. And pleasant words too! Declarative, though, to be sure. Conclusive. No room for follow-up. Lukas flailed around trying to find an avenue to take from there.

"Um, have you heard her before?" he asked.

Leo's expression dropped, saying nothing. He pushed himself off the post and, without another word, walked away, hands in pockets, head down.

∼

Leo's mech could till every acre of soil in the village in minutes. A finger pushed into the earth formed a compost pit so deep it would have taken ten people an hour to dig. It could soak up the sun and provide energy to light the whole village for weeks. It lifted wooden girders and beams as easily as a child's building blocks. It helped craftsmen assemble houses in a fraction of the time. Its presence, standing tall and strange over the landscape, kept at bay marauding bands of dieselpunks, any malicious group under the impression that they were in some other post-apocalyptic scenario.

The villagers didn't quite understand him, but they tolerated him. Smiled when he passed on the street, invited him to join games. But only, Lukas felt, because they knew he'd say no.

∼

LEO JUST SHOWED up one day. The villagers turned pale and frightened at the harsh, shrieking noise of the mech flying across the sky one afternoon. Some cowered in their homes, fearful that the war was back. Others gathered to see what was in the sky, curious where it might land, if it would even notice them.

The mech landed in the meadow where Leo would later assemble a platform for it. The cockpit opened as villagers gathered round and jumped down. Leo requested the first person he saw to speak to their leader.

Insofar as they had a leader, it was probably Kirby, a sixty-something-year-old woman who was the unequivocal best at juggling responsibilities, parceling out tasks to those best suited to perform them, and generally keeping everyone from being too complacent, from just sitting around eating rations and drinking old jugs of wine while playing music together in bombed-out cottages.

When Kirby appeared and introduced herself, Leo bowed his head down.

"My name is Leo Sternlieb," he said. "I'm responsible for carrying out the scorched earth campaign that decimated this area. My life is forfeit. I offer you to take it."

Kirby looked around at her fellow villagers, hands at her sides, her eyes wider than usual, confused as the rest. A face and a posture that said, "Well, this is a new one."

Lukas was one of many in the crowd, eyes fixed on this captivating new figure.

Leo had these strange, glassy eyes, intense in a way you could see from any angle. Brown hair parted to one side, a little silly, as if it had just settled that way one day and he kept it there. Lanky frame, wearing only shorts and a tanktop. Arms and legs covered in bruises and scars.

"I think," Kirby said after some moments of weighted silence, "that you have the absolute wrong impression of the kind of people we are."

She put two hands on his shoulders, waited until she looked up at him.

"I wondered where you boys ended up," she said. "You poor, lost things."

She returned her hands to her sides, and waited a moment longer before continuing.

"Let me tell you something I've learned about personal responsibility," she said. "You know how much I wanted to die, after losing everyone I've ever loved in the war? My mother? My children? My grandchildren? But I couldn't die, because, well, do you see these lovely people here?" She gestured to the crowd behind her. "People need people, kid. We help each other around here."

Leo put his head back down. He visibly trembled.

"Oh, my boy," she went on, "you think you're trying to make amends with your dramatics. But you're trying to find an easy way out."

Here she turned to the crowd.

"We will have a town hall to discuss, but I'd like to put this out there now: This boy wants to make amends. I suggest in lieu of death, he use his skills, his... machine, for the betterment of our community." She turned back around to Leo. "As long as you accept, of course?"

Leo didn't skip a beat.

"I'm a tool manufactured for war," he said. "I am yours to repurpose as you see fit."

Kirby couldn't resist rolling her eyes. Then, thinking better of it, she smiled a bit pityingly. With a hand at his back, she led him through the crowd to a safe place. The crowd parted around them, more curiosity than concern on their faces.

∼

From that first emergency town hall when they accepted Leo into the village to today's monthly town council meeting, Lukas was impressed by how persistently Benjamin aired his grievances.

"Why should he be the only one who knows how to pilot that thing?" he asked. "I'm telling you all, how many times do I need to repeat it? He's not one of us. He's helped us, and I'm as grateful as can be, but when push comes to shove we need our own people defending our community. This kid's absolute refusal to allow others to pilot—or even study the tech, for chrissake—is a serious security risk. I'll keep saying this till someone finally listens to me. It's ridiculous."

He slammed a palm on the podium for emphasis and backed away, sitting back down at his seat in a middle row.

Kirby, the council chair, leaned forward.

"Leo," she said, "for fairness' sake as always I'd like to offer you the chance to respond."

Leo stood in the back as always, arms crossed and head down, listening, engaging only when called to do so, neither above nor beneath. Just there.

He walked up to the podium.

"Thank you madam chair," he said. "I repeat that the mech is not a simple machine. It has biological components and requires considerable mental, physical and emotional stress to pilot, stress which I have been specially trained to take on since birth. I would not wish the burden on my worst enemy. As for studying its technology, I insist there is nothing to be gained. No good can come from reproducing such technology for a community like this. I ask that, in return for my services to this community, you respect my beliefs. Thank you."

He bowed his head and turned around. Benjamin made a rude gesture as he passed.

Lukas, in the middle of the crowd, craned his neck to see Leo in the back, leaning against the wall, arms crossed and head down.

∼

It was the kind of morning when Lukas could understand what people meant when they describe the weather as "crisp." Dewey, cool, the sun shining. Air quality above average for once, waking up and not feeling lightheaded.

He made his tea, steeped it in enough water for two cups. After a few minutes he poured it into a thermos and went out his front door.

He walked to the green meadow where the mech towered over the village.

Leo sat on its right foot, leaned back into the angle of it. His eyes were closed. He looked like he was meditating, not seeming to see Lukas as he approached.

"Hi," Lukas said finally.

Leo opened his eyes, turned to see who was interrupting him. He nodded slightly.

"Want some tea?" Lukas asked, taking a seat on the ground next to the foot. Close enough to insist on being there, not too close to risk meeting Leo's cold wrath.

He said nothing for a beat too long, then finally agreed.

"Okay," he said.

Pleased with himself for taking a risk and not getting his head bitten off, Lukas unscrewed the cap of the thermos and poured a little tea into it.

"I think it's Earl Grey. I found it while scavenging at that apothecary in that strip mall along the highway," he said, passing the mug to Leo. "Hope you don't mind it strong. I wasn't expecting it to still be good."

Leo accepted the mug. Holding it by the handle, he observed the steam rising. Then, a small sip. Lukas had expected him to wait for it to cool more.

"Tastes fine," he said.

The reply was so quick Lukas wondered if he even noticed the flavor.

Then Leo added, "Thanks."

"No problem," Lukas said.

They sat quietly together from there, listening to the wind, appreciating a nice, mild day for a change.

Lukas glanced at Leo every once in a while, which he was certain Leo noticed. Leo had this energy about him, like he noticed every detail but chose what he responded to strategically, picking only what needed to be addressed.

After a couple minutes, Leo handed the mug back. It was already empty.

"You'd better go," he said.

"Why? Do you have something to do today?" Lukas asked.

Leo didn't say anything at first. Then, "I'd just rather be alone."

"You're always alone!" Lukas snapped.

He didn't quite expect that from himself. But he realized at that moment that he was exhausted with this routine. It was like this every time he tried to engage with Leo. Don't get too close to me, oh woe is me, I'm just so dark and broody and damaged. Like they weren't all royally fucked up and so stunned by years of death and suffering.

"It's for the best," Leo said, unfazed.

"No, it's not," Lukas said. "Like, do you want to be a part of this place or not? To some degree you must or you wouldn't be here. So you gotta start letting people in. If not me then someone. But as far as I can tell, I'm the only one who wants to put up with you."

He turned red after blurting that out. He looked down, then back up. Their eyes met, Leo again looking not at but through Lukas.

"Fine," Leo said, standing up. "Stick around. But I need to run some diagnostics. I'll be up in the cockpit for a while. Then, if it's so important, you can be here with me."

∽

An hour went by without a word from Leo.

Lukas stayed, feeling obstinate about the whole thing. Unless you give me a good reason why not, he thought, I'm going to try to be part of your life, Leo.

He walked back home, sure to pace himself so his bad leg didn't start to throb in pain again, and grabbed a laptop, which was an old machine that still had USB ports, and a handful of memory sticks, figuring he should at least get some work done today.

He found some new music. Nothing great or significant, but important to label.

The big find was a stash of classic cartoons that he made sure to keep for the kids, especially one full series about a boy and his magic dog that Lukas remembered catching snippets of years ago, when he was a tween, blissfully unaware of the chain of events that would wind up destroying his entire life.

Then documents, mostly mundane, but some with the potential to be historically enlightening. There was a young woman in the community who was shaping up to become the town archivist, maybe he'd show them to her. First, he organized the documents into a spreadsheet. Tedious work without immediate benefit that he hoped someone would find useful someday.

He checked the time. Another hour had passed.

Lukas looked up, noticed the path of ladders, steps, platforms, and monkey bars that ran up and along the mech's exterior.

It had been a long time, long enough it was possible Leo was avoiding him at this point.

Maybe he'd just scale the thing a little, call out to Leo, see what was going on. Lukas figured that if Leo hadn't already decided to avoid him from now on, one more nosy act wouldn't make a difference.

He began the ascent. Lukas struggled to keep his balance even on the flat surfaces. It was a wonder Leo could gracefully climb up the way he did every time Lukas saw him here. The spaces between every rung on the ladders were huge, each a strain to reach from the last, and it felt like the mech moved whenever he so much as fidgeted.

"Leo?" he called, louder and louder as he got closer, his worry growing.

Finally, he made it up to the chest of the beast, where the cockpit lay half-closed.

He ducked underneath the lid and saw Leo, a visor over his eyes, shaking.

At first glance it looked almost like the squirming and writhing of pleasure, until, after a moment of observation, Lukas saw that he was struggling. His hands gripped on the arm rests, scratching against the interfaces on each. Legs began kicking violently against the seat, his waist pushing up and pressing against the security belt.

Not thinking, Lukas rushed to Leo, unbuckled him and ripped the visor off his face.

Leo's eyes were red and swollen. Not crying. Monitor burn eyes, the kind he got staring at his screen for too long.

"Jesus, Leo," he said. "Are you okay?"

Leo jumped at Lukas and grabbed at his throat.

Lukas, frozen with shock, couldn't fight him off. Lukas was taller but weaker, brittle really. Too unused to fighting, even to retaliate, even to defend. Leo was too skilled, too agile. Lukas struggled till his arms felt numb, till his head went cloudy. He felt weak, the light going out of his eyes.

Then, Leo's hands relaxed their grip.

Lukas gasped for air. Then, a tightness surrounded his body and he froze in place. He thought Leo was about to throw him off the mech, get rid of him for good.

No, Leo hugged him, his face buried in his chest.

Lukas caught his breath, tried to fight off the jitters of adrenaline. He didn't return the embrace, but kept one hand on Leo's shoulder and rode out the final, confusing moments of their delirium.

∼

THE SUN SET below the plains, the line of the horizon abstract and black. A certain calm always came over the village at night. Now was the time to go back to doing what everyone wanted to do, to drink wine and play music, trade stories, be merry in each other's company.

Lukas and Leo sat wrapped in blankets on the floor in Lukas's little home.

"I told you not to get close to me," Leo said.

Lukas' neck was still red and sore, his breath still uneasy.

"I thought that was all a moody tough guy act," he said, trying to sound casual, lighten the mood.

"I mean everything I say," Leo said.

So they said nothing for a while.

Lukas made herbal tea, threw together a nice hearty vegetable barley soup. The work was a microcosm for everything he did in the village. Something to keep his mind and body occupied, to keep the ghosts of the past at bay.

He expected Leo to leave at some point, just fade away into the background like he always did, but he stayed there in that meditative state on the floor.

Even when Lukas went out to get some bread from the bakery, coming back with a long baguette under his arm, because goddamnit almost dying was not going to get in the way of him making a proper supper, Leo still sat there in the same position on the dusty floorboards.

Lukas cut the bread, set a few slices aside, and carried them on a tray with two bowls of soup. He set it down on the coffee table so they could eat sitting on the floor.

"I wish you'd listened to me," Leo said.

Lukas handed him a bowl.

"And I wish you'd listen to me, too," he said after Leo accepted the food.

"You don't know this because you weren't around," Lukas continued, "but I had an older sister who used to be the problem child around here.

"We were the only ones there for each other after, you know, everything happened. Lost our parents. She lost her wife. And she got... well. She had problems before, and they got worse after. She flew into rages, she'd destroy things, she'd threaten people. Seeing the things that the worst side of herself brought her to do, I could tell what was and wasn't her.

"Whenever she was like that, I saw someone else in her eyes, something, I don't know. I almost want to say possessing her. Some malevolent spirit that feeds on human misery, exploits people when they're at their most vulnerable. I don't know. I know, in the end, it was her, that she did inexcusable things. But I also just know who she was, and I know not to define her by the worst of her.

"My whole point being, what I just saw with you... it was the same look. The same turning into something else. Whatever that mech makes you do, whatever kind of reliance you have on it, whatever the military did to you to make you and everything else this way, I know it's more complicated than whether you're a good or bad person."

Leo circled his spoon in the soup, looking contemplative.

"And I just... I don't know," Lukas went on. "Maybe you're not interested in me in the way I'm into you. But I like seeing you. You're so quiet but I like that you're quiet. So many people around here, they're good people but we all just talk and talk and talk, as if we're trying to drown out all the horrible things we've been through. And you don't do that. I feel like we could sit and not talk and just be together, you know?"

Leo brought a spoonful to his mouth. Lukas thought that, maybe, there was an expression of satisfaction on his face for a moment.

He put the bowl back down on the coffee table.

"Ever since the military took me," Leo began, abruptly, like if he didn't start now, he never would, "they worked to make me and that mech into one being. I don't know what it does, or how, but when I'm connected to it, it feels like absolute euphoria.

"But ever since I arrived here, I've been slowly reworking the system. It influences me, but I influence it back. I'm trying to teach it to dismantle its own destructive capabilities, to de-emphasize combat training. To not trigger pleasure receptors, or suggest violence. To only help your people stay alive and healthy. But I... whatever happened today, I was weak mentally and it got to me. Reminded me of what it felt like. And being torn from it the way you did... Maybe it was necessary, I don't know. But for those few moments, you were the enemy. You took me away the only thing that had ever made me feel good."

Lukas couldn't look at him, couldn't look anywhere else, so he looked at the floor.

"I like you, Lukas," Leo said. "I do. I like the way you look at things. You find awe in every little thing, like that music you found. I see you bringing everyone around here closer together. But I can't be a part of that. It's not something possessing me that makes me dangerous. It's me. It's who I've been my whole life. And I can't put you through that."

Leo stood up. He put a hand on Lukas's shoulder, and before he parted he said,

"Not, at least, until I'm ready."

∼

FOR THE MAJORITY of its needs, the village could provide for itself. Scavenging parties gathered occasionally. It tended to happen very spur of the moment. Foolhardy friends talking, realizing a child had a headache or the flu, or the half-dozen diabetic folks—who'd been stockpiling insulin for years as it was—were running out of needles or some other necessary supply. Some people were just restless and eager for adventure.

They went out this time in one of the vans that hadn't been blown half to bits or rusted between the sun and the rain, promising their loved ones with smiles on their faces to be back by supper. Off to raid one of the hospitals or pharmacies or clinics or supermarkets that one or another of the group had a feeling was still standing, hadn't yet been thoroughly ransacked.

Lukas never went, as he was never certain when his leg would act up and render him immobile, but Leo joined occasionally. Like mist, he drifted into the starting group as it rallied allies. Then he'd sit quietly in the back of the truck or van, his head down like always, eyes just barely not closed.

Rumors of what he was looking for always trickled throughout the village. The big one was some experimental drug he needed or else he devolved into a degenerate psychopath, although why a large portion of the pharmacies in the Midwest had this was never questioned.

Lukas had a feeling he knew, though. If they raided a pharmaceutical facility or a pharmacy or a home somewhere, he'd once or twice found him carrying a little bottle and needles, or a gel. Nothing so controversial as any rumor might have one think. It seemed to Lukas that most townsfolk knew, but preferred to spin yarns for the fun of it.

∽

LEO LEFT HIS MECH STANDING, unguarded.

The cockpit could be forced easily with a locking mechanism that had been broken long ago.

No one but Benjamin knew this, he was fairly certain. Benjamin had watched Leo open the cockpit from a distance through an old telescope for months, nearly every time he went into the mech. Especially that last time, when he'd attacked Lukas. That was the final straw for him. Benjamin knew he had to do something now or else real harm would come to the community.

He saw Leo pull where the handle was hidden innumerable times. One could open the cockpit door manually with it.

Benjamin saw Leo leave with the hospital raiders, that happy band, and took his opportunity.

He ambled to the meadow where the mech stood. Unbridled power just sitting there rusting, inadequately appreciated by its pilot.

It could be used. Not only for defense, but for expansion. Not only for expansion, but for travel. Wisdom. What else was going on in the world? Who else survived?

Not to mention the mech could be used to seek out those who started this whole fucking atrocity. Fantasizing at night, Benjamin could see himself tearing them limb from limb with the colossus, crushing them into dust. Pop off heads like dandelions.

All it took was one bold leap into the unknown. One chance that he needed to take or so help him.

~

THE TRIP WAS SUCCESSFUL. Lots of minor, helpful medicines, cold syrups and paracetamol. Necessary supplies like sterile syringes, rubbing and denatured alcohol. As they drove away they shared from a bowl of cough drops as a victory ritual, the smell of sweet cherry menthol rich in the cloistered air.

The van crept toward the shack on the outskirts of town currently standing in as a clinic, tires rolling along the dirt road, its surface well-flattened with assistance from Leo's mech.

Leo had been disappointed this trip. He was trying to rely less on the mech to produce his hormones, but they were getting more difficult to find in the wild.

He looked out the window, wanting despite himself to always have his mech within eyesight, expecting to see it standing in its usual spot in the meadow.

It wasn't there.

"What the fuck?" the driver said, alerting everyone in the cabin toward something in the center of town.

Leo went up front and saw his mech towering over the village square on all fours, shadowing a small cluster of straw-bale houses.

Without hesitation he rushed to the back, thrust open the rear door and hopped out of the still-moving vehicle.

The van was old, the drive neither smooth nor direct enough to get there in time. Had to run.

He made a beeline for it.

~

EVERYONE HEARD, none saw.

They gathered outside when they heard the mech's cry, a beast striking terror into the hearts of its prey. It stood up from its kneeling position, creaking all the time, and began walking forward.

Crunching, gurgling. Agonizing screams coming from the cockpit. Sounds only ever described on the pages of pulp horror novels, yellowing in the dusty shelves of abandoned houses. Sounds like bones twisting slowly, like flesh torn away, strip by strip.

No one but Leo saw the true aftermath.

The villagers were mostly older, or else suffering from one physical disability, injury, ailment or another. Or else just frozen in place by fear. Gawking up at the robot, sure it was about to crush the town whole but unable to look away, unable to move out from under its shadow.

They watched, stunned with the sudden violence, memories of war and death like lightning, their brains fried with shock. Eyes unbelieving.

∼

LEO DIDN'T THINK. He scaled the mech, jumping catlike from to its heel, running along the calf and climbing the thigh, leaping from one platform to the next, skipping rungs on the ladders, jumping up steps, finally dangling from rungs to reach the cockpit. He managed to pry it open from the side just enough to slide in.

From the little crack he'd opened, a lump of flesh dropped to the ground.

Villagers screamed and dispersed.

He sealed the cockpit shut.

The mech began to stand, motion more graceful now. Almost tiptoeing, it walked back to its platform in the meadow and took a knee.

The crowd looked in horror back and forth from the mech to the pile in front of them of what had once been human.

Lukas stood among them, as stricken with terror as anyone, but snapped out of disbelief when he remembered that Leo was still in that thing, still vulnerable to its influence.

He ran staggeringly to the meadow, fearful of what the machine might be doing to Leo, what thoughts and impulses it might be instilling.

He tried scaling the mech. He went too fast at first, falling from a rung at the ankle. The wind rushed out of his lungs as he hit the ground.

He tried again, visions of Leo, of what the mech was capable of, how it clung to that boy like a parasite.

Leo had already covered what was left of the body with a plastic sheet when Lukas finally reached the cockpit.

Only Leo saw everything. But Lukas saw the viscera, the blood splattered everywhere. Saw how the mech recognized an unauthorized pilot, and how, rather than simply shut down, instead convinced the interloping pilot that it would function, that it would obey.

At the moment Benjamin was sure he had mastered the beast. It began to retaliate.

Once, maybe last year, Lukas found an old videogame through an emulator on a laptop. He played it for hours, reached the end, only to find that it was a pirated version. It had a measure in place to prevent the player from completing the game. Almost the entirety of the game was unchanged, but it made the final dungeon impossible to complete. Waves of enemies, at far greater level than anyone could reasonably oppose, pummeling the player at every turn.

What a design to apply to war. Lukas imagined some enemy soldier on the battlefield, trying to take over a mech from its host, long since dead, only to receive such a punishment. Not just killed, but tortured, brutally. Experiments of the flesh. Information to be harvested and exploited in future battles. Then the body dropped in front of its former comrades to psychologically torture them.

What was once Benjamin was no longer visibly human. Seeing the shape under the sheet, one wouldn't assume it was a body. Just a soft, indeterminate mass.

Lukas didn't say a word.

Leo looked to him once, and they communed in an unspoken flash.

Leo didn't want him there, relying as usual on distance as protection. He knew, and Lukas's gaze suggested, Lukas wasn't going to go anywhere without helping.

First Lukas turned away, resisting the bile rising in his throat, and climbed back down, quelling the fears of the villagers who had gathered there as he passed. Sometime later, he appeared again with rubber gloves, sponges, rags, bags, and a spray bottle full of the apple cider vinegar he'd been fermenting in a 5-gallon bucket behind his house.

When he managed to climb up again, Leo accepted the added supplies. "Thanks," he said, and continued working.

They wiped down every inch of the cockpit. The bloodied panels, the nooks where little globs of what used to be the human body had settled.

They set the body down next to the mech and awaited the coroner.

∾

MANY SPECULATED that Leo would disappear. Surprisingly, though, there was no call for it from the masses. As a matter of fact, most found that despite everything they still appreciated the little bastard standing in the corner of all their social gatherings.

Far from leaving, he made an announcement in the town square that he would stay until the village had prepared an adequate punishment for his transgression.

His phrase, "punishment for my transgression."

He still didn't realize, Lukas thought, that no one in the village thought in those terms but him.

Some blamed him, yes, but generally there was an understanding that it was an accident. That Benjamin acted brazenly, falling victim to a trap well beyond what he could have reasonably anticipated. He was dead not because of an action on Leo's part, but due to a lack of precaution and respect for boundaries.

"You wouldn't dig a hole," a council member reasoned during their deliberations, "and when someone stumbles in and breaks their neck, call them a murderer. The person who fell would be called careless and you'd just get told to put up a sign that says 'Warning: Big hole' next time. And here, Leo, you've already warned us. You've been warning us."

This was the ultimate decision reached by the council.

Lukas sat next to Leo in the town hall, his heart-sinking infatuation with the boy still strong even after the unimaginable horror of what he'd seen in the cockpit. After everything, still wanting to see this strange, sad boy find a normal life in the village.

The council had come to their decision.

"We don't need any more death or pain," Kirby said, gathering the thoughts of the rest of the council into one concise sentence. "When you first came here, Leo Sternlieb, I told you not to try and take the easy way out. Punishment is simple. Atonement is hard. And I, and I believe my peers as well agree, see you still seeking punishment. And we don't even blame you for this! Leo, my dear boy, you are more a part of this village than you might think. Your punishment, insofar as it can be considered such, is to remain with us, and to continue to help us."

∼

THE COUNCIL AGREED Leo should be kept far away from the funeral and burial. Kirby actually said so to Leo—the rest of the council probably would have let it go implied. None expected much backlash. Benjamin hadn't been greatly liked, they had to admit. No family to speak of, except for the general familial bond everyone implicitly shared in the village. He had his strengths, was a killer mandolin player, and could drink the best of them under the table. But he had a sort of mundane darkness to him. Too big an ego, too rowdy and loud a spirit.

He did have a share of people who would miss him, in one way or another. And certainly others believed that Leo's mech should be better harnessed too, not just for dainty tasks like picking up logs and stirring the compost heap with a finger, like a spoon in tea.

After the wake, when villagers caught sight of the shape in the casket, the suggestion of a body beneath a pure white blanket, few spoke up with such beliefs anymore.

∼

LUKAS HUMMED and gently swung his woven picnic basket as he walked back to the meadow, the two ends of a split baguette poking out from the lid. He passed the town square and stopped to listen to the musicians, the regular four lounging on the stage, occasional listeners stopping by. Lukas's music player had barely left the stage since he found the Joni Mitchell trove. They listened to *Clouds* on low. It was in the middle of "Both Sides Now."

They were playing for themselves today, experimenting, lost in individualized soundscapes, riffing off the canned music that murmured beneath their strumming.

He sat on the edge of the stage and listened awhile.

Villagers passed by, going to and fro between their various tasks. He waved and smiled to everyone and most waved and smiled back. Some didn't. Some were apprehensive about him these days, what with how much time he was spending with that weird mech boy lately. Not hateful, not angry. Just suspicious.

The indentations in the earth, four corners on each side of the town square, permanently marked what had happened.

Lukas got up, waved goodbye to the musicians, and continued on his walk. He traced the lines of dirt where cables had been recently buried, hook-ups for new homes plugged into the mech's enormous battery.

He followed the lines into the meadow, into the shade of the mech, where he found Leo in his usual spot on the foot.

He, too, had a phone playing music. Joni Mitchell. "Both Sides Now." But not the young, flighty, hopeful version on *Clouds*. The elegiac, operatic version on her later album of the same name. It felt more appropriate for Leo, he thought.

Other villagers refrained from picnicking under the mech's shade for a few weeks after the incident, wary of the thing's grotesque power, but eventually their feelings about the machine normalized again, and they realized they couldn't resist a good picnic anymore. No longer seeing it move, no longer seeing its fearsome power. Just a statue with a convenient umbrella-opening function. They came petering back in.

A few sat on blankets now, drinking wine, reading to each other.

The former pilot had his eyes closed and head down, reclining with a hemp pillow behind his neck. Lukas sat down at his side and, hearing deep, long breaths, realized Leo was asleep.

He started taking food out of the basket, humming the familiar tune to himself.

In a minute, Leo woke.

"Hey," he said. He stretched and turned onto his side.

"I hope I'm welcome to join?" Lukas asked.

Leo nodded and scooted over to make room.

Lukas smiled. He lay down on the foot beside Leo.

As his eyes loomed upward, they were forced shut by the shine of the sun on rusting metal.

In a few minutes, he heard Leo snoring.

Lukas, too relaxed to move but too awake to drift off, lay there next to him, his eyes closed, hands cupped beneath his head.

The mech creaked in the wind, micro-adjustments in the mechanical joints. Soon, in Lukas's mind, it began to sound like rustling tree branches, like swaying grass.

About the Author: Bryan Cebulski is a rural California-based journalist from the Midwest who writes quiet queer speculative and literary fiction.

Website: https://bryancebulski.wordpress.com
Twitter: @BryanOnion

UPGRADE

ALEX SILVER

One

I tapped my temple. As if the fuzzy halo around my vision was a loose connection I could jostle back into place with a well-placed smack. I snorted at my foolishness. No, I needed to go in for repairs before I finished frying my malfunctioning ocular implant. If I went back on-grid, I would be eligible for the latest model, free. Hell, they would make me upgrade.

Under the new charter of rights and reqs, all dome citizens have a right to state-of-the-art health tech. Including regular upgrades to our implants and patches to upgrade our nanites. But that meant running standard scripts. Jono cracked my older model implant to let me run greynet scripts. Higher risk, higher reward. Which meant, I needed to drag my ass to Jono to get the malfunctioning circuit repaired.

Jono ran a legit mod clinic, licensed and everything. In legal terms, that only let him install recreational mods. Adjust a p-port for a new dick, sure. Add a little something extra to improve strength or boost speed, a-okay. Implant new mag links, fine. Even bionic limbs fell under rec-tech. But meddling with standard-issue med-tech like an ocular implant, not so much. Maintenance on an obsolete occ raised red flags. No one kept an older model ocular implant. Unless they intended to bypass the latest security upgrades. Most mod shops would report my dated tech to Oversight rather than keep it running. I paid well for Jono's discretion.

Lucky for me, the fritzing circuit didn't interfere with my control overlay. I struggled to make out much more than vague outlines of my room, but I pulled up my scheduling app. The digital assistant let me book an appointment under the guise of getting fitted out for a new hot-swappable dick. Then I caught a pre-programmed zoomer to Jono's. Heck, Jono had been singing the praises of the newest model for months now. So, if I had the credits left after the needed repairs, I'd ask about having him kit me out down below, too.

The zoomer dropped me outside the familiar clinic. A chime sounded when I walked inside. The vague outline of the register appeared vacant.

"That you Klein?" Jono's booming voice greeted me from the back.

"Guilty," I called toward the back of the shop.

"Be with you in a tick," Jono replied, "pop a squat."

I shuffled to a seat to wait. The details blurred together, but Jono always kept his clinic as tidy as his private quarters were messy. That knowledge allowed me to traverse the waiting area with reasonable confidence. I found a hard-plastic chair by touch and sank onto the seat.

Not that I spent much time in Jono's bedroom. Still, he had the big and bulky build I liked when I was in the mood for rough play. Jono might knock a few creds off the kit if I offered him a test drive of the new install.

I had more important shit to deal with than fucking my medic, but at the moment, I was a sitting duck with my occ all screwy. Thinking about banging Jono beat the hell out of wondering if Oversight was on my tail after I botched the exit on last night's job.

I pressed my palm to my temple again. That did nothing for the misaligned occ or the ache in my temples from trying to adjust to my screwy vision. At least putting my hands over my eyes gave my brain a rest from trying to unscramble visual inputs through the busted chip. I sat in darkness until Jono's shadow darkened the room further.

"You know, there's no shame in going on-grid, K."

I scowled in his general direction, my head spinning at the sudden movement. "I'm fine, thanks," I snapped at him.

"Mm-hmm," Jono hummed one of his 'I don't get it, but you do you' sounds. Like he'd do if someone came in asking for any outlandish custom mod.

I gritted my teeth.

"You want me to look at your occ first, or did you just want me to outfit you for the latest in penile prosthetics, Klein?"

"It's acting up again," I admitted, gesturing toward my eye.

"No shit. The circuits they use now are crap. Designed to biodegrade once the next-gen comes out, no one keeps the same occ as long as you, K."

I set my jaw. "Can you jailbreak the newer models yet?"

Jono let out a frustrated growl. "Why are you obsessed with the greynet? You could stop struggling if you would go on-grid and take your allotment. You'd even get the latest med patches when they first rollout. I hear the inoculation for that new flu strain is ready. Would it really be so bad?"

"I don't need a lecture, J." I scowled. "Can you fix my occ or not?"

Jono sighed, but he stepped aside to lead me to the semi-private bay at the back of the mod clinic. I felt my way to the chair and leaned back. Jono fastened the straps to hold me in place, then got to work on my occ. It was just as well I couldn't see what he was doing as he accessed the surgically installed implant port.

"This is… not great, Klein," Jono complained. "I don't want to know what you were doing to get fried this bad. I need to pop it out. See if this is even salvageable."

Removing the occ hardware meant knocking me out; if I was conscious, my brain would process the unplugging as if Jono had popped out my eyeballs. I didn't need that kind of trauma. "Gotta knock me out?"

"Yep," Jono popped the p. "Might as well do the upgrade on your p-port while you're out so it can accept the newer dick models. The bot can do the procedure on auto while I try to unfrag your occ. That should cover my ass for doing unlicensed med-mods," he grumbled the last, a grumpy reminder that he was sticking his neck out for me.

"Thanks, J, I owe you one," I said, meaning it.

Jono snorted. "You owe me way more than *one*, buddy. Was it worth whatever job did this to you?"

"Yeah," I said, voice husky as I considered last night's job. It was worth it. I *might* have fragged my occ, but I'd gotten past the Oversight drones with the new signal blocker. That meant I was still in the running for Dimech's Top Modder Challenge.

Jono's voice softened, and he was gentle as he swabbed my med-port with an alcohol wipe before injecting me with the anesthetic.

"Hope you're right, K," Jono said. As the meds hit my system, it sounded like he was talking from the far end of an air duct, the words growing fainter until I couldn't follow them. "Alright, I'll have you good as new in a tick. Time to take a nap for me."

Two

"Hey there, sleeping beauty." A familiar voice rumbled the greeting as I woke up in Jono's recovery bay. I blinked through the residual grogginess of the meds that had put me under. The cozy bunk came into sharp focus. Jono had fixed my occ.

I sat up, relieved that Jono came through for me yet again. The movement throbbed in my temples and sent a twinge of post-adjustment soreness through my lower abdomen. The ache tugged at my groin. I winced. Jono shoved the hydration tube built into the bay between my lips and steadied me with a hand on my shoulder.

"Easy there, K," he soothed.

"You fixed it?" I asked, though I saw for myself that he'd repaired the faulty connection. No more static in my vision. No more low buzz of a minor misalignment jangling at the edges of perception. Only clear, crisp vision beyond my default home overlay. I focused on the port diagnostic. A map of my body overlaid my vision; the entire map glowed with a bluish tinge used to show all systems were healthy. A slight purple tinge showed my nanites were healing tissue damage at my temple and groin, where Jono did his magic. Exactly what I would expect from the procedures we'd discussed before he put me under.

He didn't answer right away, and I dismissed the overlay to stare down my oldest friend. "You fixed it, right?"

"Klein…" Jono gave me an apologetic look as he shook his head.

"Jono," I said his name right back, voice tinged with panic and betrayal.

"Don't lose your port over it, K. You fried the chipset. It's a miracle the interface even lasted as long as it did. I upgraded you to an Ot5 I had in the back."

Okay. That could be worse. Ot5 was not the current model. It was harder to crack than my previous occ, but not impossible. I could still get greynet access on an Ot5. I took a deep, steadying breath.

"Okay." My voice only shook a little on the word.

"I imported your preferences and set up your standard scripts. It's ready to run homebrew. And it should trick the sensors next time you get scanned, unlike the piece of junk I dug out of your head. This is an upgrade, K."

"One I didn't ask for," I grumbled, even though I knew Jono was right.

"Right. Well, next time I can leave you conscious for the procedure. Then you can tell me to leave you blind rather than upgrade your occ," he shot back, jaw set mulishly.

"I didn't consent to this." I gestured sharply to the new implant.

That accusation cut deep. Jono crossed his brawny arms over his broad chest as he glowered at me. "You consented to repairs. I did the repairs and preserved your greynet access; that's what you care about, right?" He stopped short of saying it was the *only* thing I cared about. No rehashing the argument we'd had off and on since I got my first mod. The reason we'd never be more than occasional fuck buddies.

"Right," I growled. He didn't get it. That was fine. I didn't need Jono to understand. I only needed him to accept this was who I was and keep my mods working off-grid.

"Fine. I've got the latest models out back, any preferences?" Jono asked.

I shrugged one shoulder. "You know what I like."

Jono pushed away from my bedside and stomped into the backroom. He returned moments later, a dick in each hand. "I've got cut and uncut. They both connect to your wetware nerves and urethral port. And they're rated for reproductive use too, the reservoir for fake jizz can hold a viable sample."

I raised an eyebrow at that ridiculous notion. As if procreation mattered to me in the least. I pointed to the uncut dick, and Jono flipped it into my hands. The synth-skin felt silky smooth to my fingers. It was already approaching body temp from Jono holding it. I played with the foreskin. It stretched satisfyingly over the head. I imagined plugging it in and jacking it; yeah, this was the one.

"Thanks, Jono. I'll transfer the creds to your account through the usual channels," I assured him as I swung my legs off the gurney. Before getting up, I lined up my new hardware with the upgraded pleasure port. I hissed at the slight pinch as the port engaged and then the rush of overwhelm as my body accepted the new input. Ugh, instant boner from the acute sensitivity of a new bit of hardware. I shivered at the way the air played over my new synth-flesh.

"Good?" Jono smirked at me.

"Care to take it for a test drive?" I offered, gesturing at my groin. I doubted he'd take me up on it while I was still lightheaded from the meds and the adjustments to my mods.

Sure enough, Jono dismissed the notion with a flippant gesture. "You know better. No fucking for at least forty-eight hours after an occ install. And go easy on the new hardware—"

"Yeah, yeah," I interrupted the familiar lecture, waving away Jono's dire warnings. "No overexerting myself while the adjustments to my port heal or I might lose sensation, I know the drill."

"Come back next week, and I can check the alignment on the new occ. Make sure the mods are healing well." He winked at me. The occ wouldn't need an alignment that soon. The follow-up visit gave us an excuse to hook up without the risk of alerting anyone in Oversight that he was more to me than a talented mod jockey.

"Sure thing," I agreed, limping on my way to the cubby where Jono stashed my crap after a procedure. Yep, as expected, my clothes sat in a neat stack alongside the damaged occ. A few hot-swappable accessories I'd forgotten to unplug before the appointment, and the dick I'd worn here lay piled on top. Jono always unplugged everything he could when he put me under to work on my mods. That way, if he had to shock me in an emergency, it wouldn't risk frying all my favorite toys.

I plugged my removable mods back in before getting dressed. These mods all had legal components. None of them would get me noticed on a casual inspection, but each had greynet upgrades that might land me in lockup if scrutinized.

To name a few of my favorite toys, I had two extra digits attached via mag links on each hand that improved my dexterity. Those doubled as digital and physical lock picks. Skin patches placed over major my muscle groups boosted nerve signals for faster reflexes. They also concealed encapsulated doses of less-than-legal stimulants to give me an extra athletic edge in a pinch.

The chip on the back of my neck that was a grey-hacked version of a GPS integrated navigation device to steer me clear of Oversight occ frequencies. It would detect any devices operating on the Sec-Tech frequency within a hundred yards. When it detected Sec-Tech drones, it vibrated a warning. I ignored that one when I wasn't plugged into the greynet. Better not to attract attention by avoiding Oversight when I wasn't actively breaking the law.

I had other mods at home and more than a few permanent upgrades, impossible to unplug. All the standard-issue nanites that speeded healing and improved my resistance to disease, for a start. They purported to protect against UV damage outside the domes too, but no one tested that feature these days. We had everything we needed inside our domed cities. More importantly, I'd gotten greynet hacks to delete the programming that would let Sec-Tech knock me out at a distance with those same nanites. I'd even found a hacker who could disable the Oversight anti-lawlessness subroutines. The ones that hacked your own nervous system to make engaging in illegal acts rather unpleasant.

Some of my mods were more mundane. I had a few that were pure aesthetics, too. Among my favorites, the glowing purple and red bands on my upper arms. Those were for when I wanted to pull without broadcasting my profile. The colors advertised what I was packing in my pants, and who I was looking to fuck with it: a dick, and I wasn't picky so long as they didn't mind it wasn't what I was born with.

On the greynet, many of us preferred genital mods. Better sensation, less mess, no need for fertility blockers, and you could have any parts—or combination of parts—that suited you. Outside the grey, I knew plenty of people who embraced mods of every kind yet balked at getting a p-port mod to integrate with genital hardware.

Guess it made them squeamish to bypass or remove the original bits. That was a bonus to my mind, but then I'd never much understood people who wrapped their identity up in what was between their legs at birth.

Jono said it was because I was mis-classified at birth. He claimed if I'd been born with a dick, my preferred equipment, I'd have thought twice about the procedure to replace it with a pleasure port. The p-port let me swap between artificial genitals. Maybe he was right, but I hadn't thought twice—I'd barely thought once. And back then, getting a p-port required jumping through enough hoops that I'd felt like my only recourse was a greynet mod. That's when I'd first gone off-grid. The grey zone gave me a home. For me, the grey wasn't about breaking the rules or trying to take more than my fair share. It was where people understood me.

Sure, I could go on-grid and get all my routine occ upgrades through universal mod coverage. Every dome citizen had a right to any needed health mods. The nanites we got at birth protected us from disease and injury. Our health records were available in real-time thanks to those same nanites. The bots in my bloodstream relayed the state of my health to my citizen records. That data fed into a system that determined my dietary needs. The Nutri-kiosks in every home and public square altered my food allotment accordingly.

All the systems tied together, and our occs allowed us to interface with those systems. We could only access the nutrients we needed, but on-grid, everyone had access to their nourishment at any kiosk. Off-grid, you were on your own. I liked that, though, relying on my wits.

The problem with going off-grid was that it threatened the status quo. Oversight discouraged it, and greynet mods were illegal. They claim the rules are to protect us. More than one hacked mod had led to grievous bodily harm or killed an off-gridder. Any good on-grid citizen would agree making hacks illegal was for the hacker's own good. Ask those of us who preferred the outskirts, and we would defend our right to make that choice. Even if it killed us for not much gain.

There was nothing like the joy of testing a new mod and sharing it with my buddies. Nothing like the latest mod zinging along my senses. I lived for that thrill.

I used my occ to call up the zoomer app, and summon one of the solar-powered solo transport boards from a nearby charging bay. It would get me from Jono's to the Quarter, where I was squatting. Another downside of being off-grid. No citizen assigned housing. Plus side, no one tracked my every move and every person who visited me. The downside, off-grid housing wasn't luxury accommodations. Not that I cared. I didn't need luxury when I had the grey.

I plugged in, even as the zoomer whisked me across the grey zone toward home on autopilot. The new occ interface took some adjusting. The dull ache behind my eyes from the changes only seemed to get worse the longer I was awake. Still, I accessed my usual greynet haunts at a thought.

The interface showed me the job board. They modeled the grey jobboard after the one on-grid. Everyone could earn extra creds beyond their citizen stipend by signing on for jobs in the community. The same was true on the grey. But instead of data entry, remote customer service, or menial labor, greynet jobs came with more risk. People posted looking for coders or modders. Some wanted testers for new mods or hacks on existing mods. And bingo, there was a job posted a few hours ago from the mysterious Dimech. *Wanted: mod tester candidates to pass the third level of the Top Modder Challenge. Compensation: commensurate with challenge results, the greater the risk, the greater the reward. - Dimech*

The Top Modder Challenge was the reason I needed my greynet access. I refused to miss out now that I'd finally gotten on Dimech's radar. They were legendary off-grid and infamous on-grid. Rumor claimed they worked with the lead developer behind the Ot1 ocular implant. The first generation of the current model. The team behind Ot1 had revolutionized modding.

Life in the domes had been fraught until the team behind Ot1 created a fair resource allocation system. With the implants, every citizen could be sure their needs got met. When ocular interfaces became mainstream, it changed everything. Occs made nanites practical for widespread use. Food security followed the nanite powered medical revolution thanks to occs. Occ integration provided an uncomplicated way to ensure a fair distribution model for vital resources. It didn't hurt that Seed owned the whole agricultural sector by then. Nutri-kiosks were already popping up on every corner—food for all.

I was born after the global shift to domed cities. But all the history books agreed that the Ot1 smoothed the transition to globalization. Occs fulfilled the domes' promise of plentiful food and healthcare for every citizen. No one would go hungry or homeless on the grid. Everyone inside the domes had safety from the ravages of a climate that could no longer sustain us outside our protected cities.

The grid provided ample work for every citizen. Oversight had built a fair-trade system that spread work and rewards to all citizens. The chaos of the mass migration into the domes turned into a new social order. All because the makers of the Ot1 secured their patent with an ironclad non-profit stipulation. No one could ever profit from the device or any tech integrated with the occ implant. Every citizen who wished to go on-grid got free ocular implants from the time they reached the age of majority to the grave. We all contributed to the grid, and it took care of its own. In theory.

Most of the time the theory worked. We didn't have poverty the way the history books talked about it. The grid didn't allow accumulation of wealth. You earned what you needed, and anything over your credit cap passed back into the system.

Some people left the grid to escape the wealth caps. Others for the thrill of flying without a safety net. And some had political grievances. I was in the second category. I felt most alive when I was testing a new mod.

Dimech was issuing a challenge to every mod junkie out there. Take the next risk, earn the next reward. I'd just about busted my occ on the last challenge, and I was already jonesing for the next round.

I accepted Dimech's work order into my job queue. A tingle along my spine alerted me to a Sec-Tech drone making the rounds of the sector. I tabbed out of the greynet and focused on a grid-approved porn feed I enjoyed. In a stroke of luck, my favorite channel was live. A local couple who were both ported. They set their occs to stream their sex-life and earned credits for every view on their channel. I got charged entertainment credits for viewing, and I had plenty to spare. For an extra fee, this channel offered the option to plug into the tactile subroutine. Pay up and get their p-port signals synced to my port, so I felt the sensations along with the couple. Bad idea with the brand new install.

Today the couple on my occ overlay were using older hardware, Ange had a monster cock plugged in. She was giving Trel the fucking of a lifetime. Trel, for their part, was using a mod that combined a vaginal canal and a dick. Trel looked ready to blow any second. I didn't stop watching when the tingle from the drone had passed.

Instead, I explored my newest mod. I ran my fingers along the length; it was as warm and soft as my skin. The internal parts started flaccid, almost like a native cock, so it fit in my pants. As I stroked it, the smooth synth-skin moved over a harder core that firmed with my growing sense of arousal at every touch. The needy moans from the occ-stream added to my pleasure.

The stream ended with Trel spurting fake cum all over themself. Ange pulled out to finish jerking off and add to the mess on her spouse's torso. The stream cut off, leaving me with an unobstructed view of my new throbbing dick in my hand. I tucked it away, muting the inputs to kill my arousal. Jono was right that I should give the adjustments time to heal, nanites, or not, and I had a job to plan.

Three

THE THIRD ROUND of the Top Modder Challenge proved more difficult than the previous two. Round one was testing a new line of code: could the patch fool an Oversight sensor? All I had to do was access the grey in front of a drone and trust the patch to hide what I was doing. I took the leap of faith along with about a hundred other off-gridders. We all had our reasons, I'm sure. For me, it was about the thrill of the challenge. The intense rush of adrenaline at doing something so reckless.

I'd completed the task with ease. The detector chip in my neck made finding a drone child's play. If they caught me running on the grey, I'd end up back on-grid with a brand new Ot8 implant. Until the mod community broke the state-of-the-art security features, greynet access remained impossible. The grey almost always ran a few generations behind current-gen med-tech. I shivered at the thought of getting cut off from my community on the greynet.

Solution: don't get caught. Simple. The potential consequences made it terrifying. I'd done it, though. And the second challenge, too.

For that, I broke into a citizen residence and accessed an on-grid private Nutri-kiosk with an interface patch. Easy-peasy with a hack that let me copy a citizen's RFID instead of only reading their profile when we interacted. The only snag I hit came when my target walked in while my order was still processing.

When I broke off the connection after they reported a hacker to Oversight, the kiosk's anti-tampering protocol had fried my old occ. Still, I'd gotten the meal and gotten out, so it counted as a completed mission. The boards said only a handful of us had succeeded in the second challenge during the allotted time frame.

Mission three was an even higher risk. It would winnow those vying to win the challenge even further.

Dimech ran these challenges every few years, and I'd never made it past round three. This was my year, though, I felt it in every circuit connected to my occ.

All I had to do was infiltrate the governance offices. The mod from challenge one would help me avoid detection from Sec-Tech and Oversight. The RFID duplicator should let me gain access if I copied a citizen profile for someone with higher-level grid access.

Once inside the halls of governance, all I had to do was plug into an interface and upload a harmless virus tagging that I'd been there. The new Ot5's faster processing times should make the upload go more smoothly. I owed Jono a proper thank you for the upgrade, loathe as I was to admit it. First, I needed to rest.

The challenge timer gave me until tomorrow at midnight to complete my task. Enough time to scope out the public plazas around the governance building. Find the highest-ranking citizen around to copy. The higher clearance the port I tagged, the better my challenge ranking. Lucky for me, I had a target already in mind.

Four

It had been years since I last saw Xav. I scanned my old friend's RFID tag to pull up their current profile. Still went by Xav Radke, ze/zir pronouns was a change from when I'd known zir. Basic health stats were irrelevant to me, but which might save zir life in an emergency. If EMS needed to dose zir with exogenous meds or administer a blood transfusion, for example. I skimmed through zir relationship status line, considering an angle of approach. Single, not looking, and not interested in casual sex. The glow bands that we'd gotten inked together when we reached our majority were quiescent in zir upper arm. That bore out what zir profile said about lacking interest in sex or relationships.

So, if I'd been of a mind to strike up a flirtation, neither of us needed to waste our time. In fact, if I ignored zir profile and bands to angle at getting in zir pants anyway, ze would be within zir rights to report me to Oversight for harassment. The fact I'd pulled up zir profile would substantiate that I'd knowingly made an unwanted advance. The punishment for a first-time harassment charge was only a twenty-four-hour orgasm block. I'd used apps with similar code to edge myself, but it was different when you couldn't turn it off at will. That ruled out a direct approach to gathering intel about Xav's current work.

It was strange to observe Xav from across a public plaza as ze ate lunch from a communal Nutri-kiosk. We grew up together. As someone who had worked zir way up the grid hierarchy, Xav had access to the cutting edge of anti-aging upgrades to zir nanites. Xav still looked like ze was in zir early twenties. I took a moment to admire the long purple appendages sprouting from zir scalp.

Looked like even after choosing a life on-grid, Xav hadn't lost zir interest in the more eccentric mods. Tentacles in place of hair seemed a more than reasonable trade-off in my book. Most citizens didn't see body mods in the same casual way I did, so it seemed an odd choice. I was familiar with the mod Xav had chosen. Two dextrous feelers for manipulating objects. The models I'd seen also doubled as sensitive erogenous zones, a feature that could toggle off and on at will. Those had cost a load of creds at a licensed med-mod shop.

Jono installed something similar using mag links. A nanite upgrade innervated the appendages and linked them into my occ controls. I doubted I'd look quite as lovely with the long, graceful feelers. Xav had one of those vid-perfect faces that always could pull off the more exotic mods.

I was losing track of my goal here. No rekindling an old flame. Xav had no tolerance for the greynet. With zir position, we couldn't be friends as long as I was off-grid. Heck, after what I planned to do with zir credentials, I doubted ze would ever forgive me. I pulled up the subroutine that would let me clone zir RFID profile. Then I used a different citizen profile I'd copied on the way here to access a Nutri-kiosk a few seats down from Xav. Close enough to observe zir, but far enough not to attract zir notice.

I needed zir credentials to go along with zir profile if I wanted to get much further than the public halls of governance. That meant collecting a biomarker sample. The skin near a mod port lost sensitivity. If I got close enough, I had a modded digit to collect the sample from the skin surrounding Xav's port. I knew ze had a med-port on zir left upper arm. A twin to my own, from the monthly blockers we'd both opted to take from puberty to our majority when we could get legal mod work done. Ze might have had the port removed after it was no longer needed, but most people left them in since they made med injections painless. I just needed an unremarkable reason to bump zir in the lunchtime crowd. Plenty of people were eating their lunch around us. It should be simple to jostle Xav in the press if I timed it right.

A commotion on the far side of the square drew my attention. A shabbily dressed citizen plucked at their arms and twitched. Their moans sounded loud in the sudden hush around the square. My overlay blinked with a message from Oversight that someone had reported a citizen having a medical crisis near my location. The message warned me to stay out of the way when the crisis team, comprising a medic and a social worker, arrived. My overlay flashed with a vid link of the distressed citizen. The vid obscured their face, but otherwise left it clear enough to confirm I wasn't witnessing a separate—as yet unreported—incident. The blue flush to their skin was a clear sign of Synth overdose. Poor schmuck.

The victim's misfortune was just the distraction I needed. As the crowd buzzed with the emergency signal, I slipped away from my Nutri-kiosk and sidled toward Xav. Zir attention remained fixated on zir overlay. I brushed into zir arm, pretending to stumble into zir back to cover for jabbing the port site with my modded digit.

Xav spun to face me, a frown knitting zir familiar features. I gripped zir arm for balance.

"Apologies, citizen, I need to get my mod recalibrated. The old knee isn't what it used to be," I hunched my shoulders. Had to hope the synth-skin mask I'd put on before this outing would transform my features enough so that Xav wouldn't recognize me. My voice was a full octave lower than it had been when we'd known each other. No flutter of familiarity passed zir face.

"Joint repairs get more complex if you put them off," Xav lectured. "See that you get it tended soon, elder." Xav patted my hand, as though wanting to take the sting out of the admonishment. Still a self-righteous prick, then. That eased some of my guilt over using Xav's credentials. My overlay flashed that I'd gotten a viable sample. The needle retracted into my mod, nothing to betray what I'd done.

I nodded affably. "Of course, citizen. I'll make the appointment today," I lied.

Xav smiled benevolently. I made a show of steadying myself before releasing my grip on zir arm. I activated a subroutine to send shooting pain along the nerves in my leg and limped away. Not fun, but better than blowing my cover since I was not an accomplished actor. I hobbled across the square to the governance building.

The slower gait gave me time to set up a shell profile with Xav's copied profile and zir stolen biometric data. I could go home and create a more durable copy of zir data, make synth-films for my eyes and fingers to fool scanners. Instead, I trusted my success to a code breaker I'd gotten off a buddy. In theory, it would combine my biometrics and the sample I'd gotten off Xav to run an algorithm to trick the sensor. If it worked, it should take my stats and read them as Xav's. Risky. Perfect for scoring me challenge points.

I was out of Xav's sight, so I turned off the signals that helped me maintain the limp. Next, I toggled the synth-mask into a new configuration. Wrinkle smoothed away to make my appearance younger. The first security check only required RFID clearance. The cloned profile got me through. No sweat.

From the restricted area, I got on the elevator and synced my occ up to the controls. I used a greynet mod to trick the system into reading Xav's profile. Accessing the lower levels took a biometric check. The higher the area's clearance, the more stringent the bio-locks. The first genuine test of my new algos. I held my breath as I pressed the pad of my thumb to the sensor. The first bank of numbers on my command overlay lit up green.

Next was an ocular scan. Harder to trick, but I held my head still and stared into the little camera as it shot a beam of light into my unmodded eye. They equipped some security systems to turn that beam into a weapon if you didn't have clearance. The one here at the public governance building was unlikely to do permanent nerve damage if my program failed. The next block of numbers lit.

Deep, steadying breath. No celebrating yet. To access the lowest levels, I had to give a DNA sample. I held up the digit with Xav's blood in it and let the machine prick the synth-skin and collect zir blood.

Bingo. All levels access. I screen-capped the panel on my overlay as proof and hit the button for the lowest sublevel. The elevator descended.

Five

I DON'T KNOW what I expected to find in the sub-basement, but it wasn't an ordinary office. The drab hallways with uniform cubicles in neat rows seemed anticlimactic. No one glanced up at me as I stepped off the elevator and strode down the hall. There were only a handful of citizens at their workstations during the lunch hour. They all appeared too engrossed in their work to notice my arrival. No one had access to the lower levels unless they had legit business there, so they would all assume I belonged.

The glass-walled offices along the perimeter had neat name-plates next to their doors. I found Xav's name on a door along the back wall and walked in like I owned the place.

Once inside, I activated the blinds on the glass wall to give myself privacy. I synced my occ with Xav's workstation. Again, the system scanned my RFID, reading the cloned copy before granting me access. I wasted no time pulling up a command prompt and loading Dimech's file into the system with my tag. I got in. Klein was here. I smiled as the file pinged that my install had succeeded. I spared a thought for what the encrypted file did, but Dimech's challenges were only a game. It couldn't be anything too consequential.

I itched to see how my results stacked against the competition. No time to gloat, I had to exit before anyone noticed I had no business down here. I unsynced my occ and retraced my steps to the elevator. No security checks for leaving, so I rode up to the ground floor.

Everything ran smooth, until I returned to the public plaza. I opened the app to call up a zoomer, but before I stepped aboard, a greynet message overrode my overlay.

User Special-K: *Congrats, Klein, you're the first to complete the third level of my challenge.*

Achievement unlocked: revolutionary

I frowned as I set the destination on the zoomer and stepped aboard. This was only a game, I had no objections to the current social order. Revolution was the last thing I wanted. I enjoyed the status quo. As long as Oversight let us choose a life in the grey, I harbored no arguments with the government.

As the zoomer took off, I tried to blink away the message, to no avail. A second message replaced the first. This time, Dimech's handle popped into my interface. Followed by the symbol for an organization I'd thought had disappeared when the domes closed. The domed cities protected us from rising temperatures and sinking lands. Against all odds, our enclosed city thrived. Refugees from a world ravaged by greed created a novel way of life. Schools taught that the old symbol of protest died away after ocular implants remade society. The strange ancient symbol set my nerves on edge. This seemed less and less like an innocent prank. What had I gotten myself into? Then my display filled with a single word that chilled me: *Boom.*

Behind me, there was a concussive blast of heat and sound and light. With the sick realization gnawing at my gut that he'd played me, I turned to face the governance building. Instead of the stone edifice, there was a wall of smoke and fire.

The zoomer stalled. An emergency override redirected me to the nearest shelter. Alarms blared all around me. My overlay filled with an Oversight alert, warning me to seek immediate shelter. A pre-recorded voice assured me that help was on the way.

I didn't have to let the zoomer deliver me to Oversight. If I did nothing, emergency overrides would take me to a Sec-Tech checkpoint, along with everyone else within a few blocks of the bombing. Sec-Tech would ask questions about whether I'd seen anything. I could have used the greynet to do a manual override. Flee the scene. Protect my secrets. I didn't.

Turned out Jono was wrong; I cared about something more than my greynet access, after all. I couldn't leave Xav to take the fall for blowing up a building. Defeated, I let the zoomer take me to the nearest Oversight station to give them everything I knew about Dimech and the challenge.

Six

I'D BEEN RIGHT that this was the end of my freedom. Oversight took one look at my out-of-date occ, and before I knew it, they had me speaking to a support worker about getting back on-grid. Next step, getting upgraded to the latest occ model with its top-end security features. That would cut me off from the greynet.

They paused when I told them I had information about the bombing. When I dropped Xav's name, I got whisked away to talk to whoever was in charge. That turned out to be a burly Sec-Tech detective decked out in the latest model personal armor suit. It looked kind of badass, and it covered a bionic mod I didn't associate with grid citizens.

A quick scan of his profile told me his name was Harris, and he used he/him pronouns. His entire left arm was mechanical. He had sensory mods in place of hair, similar to Xav's but more of them, and smaller. Medusa mods, lots of little feelers that gave him sensory input. Bet they were sensitive to touch, too. Not that I'd be touching the imposing guy attached to the hypnotically swaying tendrils anytime soon. Or ever. Pity, if he wasn't likely to arrest me as a terrorist in the next few minutes, he'd be just my type.

"You said you have information about the bombing at the governance hall?" Harris demanded, looking down his nose at me.

"Yes," I wet my lips before plunging in and burning my bridges. "You know about the Top Modder Challenge?"

Harris grunted, a sound that I interpreted as a 'no', then gestured for me to elaborate.

"The greynet has a job board, like the one on-grid, except greynet jobs are more like games. Or challenges. You know, tag the most secure location, test a new mod to the breaking point, bypass the latest sec-tech patch. Stuff like that." I shrugged, playing it off as not a big deal. Not worth Sec-Tech's interest.

"I am aware of greynet pranks," Harris interjected, arms crossed over his chest. He didn't look the least bit impressed by me. "Get to the point, Klein."

I nodded, took a deep breath, and confessed, "Quintus Dimech runs one of the biggest challenges every year. I thought I was just tagging in. The code was only supposed to contain a tag. I swear it. If it wasn't from Dimech, I'd have confirmed that, but it seemed like a harmless prank."

"You uploaded the code that caused the generator to overload?"

"Yes. Xav Eckles and I used to be friends. Before I went off-grid. When I took the challenge, I cloned Xav's profile and stole a bit of zir genetic material without zir knowledge or consent." I hid a wince at the confession. It wasn't an act I was proud of, but it was only supposed to be a harmless prank. "Then I used that to access the secure network inside the governance building. He said it was only a tag. To show how easy it is to bypass grid security, thumbing our noses, not an attack."

Harris regarded me for a long time, then he nodded. "Okay, that lines up with what we already know. Give me a minute." Harris beckoned to the Sec-Tech guards who had escorted me and said, "See that Klein doesn't leave. I have a job for him."

I could only guess what that task might entail. Harris turned to leave. If I stayed here, my situation would get sticky in a hurry. I'd let myself get hauled in and questioned, that would make me suspect among my contacts on the grey. Once they learned that I'd cooperated with Oversight.

Something this major going down minutes after I tagged in at the governance building? Yeah, people would check up on me and it would not go unremarked that I was here instead of doing an override on the zoomer. At the least, Dimech would know. If Harris accepted my help hunting down the party behind the attack, there was a small—rapidly shrinking—window for action.

"Wait," I called out as the door slid open for him, programmed to respond to his occ. I suspected the door's programming would lock me inside if I tried to pass through it using my actual profile chip. Harris paused, but he didn't turn to face me. I had to talk fast if I hoped to get out of this mess unscathed. "I can help, if we act fast. Once they know I'm here, my contacts on the greynet may not trust me and our options shrink."

"What contacts would those be, Klein? Anarchists intent on bringing back the bad old days?"

"No. Just a few others who aren't happy on-grid. We like a little more risk than Oversight allows grid citizens."

One of the Sec-Tech goons snorted and muttered under his breath. "Right, risks like starving to death if you can't find work and spreading a plague because you're too stubborn to upgrade your nanites with the rest of us."

"Risks like free-flying a zoomer instead of taking a pre-programmed one," I countered. "The thrill of flying along the roofline on manual controls is worth the risk of falling."

"You mean dying," Harris corrected. He met my eyes with a steely determination that sent a shiver along my spine. God, that intense focus did things to me. Those dark eyes sparkled without the distant look of someone focused on their occ inputs. He was looking right at me, really seeing me. His regard sent an illicit thrill through me; if I wasn't careful, he might get under my skin.

"Yeah," I drawled with a laconic shrug.

Harris' eyes unfocused, he was checking his occ display. He frowned and then nodded to me. "Xav confirms ze knew Klein Wallace as a student. Ze says you haven't been in contact in years, though. So, Klein, tell me why we shouldn't send you to Oversight as a co-conspirator in the bombing?"

"Because I'll help you nail whoever's behind the bombing. I'm nothing but an unwitting pawn, but I can help you find the guy moving the pieces if we act fast. Now, before they realize I'm not on their side."

"And what makes you think we need you for that?" Harris challenged.

"Because I'm part of the greynet, I have connections, and I'm in contact with Dimech."

Harris regarded me impassively for a long moment. I regretted coming here, even if fleeing would have meant leaving Xav high and dry. If Harris refused my help, I saw no simple way out of this situation.

I didn't want to get sent to Oversight. Not for this crime. It would mean reprogramming; the worst punishment possible. So terrible they reserved it for treason and mass murder. The process left you a different person than before. Meek and docile. They did something similar before the domes. The primitive version risked leaving the patient incapacitated. Without consent, it was an act even most greynet mod shops refused. Only the least scrupulous shops even offered elective versions of the procedure, most often to treat Synth addiction. My insides crawled at the thought I might find myself headed for a re-programmer's not so tender mercies.

"Please," I croaked. "Let me help."

Harris's steely gaze didn't leave me as he said, "Okay."

"Okay?" I blinked, hope rekindling in my chest.

"Okay. Don't make me regret this, Klein. Come on, if you're right, we won't have long before your connections get wise to you being here, let's move." Harris turned on his heel, expecting me to follow. I scrambled to obey, not daring to test him when the stakes were so high.

Harris took me to a mod medic who jacked into my occ and uploaded a proximity alert. They explained that if I had to stay within a thirty-foot radius of my new minder. If not, my occ would transmit a signal to every Oversight drone in the dome that I was an escaped criminal. Possible to work around, given adequate time and resources. I had neither at my disposal at the moment. So I agreed to Harris' terms and followed him out of the Oversight offices. We boarded a waiting double occupancy zoomer.

"Where are we going?" I asked.

"Wherever your contacts would expect you to be, considering what happened. Let's try not to blow your cover right out of the gate."

I gave him an exaggerated once over, and said, "No one is going to believe that I picked up an Oversight drone to bring home." I didn't add the second half of that thought: 'no matter how ridiculously hot he is.'

Harris smirked at me, as though he'd read my mind. "Don't worry about that, I can blend in off-grid."

I doubted that, but he was in charge here. My fate was in the man's hands, so I mounted the zoomer with him and provided the address for my current squat.

Seven

WE STOPPED off along the way for Harris to change out of his Sec-Tech gear. Instead, he donned a mod-suit that blended better with the slums. He was still a giant of a man, but his medusa mods, bionic arm, and the colorful glowing insignia on his bare flesh-and-blood biceps fit into my world.

The colorful neon bands around his arm made me smirk at him. He caught me looking and returned my lingering gaze. Our stated preferences aligned. The realization filled me with a giddy interest. But then I remembered the smoke and fire. The explosion I'd gotten duped into causing. No sense flirting with a drone who'd be out of his mind to trust me.

My top priority had to be helping him investigate Dimech and the bombing, even if I had to skirt the law to do it.

"You can't go off-grid as a Sec-Tech operative. Don't suppose you have a spare ID you can use?" I checked.

"That would be illegal," Harris said wryly. "I can get something set up through Oversight for approved undercover work, but approvals take time we don't have."

With a heavy sigh, I offered, "I can hook you up with something if you let me link to your occ?"

For a moment, I thought he'd refuse. Instead, he nodded and dipped his head to offer me access to the almost invisible hard outline of a chip embedded under the skin of his forehead. I patched into his occ and uploaded a greynet clone account to his chip through his occ interface. That way anyone who scanned him wouldn't see Harris the Oversight drone's public profile. They'd read him as a fellow off-gridder. Big and intimidating as all seven hells, but one of us.

I admired his physique in the skin-tight mod-suit. It should protect from projectiles, energy weapons and blunt any high-speed impact, like a fall from a zoomer. I had something similar on under my more grid appropriate attire, too. While Harris changed, I ditched my business wear. His place seemed nice. Quiet. Then we were back on the zoomer, headed toward home.

I knew something was wrong before my proximity alert even pinged my occ overlay. We were a few blocks from my building still; I slowed the zoomer to check my security feeds. Someone had been inside my squat while I was out. They had compromised my surveillance feed. Whoever broke in was no amateur. They had hacked the camera to show a loop of me leaving the building this morning. My grid appropriate attire still stowed in a satchel. This was a taunt. Same as the messages on my occ display before the building blew. No telling what we'd find if we blundered inside.

"Cluster melons," I cursed under my breath. Change of plans. I overrode the nav controls on the zoomer to detour away from home. I'd miss my setup, but I'd already resigned myself to writing it all off. The heavens only knew what sort of malicious code the intruder might have installed. None of my gear was valuable enough to risk plugging back into it. At least I'd brought most of my favorites with me for the mission, including my latest acquisition from Jono. My new rig was the least of my worries.

Harris quirked a brow at me. "Something wrong?"

I nodded. "Not sure who did it, but my place's compromised. Whoever broke in might still be there. Waiting for us—er, me."

"I think I can handle an intruder," Harris observed blandly.

"You sure about that?" I challenged him, hands on my hips, and heart racing at the thought of going into my home to find it violated. "This is the grey zone. We don't play by on-grid rules here. Anyway, I have other bolt holes that will serve our purposes," I said, trying to sound unaffected by this invasion of my haven.

I swallowed hard. All my gear—gone. Even if I extricated myself from this mess, there would be nothing to salvage now that Oversight had my address. Heck, Harris could call in backup drones to raid my place even now.

Harris didn't waste more time posturing. "You're the one who said we needed your setup here. If we don't, then tell me where to go, Klein," Harris relented.

"I need to plug into the net on a proper interface. Doesn't have to be here, though. Come on, I'll do you one better, I'll show you where we're going," I said. With the way Dimech had been one step ahead of me all day, I didn't trust tech to get us where we were going. I'd led enough trouble home without bringing it to my closest friend's doorstep, too. "We're ditching the zoomer and walking from here. Hope you've got boosters in that suit." I leveled a challenging look at Harris, daring him to keep up with me.

Harris did not look happy at the development, lips pressed into a tight line, but he didn't argue. I landed the zoomer atop an abandoned building and led him along the rooftop. I activated a signal scrambler to ditch any electronic trails we'd picked up. Then I hit the muscle booster patches under my mod-suit to leap across a ten-foot gap between buildings. The extra juice pumping into my bloodstream made it effortless. Hells, *this* was why I couldn't imagine returning to the grid. Not when it meant giving up the rush of adrenaline at trying a new trick. Pushing the limits of my body and mind to come up with new mods and try them. I paused only long enough to be sure Harris was keeping up before I sprinted toward our destination across the rundown cityscape of the grey zone.

The abandoned areas near the edges of the dome still felt like home, no matter how much I'd fragged up everything. No one wanted to live within sight of the world that existed before humanity fled from a hostile climate to cower within our domed cities. The grey zone had plenty of abandoned places to carve out a life. I'd find a new squat and rebuild if Harris let me walk away after I helped him. Grid citizens preferred the central areas, so us misfits took over the outskirts, made them our own. Made the grey zone a place where modders lived—and died—as we pleased.

Eight

My heart was in my throat as Jono's shop came into view. I half expected to see a plume of smoke, or rubble where the mod shop had been. It remained unchanged on the outside. I didn't dare contact Jono through my usual channels. Not with Dimech knowing far too much about me and my routine.

I had my occ display off, disconnected from the net. I navigated by memory instead of GPS. No clues to lead an enemy here. The bell over the door jingled as I led Harris inside.

"Jono?"

"With a client. Do you have an appointment?" Jono called back, warning me that we weren't alone.

"Walk-in," I replied gruffly. "Need a consult for a buddy."

"Scan the code on the counter for my availability," Jono didn't even bother sticking his head out of the mod bay. That was fine, I scanned the code, and it synced my overlay with his appointment calendar for the day. Two more bookings this afternoon, with awkward spacing so that he'd have time to clean up between clients. The privacy filter didn't show me their deets. Fuckbuckets, I didn't have time to wait. And Jono would not appreciate me announcing to the client in the bay that I'd let myself into his private quarters. He wouldn't have played it like I was some random off the street if he considered it safe to talk in front of his patron.

I tagged in a spare cloned profile for his final appointment slot of the day and led Harris back outside to keep up appearances.

"Buddy of yours?" Harris asked once we were back outside.

"My mod guy," I replied, neither confirming nor denying. We walked to the end of the block before Harris balked.

"What now?" he demanded.

I rubbed at my temples. The ache from my recent adjustments, and the after-effects of using boosters hitting me hard now that the immediate danger had passed. "Now we find a place to lie low until Jono's free."

"The modder?" Harris asked. He crossed his muscular arms, his stony expression impassive.

"Yeah," I confirmed. "The modder."

"He help you pull off the bombing?" Harris asked.

I snorted derisively. "As though I'd tell you if he did? No, Jono doesn't know a damn thing about the challenge, Dimech, or the bombing. Come on. We need a Nutri-kiosk and a place to crash."

"We don't have time to fuck around," Harris snapped, the impassive facade cracking. That hadn't been what I meant about crashing, but hells, I wished he was wrong.

I deflected my feelings with snark, "That works, since I don't fuck around with Oversight drones."

Harris gave me his best unimpressed face and ignored the dig. "We don't know what else this Dimech has planned. Once you linked his greynet work order to the bombing, our tech team connected him to hundreds of job postings. They could be up to anything. You might face much more than mere public property damage charges by the time this ends."

That should not have sent a rush of relief through me, but it did. Enough that my knees buckled, and I'd have fallen if Harris hadn't steadied me. "No one died?" I asked, scarcely daring to believe it.

Harris shook his head. "No. Most of the employees were at lunch. So far, the medics on site have reported extensive wounds, but no fatalities."

I wasn't an unwitting mass murderer. Small mercies. I hadn't allowed myself to consider that until this moment. Did that make me an uncaring bastard? Probably, but I couldn't change what had already happened, and I'd been in survival mode. Still should be.

"Good. Come on, I have a code to get into Jono's place from the back." I led Harris down an alley and around the building to Jono's private entrance.

The rickety stairs creaked underfoot, Jono joked that it let him know someone was coming. He had a surveillance camera on the door too, but Jono always did like low tech redundancies. The stairwell was dusty and dim to discourage interlopers from looking for something nice to pinch. I keyed in my access code and used the picks concealed in my bionic digit on the old tumbler style lock.

Harris raised a brow at me as I swung the door open and gestured for him to enter. He didn't comment, and I kept my mouth shut for once. It wasn't like a charge for breaking into my buddy's place was going to mean anything. Not after the crimes he could already lay at my feet.

I went straight to Jono's gaming rig in the back bedroom, Harris trailing behind me. If he was right, we couldn't afford to sit around on our asses while Dimech hurt people.

I used fabricated credentials to log into the grey through the interface. The processing power in the stationary array made it easier to hide my traces as I accessed the jobs board. Too bad Dimech not only knew every trick in the book to avoid a trace himself, but his family had also invented the damn tech we all relied on. That was a chilling thought, considering what he'd already done. What else might he have planned with the snippets of code he'd doled out for the challenge? Code that we'd planted inside the most secure server that connected to every grid citizen's occ. The same one that housed the database that pushed out upgrades for nanites for every citizen on-grid.

Oh, hells. I hoped to all seven of them that I was wrong as I pulled up the line of code I'd recklessly accepted as nothing but a benign tag. Decryption time.

Shit and damn. There was a scheduled nanite patch going out tonight. A new flu virus was passing around the dome. The patch would upload the gene sequencing for the nanites to recognize and destroy the new disease strain. Much more efficient than the old-world vaccines. Those were a rudimentary attempt at programming our native immune response to diseases. Nanites worked better.

No wonder Dimech blew up the fucking building. If anyone saw what he'd slipped into the next update, there was no way it would make it past inspection. In all the turmoil, his minor changes to the code would go unnoticed. And tonight, when every good grid citizen uploaded their new flu patch, he'd strike. Instead of protecting them from the latest viral strain, Dimech's code would fry their medical nanites. His next attack would knock out their immune systems, leaving them vulnerable to disease and injury. That wasn't even considering people who relied on their nanites to manage chronic conditions.

Nanite tech had all but eliminated most diseases. This would be a disaster like nothing we'd seen since before the domes, back when the sea level rise had wiped entire cities off the map. It was catastrophic. The blood drained from my face, and Harris noticed. "What is it?"

"The explosion wasn't the major attack," I said, leaning sideways to crack my back. This was bad. Un-fucking-believably bad. A level of bad I'd never have touched with a ten-foot pole if I'd realized Dimech's endgame.

"We expected as much. They also back up everything in the governance building on off-site servers. And those servers are much harder to access," Harris said, missing how serious the threat was.

"No, I mean like, apocalyptic bad," I clarified. "The bombing was a cover for the actual attack. Meant to divert attention and resources by distracting everyone from the real threat. The challenge had a 24-hour window from when he posted it last night at midnight. Guess what happens tonight at 12:01?" I met Harris' gaze, and he stared back, brow furrowed as he thought about it.

I could tell when he figured out the significance by the terror and outrage warring across his features. That glimpse lasted for a second before the impassive facade dropped back into place. Fascinating. And not my biggest problem right now. We only had hours to act. No way we could access the backup servers remotely after the bombing. Every government system was on high alert and would remain that way until far too late to fix this. Still, Harris knew people. He'd be able to get through to Oversight and have them delay the patch update. Med-Tech would scrub the patch free of Dimech's code, crisis averted.

"The new flu patch." Harris sounded grim.

"Yeah. But it's fine, right? You can contact someone and get the update delayed?"

"Right," Harris' eyes lost focus as he accessed his occ display. And then he scowled. "Signal is down. I *should* be able to get through on emergency channels, but there is so much chaos I can't even access the priority channels."

"Okay, but we can just talk to someone, right? In-person?"

Harris sighed. "Sure, if the entirety of Oversight wasn't a kicked hornet's nest after the explosion, we could. But Sec-Tech's spread thin with protecting the other targets we gleaned from your job board activity. And the leadership is in lockdown since we knew the attackers used cloned accounts to plant the malicious code. They won't trust anyone they don't know personally with something like this. And I'm not at the top of the hierarchy."

"Well, no, I expect if you were, then you wouldn't have gotten saddled with babysitting me, would you?"

"Right." Harris looked unimpressed.

"So, what do we do? Try to hack the servers? I'm sure they're locked up tighter than a virgin's ass about now. And remote hacking isn't my specialty."

"No, you get off on infiltration jobs, don't you, Klein?" Harris sounded almost amused, but his expression gave away no hints to his true feelings.

"Ah. So, you *have* heard of me? I'm flattered." I batted my lashes at him, mocking, even if I enjoyed thinking of him noticing my pranks.

"You specialize in B&E," Harris replied, definitely amused. Good. "The better the security, the less you can resist. The only reason you're a low priority target for arrest is that you do nothing more than tag in once you gain access."

I smirked. "I know better than to shit where I eat. Where's the fun in giving you Oversight drones a reason to swat me when I have just as much fun being a nuisance under the radar?"

"Well, you're on our radar now," Harris pointed out.

"Yeah," I slumped in Jono's seat. Shit. There wasn't any easy return to my old life for me.

"If we can't stop this, they'll reprogram you. Dimech's attack will hurt too many people for the tribunal to grant leniency." Harris sounded almost like he regretted that.

"That's what I figured." No one who survived after getting their nanites wiped was going to feel much pity for the pawn who destroyed their way of life. Let alone the countless casualties if we couldn't stop this.

"You want a way out?" Harris offered.

"Out of what?" I asked, suspicious.

"All this," Harris gestured.

"How?"

"You break into the server farm and wipe the bad code from the patch before it goes out," he suggested. Or more like demanded.

I stared at him. "You want me to break into the most secure server in the dome in the middle of a spree of terror attacks? And then access the best-guarded data in existence at the moment for long enough to wipe whatever Dimech did to it before it goes out *tonight*?"

Harris nodded. "That about sums it up. You don't even have to wipe it. If Oversight catches you tampering with the servers, they'll suspend the update until they can verify that it's unaltered."

"Yeah, and if Dimech catches on to what we're up to, what's stopping him from triggering the patch update early?"

Harris frowned. "Can he do that?"

"I'd like to think he can't, with all the safeguards in place, but how many lives are you willing to bet on it? Because it might cost every single one on the grid if we're wrong."

"I see." Harris' frown deepened into a steely resolved as he met my eyes. "Well, then. We better not get caught."

Nine

WE. Harris had said we. Did he plan to come with me? Shit, I worked solo. No way could I pull off the biggest job of my life with a tag along. *Right?* But then Harris had Oversight credentials, he might prove useful. We needed every edge to pull off something so ambitious. There was no time to prepare. I needed Jono, he'd slap some sense into me. Terrible as it was, the patch wouldn't hurt those of us who lived off-grid. It wouldn't affect me. I could give Harris the slip, and there might not *be* an Oversight left to pursue me by morning. Not if Dimech had his way.

I missed the squeaking stairs. The door banging open took me by surprise.

"You're alive!" Jono enveloped me in a bone-crushing embrace, then he held me at arm's length and gave me a shake that rattled my skull. "Don't you ever pull a stunt like that again, you great twat."

"Sorry?" I gave him a sheepish look, but I didn't pull away and he didn't drop his hold. Not even when Harris cleared his throat, reminding us of our audience.

"Sorry? You damn well better have more to say to me than that weak-arsed apology, K," Jono fumed at me. He stepped back, aiming a gentle love-swat at my head.

"How did you know?" I asked, touched at his outraged concern.

"I have trackers installed in all my gear, I like to keep tabs on what my installs are doing in the world. It about gave me apoplexy when the emergency alert had you right on top of the explosion. I tried pinging you, but the networks are all jammed, and then the tracker died. I thought…" he trailed off. The simple tracker that would slip under the radar would die with the wearer, so he didn't have to say what he thought happened.

"I'm fine," I stepped back out of his hold and gestured airily at my unscathed body.

"They build all Sec-Tech's sector houses with materials that block GPS locator devices. We try to make it tough for the criminal element to extract our suspects," Harris volunteered. Jono glanced between us, shrewd as ever.

"You charmed an Oversight drone into your bed, K?" Jono leaped to the obvious conclusion. "You never saw a pretty flame you didn't want to touch, huh?"

"I'm a simple guy with simple needs," I drawled.

"Klein is my confidential informant," Harris corrected the assumption. "He has valuable intel about the terror attacks. He agreed to trade his aid for his freedom."

"That so?" Jono tipped his chin up, challenging the statement because I never got caught and I did everything in my power to avoid Oversight.

"It's true, J. So, on that note, we need a few mods and then we'll get out of your hair."

Jono grumbled about canceling the two appointments still on his schedule for the afternoon. Between my charm and Harris' implied threats, we wore down his resistance. Jono got us kitted out for the stupidest mission of my life.

Ten

HARRIS DIDN'T HAVE the exact coordinates for the remote server, but he knew the general location. From there it was child's play to hack the hydro records and narrow down the most likely address. Server farms the size we were talking about pulled a ton of juice and they had to be somewhere no one would notice them.

The zoomer we caught would have refused the address. Too far from a charging dock for it to go. Lucky for us, I preferred to fly them on manual. That would make it harder for Dimech to track me, too.

I opened the throttle and tore across the sky at the zoomer's upper safety limit for both height and speed. Harris clinging to me, his front pressed to my back from shoulders to thighs, only heightened the adrenaline rush. The flight was fantasy fodder, with nothing but our skintight mod-suits between us. I reveled in the flight across the slums to the outer dome. Too bad we were on a life and death mission and he was as likely to arrest me as fuck me at the end of the night. Mind out of the gutter, I muted the inputs from my new dick so it wouldn't distract me, and instantly regretted the loss. Still better than dead.

The server farm nestled against the dome wall. Near the power conduits that funneled hydro-electric, solar, and wind energy into the dome. Energy conduits ran alongside pipes carrying enough desalinated water to meet our needs. It wasn't far from Seed's algae farms that provided a base for most of the Nutri-kiosks nutrient blends. And biofuel for hybrid zoomers and any other tech that wasn't all-electric.

At first glance, there was no sign the nondescript building we'd pinpointed was any different from its neighbors. The server farm was here, so close, but too far to risk a direct approach. If Sec-Tech stopped us, the odds of convincing them we were there to prevent the real threat in time to prevent it weren't great.

It was tempting to zoom right up to the building, no Sec-Tech presence within sight. The low buzz of my proximity indicator told me the area was lousy with Sec-Tech drones told another story. The conduits in this area would make it a reasonable target. It made sense for Oversight to protect the conduits. My gut told me their concentration here was about protecting more than the conduits, though.

This was the right spot. Good thing too, we'd estimated our best bets for sneaking in would happen as night fell. When twilight made visibility a challenge. This time of year, it was almost nine when we departed Jono's place with his strict orders to return in one piece.

We left Jono trying to relay our findings to Oversight. Harris had passed along his Sec-Tech credentials so he could access priority channels. If he got through, they would delay the update. That seemed like a long shot. The fate of every citizen on-grid rested on Harris and me; no pressure.

At the first sign of Oversight drones, I dropped the zoomer behind a building and ditched it there. My occ overlay told me it was coming up on ten by then. We still had two hours, and the building was within sight. Harris looked green around the gills when we landed, but he didn't complain. I'd come up with our brilliant plan, using the extensive grid of ductwork access tunnels to get to our destination. Harris and Jono had worked out the details. Jono, ever the nerd, had old maps of the grid stashed in a dusty relic of an ancient book about the founding.

I got us into the first empty building we came across and we found the duct access in the basement where it always was. From there, Harris navigated the cramped tunnels toward the server farm with an overlay he had uploaded onto his occ. The Ot8 came with that as a standard navigation feature.

The founders built every building in the dome on the grid. The dome's denizens left the outskirts as the population contracted from dropping fertility rates. That didn't remove these outlying buildings' the physical connections to the grid. They all had duct access to power their outlets, run their water, and access their nutrient allotments.

Everyone avoided the tunnels. It was taboo to even talk about them in polite society. They carried the guilty lifeblood of our society—our inability to cut the umbilical cord of modern tech forced us into the domes. It didn't matter that we'd adapted to using renewable sources; the damage had already occurred. We'd already stranded ourselves within our domed cities by the time we acted. So, acknowledging the power grid was like talking about shit. We all dealt with it. Considered it a necessary part of daily life, and *no one* cared to look too closely at the details.

Not only were they the social equivalent of a latrine, but the narrow tunnels felt as cramped as all seven hells. And were just as uncomfortable to traverse. We had to walk hunched over. I didn't mind the view of Harris' ass, but it looked like the tunnels were even less comfortable for him than me.

We paused whenever my proximity sensor showed signs of Sec-Tech above us on the sidewalk. It took longer, but was worth ensuring no small sound carried and alerted them to our heat signatures in the tunnels below their feet. That made our progress painstakingly slow, but we arrived at our destination undetected. The low hum of electronics around us because more of a dull background roar of cooling fans as I took point again. I wasted no time unscrewing the grates to let us into the secure facility. A glance at my overlay showed we'd burned an hour crawling through the tunnels. Nothing ever came easy. As soon as we stepped out of the tunnel, a claxon sounded in the bowels of the building.

Eleven

SHIT AND DAMNATION. The timer to annihilation kept ticking down, less than an hour until the patch went live. It would go out in batches not long before Oversight sent the activation sequence. We had to finish this in the next forty-odd minutes. There was a slim hope that the overtaxed communications networks might delay the patch, but I wasn't ready to gamble lives on that hope. We had to act fast. Harris looked grim as we followed the only path from the conduit tunnels up into the main floor.

The whirring fans got louder as we approached the endless banks of servers. The blaring alarm blended with the noise; strobing emergency lights flashed. I had to toggle off the Sec-Tech proximity sensor since they surrounded us at this point. I looked for the first machine with an accessible data port and plugged into the closed system. It must have taken Dimech an age to perfect his encrypted line of code. Then figure out how to get it uploaded to the servers storing the latest nanite inoculations. His virus was in the system now. Transmitted as part of an emergency system dump when the attack at the governance building shut everything down. It would take a better tech guy than me to erase every trace of Dimech's malicious code. But I knew my strengths, I needed to plug in and, at worst, fuck things up enough to delay the flu patch rollout.

I ran the subroutine on my occ to find a machine that would let me jack into the system and wasted no time plugging in. Harris clapped me on the back and grumbled something about buying me time. I was already in a race to access the system through layers of protections. Once inside, I needed to sift through files seeking what we needed. Good thing Jono knew his shit. The scripts he gave me before we left got my foot into the metaphorical door. From there, all I had to do was find the files with the deadly code I'd unwittingly introduced to the system.

The timer on my overlay kept ticking down to doomsday. Jono's algorithm scanned through what felt like the unabridged collected health data of every citizen ever to have been on the grid. It was a daunting task. At this rate, I'd get through everything in a matter of days. I didn't have days. I didn't even have hours. That left our backup plan; Jono was going to be pissed. I left the algo running in the background and toggled to another interface window.

The data packet I needed was the highest priority on the server right now. No time to crawl through every scrap of data scraping for any sign of Dimech's code. A surefire methodical approach took too long. Instead, I threw caution to the wind and plugged back into the grid. That made for a jarring transition. As predicted, the prompt for an automated nanite upgrade overrode my occ's overlay.

It crossed my mind that Dimech's virus might have piggybacked on the generic nanite updates, too. No time to worry that I'd become patient zero in his planned synthetic plague. An annoying warning icon popped up, reminding me to upgrade to the latest supported occ implant at my earliest convenience. Screw that. I ignored the stupid flashing annoyance and ran a back-trace on the automated on-gridding upgrade the system had loaded onto my occ. I'd gambled that Oversight stored the patch along with the automated upgrades, and now I'd pinpointed it, I was in. The only problem was, running greynet algos on-grid fucking hurt. My nanites no longer lacked the coding that Oversight used to keep good citizens in line.

The protocols built into the programming made it physically painful to act in ways Oversight deemed too dangerous. Or otherwise made illegal. So, uploading Jono's greynet security key to let me alter the server sent white-hot pain shooting along my extremities. And that was only a warning. I gritted my teeth against the pain and did what I had to. It might not be a permanent fix, but the tricks up my sleeve would delay the update. At least until someone from Med-Tech could wipe Dimech's grubby fingerprints off the flu patch.

Too bad that breaking into the nanite control servers surpassed my usual shenanigans. It was a crime that got you sent off for reprogramming. So, the helpful on-grid nanny protocols didn't stop at tingling arms and legs to deter me. No, the unbearable pain wrapped around every nerve ending, until it felt like it bathed my skin in flames and stabbed my flesh with knives. The agony became an endless sea of misfiring neurons and nanites turned against me as I clung to my resolve. I only had to hang on long enough to disrupt the update… and there, I'd tripped the anti-tampering protocols. The servers entered lockdown mode. That ought to trap the update offline until Oversight reviewed the situation.

"Yes! Got it!" I whooped, triumphant despite the searing agony. The timer in the corner of my overlay ran down. But that was fine—no one was getting their flu patch tonight. The sensation of my own nanites devouring me from the inside overshadowed my moment of victory. The excruciating pain was too much to endure any longer. I let go.

Twelve

"Rise and shine, sleeping beauty," Jono drawled his familiar line as I came to awareness in his familiar med bay. An abnormal note of relief in his voice tipped me off that I wasn't rousing from any routine procedure.

Recent events came back to me. My memories of how I got there were fuzzy and featured Harris' powerful arms hauling me out of the server room. Had he dragged me back through the tunnels?

"No," Jono answered. Oops, guess I said that last part out loud. "Your big strong drone didn't drag your half-dead ass out through the tunnels. Once you gave the all-clear, he turned you both in to Oversight. Took them most of a day, but they got through to his supervisors to explain the situation after you fainted."

"How'd I end up here, then?" I was sore enough that I didn't attempt moving yet.

"Your drone pulled some strings to get you released to medical supervision. And some more strings to have me named as your medic of record, since I handle all your upgrades. You owe me the creds to pay the fine for med-modding without a license, by the way."

"Thanks, J. I couldn't have done it without your help," I said, meaning it more than I'd ever meant anything before. I hesitated to ask the next part, but better to know than wonder. "Am I…"

"You're off-grid. The nanny protocols did a number on you, but no lasting harm to the wetware. Fried a few of your greynet implants, and you needed a new nanite injection since the old ones got corrupted. I replaced what I could while you were out." Jono patted my arm.

"How long?" I asked.

"The medics at Sec-Tech kept you knocked out until they knew what to do with you. Once I got you, I kept you under for a week to heal. Don't glare, you needed it after the number you did on yourself," Jono chastised me, not the least bit remorseful. I couldn't argue. I must have been in rough shape. Really, I considered myself lucky not to be waking up in a reprogramming center.

"Okay. What's the official line that kept me out of the queue to get a new personality?" I asked to distract myself from asking questions about Harris.

Jono squinted at me, suspicious of my easy acquiescence. "Oversight nailed Dimech. They nailed him as the mastermind behind the terror attacks," he explained.

"Wait, attacks, plural?" Shit, had we failed? I'd been so sure it worked.

"Yes. Relax, no one died. The bombing at the governance building and a second failed attempt at the conduit relay station. Harris got you cleared of all charges as his informant. There will be questions once you're well enough to answer them, but you aren't being charged with anything."

I breathed a sigh of relief. "Good. That's… Good. Um, and the flu patch?"

"Med-Tech got the flu patch scrubbed and sent out last night. Oversight blamed the delay on the network overload after the terror attacks. Most people will never learn how close Dimech came to succeeding with his revolution. Sec-Tech is beefing up the protocols to protect future updates. You did good, K." Jono clapped my shoulder approvingly. With a wicked twinkle in his eye, he added, "Who knew you had it in you?"

I scowled at him.

"I had my suspicions," Harris drawled from the recovery bay's door. And didn't that just release the last knot of tension from my muscles? The question I couldn't ask Jono, 'Will I see him again?' answered in living color. "Glad to see you awake, Klein."

"Glad to be awake," I shot back. "You here to arrest me?"

Harris snorted, and Jono rolled his eyes. "Not unless you broke any new laws while I've been dealing with the fallout from your last 'prank'."

"More's the pity," I pouted at him, eyeing the big man with appreciation.

"Is he cleared to leave?" Harris directed the question to Jono, ignoring my needling.

"Sure, if he has somewhere other than his old squat to go," Jono agreed.

My heart sank at the reminder I needed to find a new place. My old squat would never feel safe again after Dimech violated it.

"Good, he's staying in my guest room until he's back on his feet," Harris declared. The unilateral pronouncement should have outraged me, but all I felt was warmth. Blame the warm fuzzies on being alone too long. It felt nice to have someone other than Jono to watch out for me. Someone I could rely on, even if he was Oversight.

"When can we leave?" Harris asked.

"Whenever he drags himself out of bed. I'll go grab his personal effects." Jono turned to me, patting my hand with affection. "Don't break yourself again, K."

I grinned at Jono. "No promises."

Jono grinned back, shaking his head as he sidled past Harris, giving us the illusion of a moment's privacy. Jono could still hear every word.

"We should talk," Harris said when we were alone.

"Or," I drew out the word, "do something more interesting than talking."

"Thought you didn't screw Oversight drones," Harris shot back.

"I can make an exception for the drone that saved my ass," I replied with a leer.

"Take the foreplay out of my recovery bay," Jono groused, returning. He thrust a bag full of my fried implants against Harris's beefy chest. Harris slung the strap over his shoulder without a complaint and offered me a hand standing. I wobbled, light-headed, and unsteady on my feet at first.

I leaned on Harris as he guided me out of Jono's shop. We caught a zoomer back to his place. My flirtations at Jono's were all bravado. I wasn't up for much more than hobbling to his guest bed once we got there. Harris didn't object. He helped me to his on-grid apartment and tucked me into a soft bed, alone.

Disappointing, but the guy was right about talking, much as I preferred to avoid heavy conversations. It would have to wait until I wasn't nodding off after being awake for all of ten minutes. My thing for Harris seemed mutual. That didn't mean it would lead to anything, but it might. Everything had changed; I had an entire life to rebuild. But for tonight, my Oversight drone had secured me a soft landing. That was a solid start.

About the Author: *Alex Silver (he/him) grew up mostly in Northern Maine and is now living in Canada with a spouse, two kids, and three birds. Alex is a trans guy who started writing fiction as a child and never stopped. Although there were detours through assisting on a farm and being a pharmacist along the way.*

Website: https://alexsilverauthor.wordpress.com/
BookBub: https://www.bookbub.com/profile/alex-silver
Facebook group: @alexsalcove
Newsletter: http://eepurl.com/dNcScQ

RISE

J. SCOTT COATSWORTH

Cinzia grasped Kendra's hand, pulling the child away from the edge of the *traghetto*, which floated in midair fifty meters above the waters of the lagoon. They'd have one of the best views of the Rise. *Being old has its advantages.*

Her granddaughter was a little *chiacchierona* today, chattering up a storm, unaware of the monumental undertaking finally coming to fruition below.

Solar-powered buzz drones zipped through the crowd, beaming images to the news corps and the huge tri-dee sky board hovering above the lagoon in front of them. Around her the crowd murmured, sharing a communal sense of awe.

Satisfied that Kendra wouldn't get too close to the edge of the airship, Cinzia let her go to pull out the golden ticket from her pocket. She stared at it, still amazed that she'd been chosen as of the first hundred to enter the lost city. Along with one guest.

For Italians, it was a moment of fierce national pride, a reclaiming of the *spirito nazionale* that traced its heritage back through greats like Da Vinci, Galileo, Mazzini, Dante, and Beneficio. To the gathered masses from the rest of the world, real and virtual, it was a spectacle of the likes of which they'd never seen. A symbol of hope in a world starved of it for far too long.

Cinzia put away the ticket and knelt next to her granddaughter, her old back protesting. She brushed the little girl's kinky hair from the tawny skin of her forehead, her own spotted olive skin reminding her of the seventy years that stretched behind her. "*Calmati, bambina,*" she said through the thin, clear rebreathing mask that pulled compressed oxygen from the air. "This is a great moment, one you will remember when you're as old as I am."

The little girl frowned, reaching up to touch her face. "How old *are* you?"

Cinzia cackled. "Old enough to know when to be quiet. Come here. I'll lift you up so you can see."

Though Kendra was only five, she was a handful, and Cinzia's aching back protested as she lifted the girl onto her hip.

Lucia, where did you go? Cinzia wished her daughter were still there. She'd run off with that scamp Hassan, the girl's father, *chasing happiness.* Or whatever her *menthe*-addled mind thought of as happiness now. Apparently, it didn't include family, home or a steady job.

The sky board cleared, and the young Prime Minister Enzo Speranza filled the sky. They looked sharp today, in a silver Italian suit sparkling like sunlight off water. "Welcome to the day of the Rise. We have worked long and hard for this. As a nation, we survived the Dark Decade of the twenties and the rise of the Mediterranean Sea. We weathered Hurricanes Diego and Lorenzo, and the flows of refugees from Africa and the Middle East that transformed our identity and culture."

Cinzia snorted. *And not always for the better.* She squeezed Kendra's hand. *It's not all bad.* If only Lucia were here to see this.

"Today, we reclaim our history. Our pride. Our Nation." Speranza raised their arms. "*Viva l'Italia!*"

"*Viva l'Italia!*" The shout went up from the hundred people gathered on the traghetto, and from hundreds of thousands gathered along the distant shore with their silver tickets. And from the throats of Italians across the country too, relayed through the sky board. Bug drones showed the view from the Colosseum, from Piazza della Signoria, from the slopes of Mount Etna, and from places around the world, even the drowned city of New York.

"What's going to happen?" Kendra's eyes darted back and forth, from person to person and up to the sky board and back. She was squirming in Cinzia's arms, so she put the little girl back down.

"A miracle." They'd discussed this the night before, but Kendra had a notoriously short attention span. "Just wait. We're almost there."

Cinzia grasped the railing again with her free hand and closed her eyes, remembering how her own mother had led her through the city streets.

Mamma waved at the shop owners they met along the way. "Marco, did you get those new shoes in yet?" "Paolo, I'll be by later to pick up some steak." "Elena, I hope you'll stop by tonight. I made some limoncello for you!"

And always, the return calls of "Certo, Signora Russo!" Everyone *knew* mamma.

"… and now, across the city, the injectors are about to do their work."

Cinzia opened her eyes in time to see the Prime Minister step aside to allow their Minister of Reclamation Sciences, Francesca Horvat, to speak.

"For twenty years we have planned for this day." In the background, divers swam through the lagoon, checking equipment and removing debris. "Advances in regeneratic biology have made possible what we will do today, but we had years of work to stabilize the most important buildings, and to prepare the city first. Our workhorses, the genetically modified coral polyps that will do the lifting, have been time-limited…"

Cinzia tore her gaze away from the sky board to look out at the water. Its placid surface belied what lay below, outlines barely visible through the rippling green waters. "I grew up there." She pointed at the lagoon.

Kendra followed her gaze. "Underwater?"

Cinzia laughed. "No. It was a different place back then. Totally above water." Except when the seasonal floods had come, with increasing frequency and fury every year.

Doctor Horvat had gone silent. Cinzia glanced at the sky board.

Both Doctor and Prime Minister were staring ahead intently.

There was a deep thumping sound, and the world below *rumbled* and *purred* like a stirring dragon. The sea water bubbled, obscuring the view.

It's beginning. Cinzia leaned forward to watch.

"You lived here?" The young man next to her, with dark hair and two curling rows of effervescent tattoos across his face, was about her daughter's age—maybe forty? *Youth* was such a relative term anymore.

Cinzia nodded. "In the *Cannaregio*, near the northwestern edge. Such a beautiful place." She closed her eyes, seeing it as if the intervening sixty years didn't exist. "Mamma used to take me to *piazza San Marco* for lunch. We'd get a pastry and find a spot at the edge of the piazza to watch the tourists go by, faces buried in their screens."

"You were so lucky. To see it back then." The man grinned. "I'm Gio."

"Cinzia. And maybe so." She bit her lip—he didn't know the half of it. She'd lost her mother in the Great Flood and the city evacuation after. "Where are you from?"

"Forlì. But my grandparents were from here."

She nodded. "I've been living in Imola with my granddaughter."

He nodded. "I wish I'd seen it in its prime. Before the Flood—"

The rumbling beneath their feet suddenly increased in tenor. She set a hand on his shoulder. "I think it's about to happen." The world went silent, save for the grumbling of the Earth. All eyes were on the lagoon below. Cinzia took a deep breath, reaching up almost unconsciously to touch the breathing mask on her face.

Kendra peered over the railing. "What's happening?"

The waters were stirring. Something was churning in the depths.

The new shoreline, established with seawalls after the Flood, was almost ten kilometers away. The domain of the Mediterranean had vastly expanded since she'd been a little girl, like Kendra. "Little creatures are building new shells under the old city. Billions and billions of them."

The girl peered over the edge, as if she could see those tiny polyps.

Cinzia smiled, remembering how new the world had been when she'd been little. Hard to believe the big day was finally here. The government been planning this for decades.

She'd seen the little genetically engineered creatures that would convert salt and sea water to cement in a grand magical alchemy. She understood almost none of it—this world was as different from hers as that time had been from the 1950's when her own grandmother was a child. But Cinzia had *chosen* to believe in this grand project. Her hand sketched out the sign of the cross on her chest as she said a prayer for the dearly departed.

"Look!" Gio pointed at the lagoon.

There was a dark spot just below the surface.

Cinzia held her breath.

"Look mamma!" Her hands stretched out like a scarecrow, but the pigeons weren't scared of her. They perched on her arms.

Mamma laughed. "Come on—let's get merenda. Want some gelato?"

The rumbling increased to a roar, and more dark patches appeared in the green lagoon waters. So expensive. So laborious to stabilize what was left. But every bit worth it, in this moment.

A great spume of water sprayed high enough to throw a shimmer of mist across her face as the first part of the old city broke the surface. As the spume cleared, the top of the *Campanile di San Marco* rose above the water, green roof gleaming like new. *A nice touch.* The Restoration Guild must have worked overtime on that one. Its golden weathervane was gone, but the bas relief of the lion of St. Mark made her clutch her heart.

"Mamma, what's the lion for?" She licked chocolate off her hands, desperate to make her afternoon snack last just a little longer.

"It's the symbol of the city." Mamma put her hand on Cinzia's chest, patting it—boom boom, boom boom. "The beating heart of who we are."

Cinzia stumbled. It felt like yesterday.

"You okay?" Gio's brow creased.

"I… sorry, yes. So many memories."

Skipping over the bridges. The bad days of the quarantine. The corner market where mamma used to do her grocery shopping…

The Flood.

Another building broke the surface nearby—the *Santa Maria della Salute*, the beautiful basilica. Water poured off the gorgeous green domes in a thundering flood. They were mostly intact, though one of the smaller ones had a gaping hole—water poured out of it, cascading down to the lagoon like a waterfall, joining the general uproar of the Rise.

"Look, Kendra. You can see the outlines of the *Canal Grande* now." The old waterway—the pulsing artery of the city—snaked away from them like a backwards 'S.' In the distance, she could make out the edge of the Sestriere Cannaregio, the district where her mamma had lived in a modest apartment in an old stone palazzo that looked out on a concrete courtyard.

Waters rising, as it rained for close on a month, coming ever closer to their own second-floor balcony.

"What if the water doesn't stop coming?" Cinzia stared out at the concrete courtyard, where the seawater swirled and churned.

"Don't worry about that, *tesoro*. The water always stops, eventually. Now come here and help me with dinner."

She *had* been lucky. She had survived.

All across the lagoon, the buildings of Venice were rising from the water. Many were broken, piles of bricks and debris covered with algae and surprised fish that flopped around on suddenly exposed land. The outlines of the city were becoming clear as water poured out of the buildings, churning the lagoon into a muddy, frothy mess.

A row of *palazzos* along the edge of the *Canal Grande* collapsed, sending up a deafening roar as they crumbled into rubble. Cinzia stepped back instinctively, pulling Kendra with her as the platform rose thirty meters into the air to avoid the cloud of debris that briefly rose above the lagoon before settling back to earth.

"Nothing to be alarmed about. Not all buildings were stabilized prior to the Rise." Doctor Horvat's lined face nodded reassuringly from the hovering screen before them, her voice broadcast across the world and to the Lunar colonies far above. "We expected some collapses. We will keep you away from the dangerous areas."

"What if the city doesn't stop rising?" Kendra grasped the railing, her gaze locked on the scene below.

Gio knelt next to the girl. "There's no chance of that. The polyps have a very short lifetime…"

Cinzia was grateful to him. He probably understood the science behind all of this far better than she.

Her mind drifted.

They ate the last of the almond cantucci, *savoring the hard cookies even though they were stale. Cinzia was still hungry, but she knew better than to ask for more. There was no more.*

Outside, the rain had finally slowed to a constant drizzle.

Mamma ruffled her hair, managing a wan smile. "I need you to stay here, Cinzia. Someone will come for you, I promise. I will find us help."

The helicopters had stopped coming days before, and the boats that had been plentiful the first few days, with men telling them to stay put, had bypassed their part of the city ever since.

The rumbling subsided.

Cinzia opened her eyes and looked around. For just a moment, there was absolute silence on the traghetto, along the shore, and on the sky board.

She looked over the railing.

Venice—*her* Venice—lay before her. It was in sad shape. Many of the landmarks she remembered were tarnished or broken. Whole zones of the city had collapsed, and except for Piazza San Marco, a green film covered the risen city. She was a ghost of her former glory.

But she was *there*, as solid and real as the hand before Cinzia's face.

Gio raised his arm. "*Viva Venezia!*"

Everyone on the traghetto picked up the rallying cry. Cinzia raised her own arm, shouting "*Viva Venezia!*" as a thrill raced up her spine.

The call was picked up by those on the distant shore, seen through the sky board, and soon everyone was chanting it in unison. "*Viva Venezia! Viva Venezia! Viva Venezia!*"

Pride flared in Cinzia's breast, something she'd not felt in fifty years.

The traghetto slowly descended toward the *Canal Grande*, and Cinzia watched raptly as the city rose around her. A heartrending grief threatened to overwhelm her, followed by a profound sense of homesickness. *Mamma.*

The platform settled into the water next to the edge of Piazza San Marco. The chanting died out.

A hundred bug drones hovered above them as the railing in front of her lowered and disappeared. All eyes turned to Cinzia, the oldest person chosen among the one-hundred.

"What?" She blinked in confusion, looking up at all the faces staring at her.

Gio pointed to the ramp that led down to the piazza. "This was your home. *You* should be first."

She looked around.

Everyone nodded solemnly.

Cinzia turned to face the plaza. The underwater restoration teams had scraped it clean. Though the ground was not the uniform gray it had once been, it was still recognizable.

Her eyes filled with tears.

"Come on, *nonna*! Let's go!"

Kendra was tugging at her arm, her beaded braids swinging in the air.

Cinzia followed her down the ramp, taking a step, then another toward the wet tiles of the plaza. When she and Kendra stepped onto not-so-dry land, the cheer went up again.

"The old Italy and the new, together," the Prime Minister's voice echoed through the air above her.

Cinzia didn't hear them. She looked up, and her mother was there just like Cinzia remembered her, electric-red hair pulled behind her ear, wearing a checkered black and white dress. Cinzia looked down. She had her yellow Sunday dress on, and her hands were small, the skin unblemished.

She peeled the breathing mask off her face and let it fall to the floor, and took in a lungful of sweet, fresh morning air. "*Mamma!*" She threw herself into her mother's arms. Mamma smelled like yeast and rosemary and pasta sauce.

Cinzia let go. "Why didn't you come home?"

Mamma pulled out a tissue from her pocket and wiped Cinzia's cheek. "I wish I could have. The flood… it was too much. But I always knew you would be okay."

Cinzia sniffed. "I've missed you, mamma."

"You're home now. That's all that matters." Mamma hugged her again, kissing her cheek. "I love you, *tesoro*."

"*Nonna*." Someone squeezed her hand.

She opened her eyes to find Kendra there, staring at her expectantly. She lifted her other hand—covered with spots, the skin aged and wrinkled.

The smell of her mother lingered. She closed her eyes, willing *mamma* to return.

"Everybody's waiting." Kendra sounded annoyed.

Cinzia sighed. "Of course." She reopened her eyes and turned to find the ramp crowded with her fellow passengers staring at her. "So sorry."

Cinzia's breath was ragged. She picked up her mask and reattached it to her face, and the compressed oxygen began to flow again. She took a deep breath and led Kendra off to one side. She looked up at the *Campanile*, towering over them in the afternoon Italian sun.

She began to cry again. This time it felt *good*.

"*Nonna*? Why are you sad?"

Cinzia squeezed the little girl's hand, tawny against her own almost translucent skin. "I'm crying because I'm happy."

Kendra frowned. "You cry when you're happy?"

Cinzia laughed. "No. I'm crying because I'm home." She leaned over, ignoring the ache in her back. "I love you, *tesoro*." Her mother's words echoed in her head.

"Love you too, *nonna*."

This was Kendra's world now, a future ahead of her that Cinzia could only imagine.

The image of her mamma's face in her mind was as clear as on the day she'd left. Cinzia took another deep breath and laughed. The air still smelled of yeast and rosemary and pasta sauce.

Kendra was staring at her.

She touched the little girl's cheek. *So smooth and soft.* "Let an old woman have her secrets." Kendra clearly didn't understand what she was talking about. *You will someday.*

She took her granddaughter's hand, just like her mother had so many years before. *We're finally home.* "Now come on. I'll show you where your *nonna* used to get the best *gelato*!"

About the Author: *J. Scott Coatsworth lives with his husband Mark in a yellow bungalow in Sacramento. He was indoctrinated into fantasy and sci fi by his mother at the tender age of nine. He devoured her library, but as he grew up, he wondered where all the people like him were. He decided that if there weren't queer characters in his favorite genres, he would remake them to his own ends. A Rainbow Award winning author, he runs Queer Sci Fi, QueeRomance Ink, and Other Worlds Ink with Mark, sites that celebrate fiction reflecting queer reality, and is a full member member of the Science Fiction and Fantasy Writers of America (SFWA).*

Website: https://www.jscottcoatsworth.com
Twitter: @JSCoatsworth
Facebook: @JScottCoatsworthAuthor
Instagram: @JScottCoatsworth

A FOREST FOR THE TREES

RACHEL HOPE CROSSMAN

Once, people used to hug trees. But that That was before we started randomly falling over and killing them. All of a sudden, the Family Tree was accused of being homicidal maniacs, perpetrators of assault and battery and the sooner all of us trees were cut down the better, said the Humans. They didn't care whether it was Elms, Redwoods, or Christmas trees falling, . the The carnage had to stop and that meant we had to go. So, they put a bounty on our heads and the good people of every community fired up their chainsaws for the public good. And we We had no way to run, no place to hide, and no idea how quickly life on Earth was about to change.

At least that's what everyone said.

I think they should have known better; the signs were there. Centuries of war and human dominion over the planet had taken such a toll that even a city tree like me, growing in a foggy backyard, could feel the effects. Could look back just a very few years and know that something was amiss. Could realize that when the time came, when the world as I knew it transformed into chaos, it was going to take radical action to survive. So, when nature let the dogs out and human infrastructure began to disintegrate, I just pulled up my roots and ran.

Don't ask me how. All I know is that it was either a miracle or some property of the fact that the all laws of the universe seemed to be in flux. But I wasn't the only one running; Yoshiko, a Yew Tree from Petaluma, could run too. She'd been growing on the grounds of a grocery store parking lot, and when that last storm hit, she took off on both of those contorted little trunks of hers and zoomed out the driveway like so many of the drivers she'd watched over the years.

She was moving so fast she ran right into me. Neither of us understood what had happened but when she slammed into my trunk it was love at first sight. Together, we pressed on.

But I'm getting ahead of myself, though. I was telling you youngsters about the catastrophic changes on Earth in the Year of Mud and how I helped to found this Grove."

Rumbling from deep inside his massive trunk like the sound of distant thunder, the voice of the Redwood continued, and rows of little saplings shook their leaves and shivered their twigs.

"Climate change had already forced adaptations from every living thing by then. The heat was awful and the flooding had been worse but when the bond between Human and Tree was broken, something very precious was lost. Do you understand, children?"

The young trees did not understand about floods or chain-saws or maniacs. How could they? They knew only life under the soaring roof of their arboretum, beneath the filtered light and measured drip. Here, the bond between Human and Tree was as sweet and simple as the love between mother and child. As solid as the ground beneath their feet.

"Between my backyard and Humboldt State Park, Yoshiko and I met almost two dozen other trees on the move. There was an apple tree, complete with pink blossoms and a nest of finches. A palm, a eucalyptus, an ash with a murder of roosting crows.

I have said that the Human-Tree bond was broken. Splintered is more accurate, because the bond wasn't completely severed. Volunteers from the Svalbard Seed Bank – the kind of Human who still hugged trees- cared for us when we arrived at the state park, in varying states of shock and dehydration. They took grafts from all of us who made it to the park, as well as from the pedigreed Redwoods they had come to sample in the first place. We were a bunch of mutts, a group of random city trees burned by sun and salt, in need of emergency TLC. The arborists from Svalbard saved our lives. You, children, all come from either the Humboldt stock or us City Sliders as we came to be known. If not for the loving care of those Humans, none of us would be here today."

The young saplings whispered and murmured, nudging each other with their twiggy elbows. Their fluttery voices mingling with the *kit-kit-kits* of the sparrows and nuthatches that fluttered amongst their branches.

The redwood continued.

"If you'd asked me ten years ago to believe all that's happened since, I would have said you were nuts. Would have told you that trees don't walk, can't talk, and could never have made it this far. Yet here we are."

Sliding his roots through the gritty soil as he strode deeper into the rows, the speaker paused in front of a ring of meter-high redwood buds. Linking boughs, they stretched their new green needles towards his furrowed trunk, bending their crowns like puppies nudging for a scratch and the great tree ruffled them with his lower branches as he passed.

"We didn't mean to fall on people; Humans have always been our friends. For more than a hundred years I myself stood guard over a playground and watched four generations of children share secrets under my leaves. Surreptitious lovers conjugated their bond on a soft bed of my mulched bark, secure behind my living curtain. Trust me, when trees started randomly falling over on hikers and picnickers, we were as horrified as the Humans.

It wasn't our fault though. Everyone's roots were shriveled and weak, and much of the topsoil had eroded by then from the non-stop winds that blew harder and carried more grit than I had ever seen. On the hillside behind my home I watched young trees no older than yourselves struggle to spread their root balls wide and hold on for dear life. More and more of them lost that battle and the land became barren, the birds who had flocked there since forever gone who knows where?

Flexing the full two hundred feet of his trunk and branches, the big tree shook like a dog, sending a spray of water droplets and tiny barrel-shaped seed cones in all directions. From a catwalk thirty stories up, gardeners entering data on winking clipboards glanced down and waved. Bobbing a greeting to them, the tree continued.

"Most of you know me as Dave. I have another name, a scientific one:

Sequoia *sempervirens*. That's my family name and our species has been around for almost 240 million years. *Sempervirens* means living forever, and some of my ancestors made it to more than three thousand years old, which is about as close to forever as you can get, children. We were here when the dinosaurs came and here when they left. As Homo Erectus stretched his back and looked up at the moon, as Homo Sapiens was busy learning cuneiform, our family grew and prospered. By the time Zoe reigned as Empress of the Byzantine Empire and Sir Isaac Newton was developing his three laws of motion, the Family Redwood had formed a dark green band of oxygen-producing primeval forest along the Pacific coast.

We were the tallest trees on Earth and thought we were invincible. Why wouldn't we? It seemed that our family really would live forever because when one of our old ones finally died, there were already new generations of buds thrusting upwards from their roots. Proud new stands of vigorous greenwood claimed territory, and communities of creatures lived among our branches. In those days no one would have believed that good old Mother Nature could be brought, weeping, to her knees.

It was midwinter, that time of year when everything is raw and cold and the world seems to move in slow motion that it began. That's when, suddenly, three things happened in rapid succession that took us all past a milestone and into the beginning of what we now call The Year of Mud. The year when everything changed.

The first thing to happen was that it rained as it had not done in a decade, causing flooding, and then mudding that you had to see to believe. There were flash floods, with rivers of thick, brown goo sweeping over the west coast of the United States and rendering parts of it unrecognizable. The mud wiped out homes and habitats alike. As it dried, it left a crust four feet deep of soft, sticky mud, trapping animals and suffocating plants and raising a stink of death for the ages.

The second thing that happened was a lightning strike in February that killed the Grizzly Giant, splitting her heart asunder and killing her entire root structure. She had been the queen of the Mariposa Grove in Yosemite, standing two hundred ten feet with a girth of thirty. When she went down, every remaining Redwood on the coast shivered in sympathetic shock. Some of our Old Growth were already so weakened and sick they simply folded their branches and lay down dead in sympathy.

More was yet to come, and it was the worst. Yes. The Denman Glacier in East Antarctica, melted, causing a global sea rise of sixty meters. That's what two hundred seventy billion tons of suddenly liquidated ice will do, . Apparently, and human scientists had been predicting it for years, apparently. But predictable Predictable or not, it came as a nasty shock to us all and was the third major event that triggered my flight.

Millions of people were living along the coasts of every continent on Earth at the time, including those in my Northern California town of Half Moon Bay. Surf was up like never before, and when Quellcaya Ice Cap in Peru began to leak too, . things Things got really crazy really fast here on the West coast. In Southern California, where soft sand shores had been for a thousand years, there was, all of a sudden, only churning water. Roads that people had traveled on for decades were washed out to sea overnight and the beach, once separated from the Human residential areas by miles of land, was now at their doors. In many cases it washed away their doors, and their houses too.

In my town, I saw bizarre combinations of animals swirling around as the rushing water passed my street. Alley cats and jelly fish shared space for a frenzied minute until the fish dried up and the cats drowned. Thousands of beings, Human and otherwise, died in the flood. Dogs and cats, birds and insects, barnyard animals and wildlife were swept out to sea, borne away on a super-wave a hundred feet tall.

Geography and human society were both transformed in the aftermath of sea-rise, and intellectual constructions about the way people and nature interact were shattered. Along the coast of Pt. Reyes National Seashore, the traumatized farmers and cheese-makers still clinging to residence could only marvel as the elephant seals who once gathered on the rocky sand below the cliffs suddenly floated all the way up to the sodden dairy meadows. The seals wobbled among the cows, who eyed their new neighbors suspiciously, mooing and bah-ing. It was an uneasy juxtaposition: . Bovines had chewed their cud and watched the surf crash below their fields for generations and they did not welcome the new placement of the sea or the massive, tusked intruders who stank of fish."

Dave stood still, lost in thought. For a moment, he was frozen in place, a tree like any other. A pair of slippery elms, seed pods bulging, nudged each other with their shaggy branches and slouched deeper into the soil. Next to them, a cluster of Yews thrust their light green needles up towards the sky, angling their crowns towards the light.

High overhead, gardeners in white coveralls monitored control panels, adjusting parameters for moisture and warmth in the ambience of the glassed-in Grove. Rising thirty stories high, the greenhouse was an enormous structure of white painted frames and twisting staircases. It rose like the tiers of a cake as though it were a Victorian glass house, with a spiral staircase in the huge building's center. Gigantic solar arrays fed power to the arboretum via an electric panel and heated the water that misted overall. In the tranquility, squirrels and chipmunks scampered over the soft floor and birds swooped in the fragrant air.

Dave flexed a few layers of his branches, crackled his twigs, and resumed the story.

"When countries started having to choose which species of plants and animals they could protect from extinction, people rallied around their favorite trees. In Greece, it was the Olive, in England the Oak, and in the U.S, Redwoods and Elms. Groups of all kinds from Girl Scout Troops to Kiwanis Clubs to University botanical gardens stepped in to help set up arboretums. Hundreds of thousands of cuttings were taken and nurtured into clones, kept safe from disease and climate extremes. From them, still more clones were made, guaranteeing the survival of trees.

But the death of another human by a falling tree that winter of mud was the last straw. This one had been an arborist working to save a two-hundred year old elm named Herbie, and even the park rangers and Girl Scouts who had defended us up until that point turned on us, as they claimed Herbie had done on them by killing that arborist.

I knew then that something terrible was going to happen.

Rain fell and kept on falling, through the winter and into the spring and my roots were washed bare and my tenuous grasp on the slippery soil got weaker and weaker. And then one night, a zig-zag bolt of blue electricity sizzled down at me from the darkened sky, shearing off half my trunk. It sent a shock through me and knocked me right out of the ground.

But I didn't fall, I ran.

My roots lifted and next thing I knew, me and a dozen other trees were on the move. We had no idea where to go; none of us had ever been out of our own patch of ground before so we followed the highway inland, away from the churning surf and surging detritus, hugging the glittering flood walls as closely as we could.

The flood walls were built of cars.

When humans had phased out their combustion engines for electric vehicles, it caused millions of automobiles to become so much useless steel. Then, desperate to wall out the floods, communities got the idea to crush the old cars flat and stack them like bricks. It had been pretty effective for about a decade, but now they were beginning to seep salty water and the road was flaked and cracked. Our roots burned from the saline and our bark was ragged but we struggled on, huddled together like penguins against the wind.

When we saw the signs for Redwood City, we thought we'd found our new home, hoped it would be an enclave where we could grow into some kind of a forest and live in peace.

Our disappointment on finding that it was nothing more than a dreary suburb, filled with nondescript strip malls and pizza shops was devastating.

We had no choice but to struggle on, and so we did, following the moon as it waxed and waned, always heading inland trying to get away from the coast. The few Humans we encountered were so shell-shocked by recent events that the sight of a group of rag tag trees on the road gave them no pause. The only living things that noticed our passage were the little rodents and the occasional mangy dog that scrabbled past.

Dave sighed, whiffling the little trees with his piney breath, startling a crow from his branches with a loud CAW.

"There were warning signs long before those final buzz-saws came.

The Old Ones say that gentle people lived amongst us for many thousands of years, harvesting our bark, cones and needles. They prayed and sang beneath our boughs.

But then came a time when most of the Singers and Gatherers died, and new people arrived. A few at first, then more and more. The trees paid them no mind; after all, our kind were many and human beings few, we were large, and they were small and their scurryings seemed as insignificant to us as the beetles'. But the new people had no time for prayer and no use for our cones or boughs, only our trunks.

How could anyone have known that those soft little Humans would multiply so quickly, or that once they began to cut us down they wouldn't stop? Our elders were slain, our youngsters flattened, the infant buds crushed and buried. Roads were built for the trucks the new Humans drove and next thing we knew their clear-cuts and bad smells stretched for miles. More people came and more trees were killed and new roadways sliced our homeland into ribbons. We were being exterminated."

Dave roared in anguish then, raising his roots high and stamping through the Grove, the weight of his step reverberating along the iron rails. A gardener hurried down the walkway as the tree's massive girth swept against the glass walls.

"People reaped from the Earth with no thought for its health, took all they wanted with no care for other living things." Dave stopped, bending his crown nearly to the ground, cradling a cluster of wee live oaks in his rough arms. Droplets of water rivuleted down his branches and he stood still again as he wept. Then he drew a deep breath and spoke again.

"Well, there were some Humans who gave a thought to the future, some who cared for beings other than themselves. The seedbank at Svalbard had been built decades before I fled. Its location in the farthest reaches of Norway, guarded by heavy locks and the last of the polar bears, kept it secure through a couple of generations of human upheaval. Ambient temperatures in northernmost Norway, ranging from freezing to twenty degrees below zero, helped keep out the riff faff and it served as a store house for botanicals from all over the planet, a kind of insurance policy for global food production. More than four million kinds of crops are still catalogued there, and over three billion different kinds of seeds cached, from every inhabited continent.

Creating an arboretum to safeguard the world's trees was the logical extension of botanical conservation, but the technology to do so lagged behind. After all, safeguarding trees is a lot harder than safeguarding seeds. You can't store trees underground: . we We have needs for light and heat and water. We grow slowly. Also, to create the kind of arboretum needed, trees would have to be brought in from great distances. All in all, our Grove is a most unlikely reality.

Like so many truly great innovations though, the techniques to create it sprang from calamity. Necessity truly is the mother of invention children, and as Earth reeled from the catastrophic events of the 21st century, ensuring the viability of forest habitats was suddenly imperative. The first arboretum was built at Svalbard, housing fruit trees and those with medicinal properties.

Taking grafts or cuttings from a plant and generating more via use of their growing tissue was nothing new but the process of homonculization changed everything. You all arrived here as little homunculi no bigger than one of my cones but already the very image of your parent trees.

The concept of a homonculus was first conceived by Leonardo Da Vinci, around 1500, as a theory of human reproduction. The idea was that at conception, each human became fully formed, if microscopic, and that it grew into its full size but otherwise was complete from the first. Transporting fully grown trees to an arboretum is hard and expensive so the technology to create teeny-tiny fully formed trees was a game changer, the very reason for our presence here.

As Earth morphed from a friendly planet to one riven by a nature gone completely out of control, it became clear that the Svalbard Arboretum would not be enough. Trees needed to be sequestered somewhere safer, but where?

Where indeed, my little saplings?

The first ice mines on the moon were built soon after the discovery that the asteroid's regolith is forty-two percent oxygen by mass and that enough ice exists in its polar regions to sustain Human colonies. Besides providing a steady source of both water and oxygen, the mines opened many possibilities. Propulsion using liquid oxygen meant that coming and going from Earth to Luna was now an easy commute, and solar arrays to power the new cities here were up and running in no time.

Building an arboretum on the moon was suddenly possible, and with so many craters to choose from, the idea was a no-brainer. Look up, children, and tell me what you see."

Dave's voice was serious now, and every little tree did as he said, crooking their crowns to look up. Past Dave's shaggy head. Past the white stairways. Past the gardeners high above all, to the panes of crystal clear ice roofing their Grove. There, solar arrays twinkled in the sun and giant mirrors ringed their crater, reflecting the light that illuminated their glass house.

"Here in Svalbard Crater we can live in peace. We're safe from radiation down here, sheltered from the cold and the wind. The Volunteers cherish us as they do their own children, my beloveds, and for that we must give thanks. Rejoice and be delighted, for you are treasured beings."

The young trees sighed in pleasure: Their branches were warm, and their roots plump The regolith beneath their toes, criss-crossed with hydronic pipes was just right to support their growth.

Outside, in the brilliant light high above them, Earth glittered in a black velvet sky.

About the Author: *Rachel Hope Crossman grew up in Athens, Greece and Berkeley, CA as the child of a linguist and an actor. Her imagination, marked by the stones of the Acropolis, the granite slabs of the Sierra Nevadas and the blues of the San Francisco Bay, is the all and everything that fuels her engine. A preschool teacher, then substitute teacher, Rachel ultimately followed her Montessori bliss to teach elementary. Mother of four grown children and author of Saving Cinderella: Fairy tales & Children in the 21st Century, (2014 Apocryphile Press), Rachel currently writes eco-fantasy and science fiction stories.*

Author site: http://www.rachelcrossman.com
Author blog: http://www.365cinderellas.com

AS NJORD AND SKADI

JENNIFER R. POVEY

The mules picked their way carefully up the trail. For situations like this, Deborah had always preferred mules.

Especially when it came to getting the equipment up to the higher camp site. Maintaining the trail was not easy, and there had never been a more efficient vehicle created for this than a good mule. She sat her own lightly, barely touching the hand mule. She trusted the animals, whom she had had for years, to do their job with little human intervention.

Sometimes she envied the mules. All they cared about was getting to camp and the prospect of apples or melon rind.

They didn't care about what was going on with her and Steffi. They didn't know what was going on...

Mules were not, after all, creatures known for romance. She was sure, though, that they were capable of friendship.

Right now, she needed that no-nonsense animal version of it. Maybe everything would blow over while she was on the trail.

Maybe.

She reached the top of the pass, started to come down the other side. The land had been a park for a long time, flourishing far more as part of the Managed Area. She could see where they had planted the new trees, the native grasses. Burned out the invasive Spanish grass.

People didn't litter any more.

People just didn't litter. Fines and laws and talks about bears had not stopped it.

What stopped it was making it unacceptable, a thing no right-thinking human being would do.

The camp was already set up as she led the mules into it and slid out of the saddle. Wyatt and Tricia came to help her unload. She was glad for it; three mules would have been a little much to do on her own and that was not counting the saddle mule who bent her head around and blew hot breath practically in Deborah's ear.

A sign of affection, that.

Friendship, as mules defined it. Whatever that definition truly was.

She tied him up quickly while she unloaded the pack mules, then removed her saddle and gear.

"Still fighting with Steffi?"

She turned to face Wyatt, studying the man's dark face. Finally, "Yeah."

He wasn't the person she would ask for advice. His wife had left him two years before. No matter how much better the world got, people still fell out of love.

Or married the wrong person in the first place.

Had she fallen out of love? She didn't know.

∼

THE DOLPHINS DANCED in the bright, clear water. Steffi wished she could share their joy.

She wished a lot of things right now. She and her wife had…

Had fought.

Had had the worst fight of their marriage. And now Deborah was up in the park doing trail maintenance for two weeks.

Steffi could still call her; the satellite coverage was good.

She was afraid to.

She was afraid something would happen but even more afraid that they were one word, one thought, one emotion from something terrible and potentially irrevocable.

Which was why she was hiding on the beach watching dolphins. The dolphins were exactly the kind of company she needed right now. Silent and nonjudgmental.

Not, like her brother Alex, about to tell her she was making the worst mistake of her life if she let Deborah and all she represented slip through her fingers.

She didn't need him to tell her that.

But she didn't know how to fix things. Maybe she couldn't.

Maybe they just needed time, but would that leave the wound to fester?

After what had been said, maybe it was already over. She turned her wedding ring around her finger, turned and turned.

Then turned back towards the city. Green flowed over the buildings, reducing the heat island effect to tolerable, although never to as cool as it was before. The slopes beyond were green once more, no longer blackened with the memory of fire.

She'd seen pictures. Back then she had been a child, living on the east coast. The fires had been academic until they got so bad as to affect the sky in Washington, D.C. That surreal summer and fall when it had seemed as if the world was ending at some bizarre distance, the slow-motion apocalypse in which so many people had still had all of their creature comforts.

The turning point.

Now the Spanish grass was gone, removed from the thousands of acres it had covered, replaced by native vegetation that did not burn so easily.

The thousands of redwoods would take many years to become giants, but the largest of the giants survived to mentor them.

And all they had needed to do was shut up and listen to those who had come before.

There was a lesson in that.

She needed to shut up and listen to Deborah.

It felt as if it went both ways, as if Deborah was equally not listening to her.

They needed to *sit down* and listen.

The dolphins were still playing in the clear water off Huntington Beach.

THE EQUIPMENT WAS OFFLOADED, and the mules properly secured. They couldn't be allowed to graze freely here, due to a rare species of frog.

The humans and mules were visitors. The frogs *lived* here. The mules could live with being high-lined for a couple of days.

Deborah stood at the edge of the meadow, breathing in the cool air. It was as if nothing had ever touched this place. She could pretend for a moment that she was the only person on the planet.

She had to bring Steffi up here again.

Steffi.

Would her wife even be there when she got back? Or would she find an empty...or locked...apartment?

She didn't know.

She worried. But it was hard to stay worried up here. This was the kind of place that reminded her that everything they had changed and sacrificed was worth it.

This place might never have been touched, but had it been, it might have been destroyed. There were still trees up here, and some of them were old. Cedars could live for up to a thousand years, and they mingled with faster growing pines.

The trail would be ready soon, for those who would come up here in the summer. The season was longer than it once had been.

They hoped it would become shorter again as things got better. Things were getting better.

Was it easier to fix the world than to fix her marriage? No.

So, she reminded herself, things would get better. They always did.

She reached for her phone, afraid to call.

Steffi needed space.

She needed space.

She needed Steffi and that was not going to change. Her wife's long black hair and familiar scent drifted into her mind.

A mule made a half braying sound and she turned to eye the animal. "No, you don't get to wander."

The mule snorted.

"I know."

Somehow his ears said it all, with their particular angle of annoyance. Mules could communicate so much with their ears.

Unlike humans, they didn't mind the heat and the droughts. Horses did.

It was taking so long to fix it. The temperatures were coming back down, slowly, but so much damage had already been done. There should still have been snow on these mountains. The sky to the west faintly glittered, the slight visual effect of measures taken to cool the upper atmosphere. It worked. It didn't work fast enough.

She could give Steffi a week.

∼

The car rolled smoothly along route 1 towards Malibu. Steffi saw no more dolphins, but what surrounded her was the state park, the open space, the green of it. It was spring, and the world was at its most alive. She waved to the workers planting trees, restoring native vegetation, even though they couldn't see her. That area had burned last year, as it was supposed to, the fire controlled but not suppressed.

As it should be.

She felt at her most alive. She wanted to share it with Deborah, and she didn't. She wanted her lover, and she wanted the freedom of being alone.

The ability to make each choice herself with no input from anyone else was sometimes dizzying, but the price for it was too high. The cold bed.

She reached Malibu, she pulled off and looked out at the water. She was not even sure what she was doing here.

Sea person and mountain person. Maybe that was it. Maybe what Deborah needed was somebody who would hop on a mule and go mend trails with her.

Steffi didn't trust the mules. She didn't *understand* the mules, their shifting weight, their hard hooves, the snorting and the noses trying to get into her pockets and any place she might remotely be keeping a pocket.

Deborah had tried to teach her, but she just couldn't cross the divide to that alien mind, and the divide to Deborah.

The divide between them that kept them apart was also what drew them together.

The sky clouded a little, spring rains on their way. The rains were coming back, slowly. It would take centuries for the climate to return to what it had been, but there was equilibrium now. Balance.

The rain started, dripping warm from the sky.

Deborah occasionally saw snow, high in the mountains and Steffi wanted, suddenly, yearned for something she could not have.

She pulled out her phone and tried to call her. No answer.

She left her a text. To call when she could. She couldn't leave the silence hanging between them anymore, the silence that threatened their equilibrium.

Could they still have a relationship? Sure, they could forget the arguments, but sometimes she thought they were Njord and Skadi. The ones drawn to the sea and the other to the mountains forever.

She had made the call, had reached out. And now she had to get back to the sealife center.

She could reach the alien minds of the dolphins.

Those made sense to her.

~

They were on the move again. One hand on the reins, the other on the hand mule's lead.

Deborah's phone vibrated, but she could not answer it right now. It vibrated again.

She would check it when they stopped for lunch. Soon, the trail would be ready and soon they would be taking this trip with guests. And Steffi would not be one of them.

She'd tried.

It hadn't worked.

That was the thing below the fighting and the arguments. They were profoundly mismatched.

Steffi was afraid of horses.

Deborah got horribly seasick.

Measured that way it could never work, but oh gods, when they were together. They had the winters, and the winters were good. The winters were when they remembered how much they loved each other, when the mountain passes were closed and Steffi stayed mostly on land.

They were as Persephone and Hades, Deborah thought.

She reached lunch, got off. Picketed the horses.

Called Steffi, standing at the edge of the clearing to do it, picking out signal amongst the peaks. It was a little staticky.

"I love you," Steffi said.

It was okay. No, it was not okay. Those words should have made it all okay, but they didn't. "I do too, but this isn't working."

"I know."

Deborah couldn't do this like this. Or she could.

She loved Steffi. She would always love Steffi. "Dinner," she said, "Saturday night. Seven pm to give me chance to shower."

"Dinner."

Steffi hung up and tears started in Deborah's eyes. The world was better, but not *her* world.

Once there had been snow, at times, in June. She looked up towards the dry peaks.

They were never meant to be together and she was only fixing what was broken. That was all she was doing.

So, why did it hurt so much?

It wasn't what had been said. That hurt.

This hurt.

She sat down on a rock, turned her back on her coworkers, and ate her sandwich. Ate her apple. Gave the core to her saddle mule; mules were large enough that the little bit of cyanide in the pips would not affect them.

The mule, being a mule, hunted for more.

That was it.

She wanted more.

More than Steffi could give her.

It wasn't Steffi's fault.

It was hers.

DINNER.

Steffi sitting across from her with her hair in a style she never wore for dates.

It was the last thing and Deborah reached across the table. "I'm sorry."

"I know, but I can't do this anymore. I can't be your winter lover."

"And I can't be yours."

It had been enough. For a few years, it had been enough.

Then Steffi took a deep breath. "And we can't raise kids like this."

The argument.

Deborah calling Steffi something unforgivable.

"And I can't raise kids at all," Deborah said, finally. "But I will gladly watch yours when you find the person who can."

That felt like a shift within her. To finally acknowledge that some people *did* want to bring children into this world.

To acknowledge that it was okay, even if she couldn't be the one to do it.

"I love you," Steffi said, finally, twining fingers one last time. "I wish it was enough."

"So do I. But it isn't, and the only thing we're doing to each other is causing pain."

This couldn't be fixed. This couldn't be solved.

Deborah couldn't, though, say those three words.

She couldn't.

She would be up in the mountains with guests, and they wouldn't ask why there was no longer a ring on her finger.

Wyatt wouldn't ask either.

He would just kind of know, in that way they knew, the way they understood each other. If she wasn't strictly girls only, she would ask him out.

She was, she wasn't attracted to the male form or presentation at all. Maybe that made it easier.

They ate dinner.

They parted as friends. She called her lawyer once she was at home. They would get a mediated divorce. Not many assets to split anyway, just the money they had been saving for the house they would never buy together.

But they would, could be friends.

That would have to be enough.

∼

THE WAVES PASSED under the boat. The numbers were good; they were just so good and it lifted Steffi's mood. The algae project was sinking carbon and reducing acidification. It would take time, but it was *working*. Unlike her marriage.

She had done the right thing. They had done the right thing. She was free to find somebody to co parent with or to do it on her own so she would have full control.

No.

That was why she needed a partner, so she would not take her control freak tendencies out on her child without any buffer.

She knew herself better than that. But for the next few weeks, she was going to do everything she wanted to do, without worrying about what *anyone* thought about it. Call it a vacation. A vacation from relationships before she made a new commitment.

Besides, she still loved Deborah. It could not work, but she would not disrespect her by dating before the divorce went through.

It would be...rude was not a strong enough word.

So, she focused on the count, on her job. She remembered when the summers apart had felt like freedom. When both had felt like a vacation.

Until it got to be too...too whatever it had become.

She wasn't sure what that was.

The boat glided back towards the dock, and she shook herself a little. She was brooding instead of working, and that did not make her look like a good person at all. It made her look lazy.

They reached the dock and she jumped ashore with the painter, helped secure the boat. Took the laptop and headed for the lab. There were few words spoken.

She could feel the way people were giving her space. The d word was kind of ugly, even if it was amicable and mediated.

Even if there had only been the one shouting match and then a determination not to have any more of those. Not to hurt each other the way only long-term lovers could.

She would find her true partner, but Deborah would always be her first wife. Nothing could change that, nothing could weaken that.

Her phone rang.

She picked it up to answer.

∼

THIS BATCH of guests was mixed. Two of them rode pretty well...actually, one of them rode *very* well, almost as comfortable in the saddle as Deborah was.

Almost.

Equal in skill, perhaps, but not spending her summers up here, not as fit and experienced.

The rest were the typical batch. A couple barely knew anything of what they were doing and clung to their quiet packers with beginner nerves.

These were not trails for beginners, although she hadn't lost one yet. She also had not lost a horse and two pack mules going up to fix a camp, like *somebody* she knew.

The poor guy had yet to live it down. The animals had eventually shown up at the ranch. Their unfortunate handler had done the walk of shame all the way down the mountain. Nobody was about to help him.

She had never done *that*. And she had never had a guest injured. Had to take one back because of altitude sickness, a couple of times.

She frowned at the thought. Touched the front of her saddle, for luck. There was no wood she could touch, but there was wood in the saddle.

It was still better than fiberglass. Lasted longer. A lot longer. A thought like that, though, said how dull her thoughts were.

She was regretting leaving Steffi. Or being left by Steffi. She wasn't even sure which it was. She was never going to be sure which it was.

There was nobody waiting to hear of her adventures, and she felt the lack like a missing shoe. She was off balance.

Trusting her second wrangler to keep an eye on the novices in the back, she led them up the winding trail to the first campsite. As always, hail struck them as they crossed the pass, annoying animals and riders alike. Her mule expressed irritation with a particular angle of the ears that said "Again?" as clear as any words.

Okay, it didn't *always* happen on this pass.

Just most of the time, and it was reassuring that it did. It spoke of stability and of the way things were and would be forever. The kind of stability they had lost and fought to get back, fought with everything humanity had. Right now, it was a new, poor equilibrium. The hail reminded her that it was slowly returning, if not to what it was, then at least to a livable world.

They were descending into the camp when it happened.

So close.

So close to where they should have dismounted.

So close.

∼

"Your wife's in the hospital."

Steffi registered those words. She didn't say she was separated.

She didn't say they were starting to negotiate the divorce.

None of that mattered in this moment.

"What happened?"

"An accident at work."

She'd fallen off a mule; that had to be what had happened. The creatures had finally got her.

Which was unfair of Steffi, but for a moment she could envision them, snorting and stomping.

Deborah insisted that they were safer than a speedboat.

Steffi wasn't sure and now it was all reinforced. She didn't ask any more questions.

She ran to the car. She was renting a studio, had left the apartment for Deborah, who had more stuff.

Deborah accrued stuff. Steffi didn't feel the need to fight her for any of it.

She accrued stuff and now she was hurt and she might *die* and Steffi had to get there.

She didn't trust herself on the drive; she let the car do the driving while she sat in the front seat, tears streaming down her cheek.

Regretting all of it.

Regretting leaving her, the separation, the argument.

All of it.

Regretting even the relationship in dark moments as the car turned a corner, the entire idea of loved and lost in stark darkness under the California sun.

Then she was at the hospital. Running through the doors.

"Deborah Wicket. I'm her wife. Stephanie Charles."

She'd managed to put her wedding ring back on. Legally, she was still the wife. Legally, she still had the right to see her.

The receptionist fiddled with her tablet. "If you can go to the relatives' waiting area."

She did, of course, pulling on a mask as she did so. Even in her current state...it was just a thing that you did. You covered your face in medical waiting rooms where there might be sick people, or you might be sick people.

It helped.

She didn't want to be sick people.

"Ms. Charles?"

Not Mrs. She didn't mind Mrs, but he was probably assuming because she was married to another woman.

Not unreasonable.

She followed him to a private room. "How is she?"

"Broken leg, three cracked ribs, broken collarbone, mild concussion," the doctor said. "And from what I can see royally mad about it."

She *had* fallen off a mule. And she would be out for the rest of the season.

"I need to see her."

"She's awake, but she might be a bit goofy."

Pain meds. Concussion. "Will she see me?"

She had to ask.

The doctor turned away, fiddled with his tablet.

"Yes."

Everything hurt right now. What hurt more, though, was that she had ruined the trip for her guests *and* was out for the season.

She would still get paid. It didn't matter.

Steffi's face drifted into her vision. "You...fell off?" She sounded an odd mixture of incredulous and unsurprised.

"I did *not* fall off a mule!" Deborah said, defensively.

"What happened?" Steffi seemed to relax, as if she felt that the defensive tone was a good sign.

Maybe it was. The surge of energy cleared her head a little. "I fell off the *trail*."

"You..."

"I had a couple of inexperienced guests and one of them broke the rules and got off on the trail," Deborah relayed. "The rear wrangler had his hands full because he was on a green horse, so I *stupidly* tried to walk down the trail to get her back on."

And fell off. Thankfully, it hadn't been that far of a fall, but it had been enough. And she had known better, and *that* was the real reason Deborah was so upset. "I ruin everything," she said finally, little above a whisper. "I ruined the trip, I ruined my summer, I ruined us."

Steffi opened her mouth. Closed it again. Deborah felt her hand close around hers.

"I don't want to let you go. But I should never have had you in the first place."

It was a cliche, and she could feel it building. They would get back together because of this, would pretend to be happy because of this, but nothing had changed.

"I'll.." Steffi tailed off. "Can I move back in until you're better? I'll sleep in the living room. As a friend."

As a friend.

It was dangerous, it might lead to something, to things that they would regret. "I don't know."

She really didn't.

Would the judge say they hadn't really separated?

But she knew they could not get back together. Even in the state she was in, even with the dull throb in her leg and shoulders.

She couldn't.

"I want you to, but I don't want you to. I'll..." A pause. "If not, then I know somebody."

She did.

She could get somebody to stay with her.

She would not let Steffi be her nursemaid.

Not even as a friend.

~

Deborah was right and wrong.

She had not ruined everything.

Steffi had...

...neither of them had. They had just been so close to right for each other, so close to working out. If it hadn't been so close, then it wouldn't hurt.

She had heard about a couple who had gone on the first colony ship for Mars and broken up during the voyage. It had been a mess.

Steffi never wanted to leave Earth, she understood the urge but did not and could not share it. She wanted to *fix* Earth, to restore the seas, to do her small part. She wanted to see the sunshade project working. Worlds took time to fix. Relationships?

Deborah was right. They broke up, they could not live together. Some things were not *supposed* to be fixed.

She had had to make the offer, she had to say it. To speak those words. Because Deborah was going to need help for a few weeks.

Was going to...

Steffi needed help.

A counselor, maybe, a real one and not the stupid AI therapy platforms that helped with only the most minor issues. The most straightforward.

Although they did remind people to do things like eat and sleep.

Steffi realized she was hungry. She stopped instinctively at the little diner Deborah loved, the one which sold only meat substitutes, but which prepared them properly.

Ordered food.

Deborah would get back on the mules, go back to the mountains. She would recover, and be teased about it forever, like the guy she always joked about, the walk of shame.

But she would go back, Steffi knew that. Nothing short of being disabled permanently would change Deborah and it made her love her more and it made her remember that she couldn't love her at all.

The waiter set her food down in front of her. "Need to talk about it?"

Steffi shook her head. "Marriage troubles."

Her marriage was over. She took the ring off again. They could, if they wanted.

They probably wouldn't.

Humans were complicated, AIs would never properly substitute for them.

Humans were complicated and messy, and she was complicated and messy.

She overheard somebody at the next table talking about horses. She tried not to listen.

She could not help it.

∼

Deborah was on crutches and hated it. She wished she'd taken Steffi up on her offer.

She was glad she hadn't.

They said she might be able to ride again before the end of the summer. New treatments, new ways to make bones heal faster.

Wyatt sent her a Get Well Soon card that had a sketch of somebody falling off a cliff inside.

He wasn't going to let her live it down and there was something warm about that.

She sent back a note saying she still had all of her mules.

The guest had, of course, been fine. She was upset about ruining the trip...but not for the person who had caused this.

They deserved a ruined vacation.

Then she called Steffi. She knew she shouldn't, but she did anyway. Called her to reassure her she was okay, just frustrated and a little bored.

More than a little bored.

She amused herself by daydreaming over mules for sale; she could in theory buy her own and keep it at the station, but knowing her luck the beast would promptly go lame.

Horses were a bit cheaper, but at 10,000 feet she preferred a mule.

And that made her think about the summer she was missing and the fact that she didn't even want to cheer herself up with chocolate ice cream.

Not when she couldn't exercise.

One day they'd have the instant bone fix things from Star Trek.

One day.

For right now, all she could do was rest and fret and...hear her doorbell ring.

Steffi?

Part of her hoped, hoped against hope that it was, she wanted her back, she wanted to hold her. She used the remote to unlock the door.

It wasn't Steffi.

It was Wyatt.

He brought flowers and a shed mule shoe. She laughed at the latter.

Hugged him when he came over.

"When you...you *are* coming back, right?"

"I'm not letting this stop me."

"Did you and your wife?"

"No, we didn't fix things, we're not going to fix things. This *is* fixed, because what we had was broken."

It took putting it into words for her to understand that.

What they had was broken.

What she had now was the fix. She would not stay alone any more than she would stay off the mountain.

He paused. "Good."

"I wish it had worked. But it didn't and it won't."

The mountains called to her. And she would find the one who was called with her, one day.

∼

THE MULE CLIMBED the mountain pass. For once, there was no hail. The skies were clear and the air thin. Deborah glanced over her shoulder at the guests. Her left leg had developed a slight bad weather twinge, but perhaps all cowgirls needed one of those.

They all seemed happy, although she heard Bruce, from the back, "Loosen your reins on that mule."

She laughed a bit as the guest obliged. Somebody who rode English, no doubt, not used to riding this much on the buckle.

Then she rode down towards the camp. She flinched inwardly as she passed the point where the accident had happened. She always did, every time.

It happened and it was in the past, just like Steffi. Just like the fires that had blackened so much of the West.

Now there were people up here managing the land the way it should be managed. And it hadn't stopped anyone from having their fun.

The tents were being set up by the pack crew. She grinned at the entertainment that was about to ensue.

The guests never found setting up unfamiliar tents at 10,000 feet easy.

One of the pack crew called over to her. She led her mule over, tied him up quickly and hugged the woman.

She was the fastest they had, she was on their team for Mule Days.

She was the one Deborah had wished she'd found sooner. They both believed in this place.

They both believed in what it was and could continue to be; not the greatest roadless wilderness, because there *were* roads here, if you knew how to find them.

If you knew what a road truly was you could find them.

The road that had led her here was a good one. Later, around the fire, she pulled out her phone.

Steffi had sent another picture of the twins.

Life was good, the world was fixed, and sometimes...sometimes you had to let go of what you thought you needed to hang onto.

Whether that was land.

Or a relationship that could never have worked. They had been as Njord and Skadi, separated by the things they loved and the goals they had.

Yet they had been good.
Sarah slipped an arm around her, and she leaned up against her wife. Life was good.

About the Author: *Born in Nottingham, England, Jennifer R. Povey now lives in Northern Virginia, where she writes everything from heroic fantasy to stories for Analog. She has written a number of novels across multiple sub genres. Additionally, she is a writer, editor, and designer of tabletop RPG supplements for a number of companies. Her interests include horseback riding, Doctor Who and attempting to out-weird her various friends and professional colleagues.*

Author site: http://www.jenniferrpovey.com
Twitter: @NinjaFingers
Facebook: @JenniferRPovey
Tumblr: https://jenniferrpovey.tumblr.com

THE CALL OF THE WOLD

HOLLY SCHOFIELD

Pedalling out of the shade of the Douglas firs, I heard the farming collective before I saw it. Squawking, bleating, angry barking—and that was just the people. I ground to a stop in front of the gate, careful to avoid the wild sorrel poking through the damp, crumbling pavement. "Olly Olly Umphrey!" I called over in my cracked old woman voice. The nearest person, a lanky man with a brown ponytail pulled exceptionally tight, frowned at my shout. His foot rested on a rusted cage with something brown and feathery in it.

He glanced at me, my bicycle, the small bike trailer that held my possessions, then back at the other two. The woman was waving a large and shiny cleaver in the face of a stocky, acne-scarred man. I wasn't one to judge—well, I *was*—but my calves ached, and my stomach was tired of deer jerky. I raised my voice a notch or four. "I don't want to join your discussion, I was just hoping I could do a few chores—"

"We don't need any trade goods," yelled the cleaver-wielder. "Go away, old woman!"

"Ageist, much?" I yelled back. The driest summer in Vancouver Island's recorded history meant my scalp itched continually, and a guest bunk sure beat out a dusty tent, but I didn't let such comments slip past me. Not since I turned seventy last year.

"Let her in," the lanky man said.

I pushed my bike along the high chain link fence—the height of it intended to keep out the overly-numerous deer rather than human intruders—until I reached the gate.

Neither of the other two had moved.

The lanky guy sighed long and low. "By the power vested in me by Henkel's Wold, let her in." At his feet, the caged guinea fowl backed him up with an ear-piercing shriek.

The short guy moved first, walking up to the lock and looking into the biometric screen. It gave a loud click. My heart did the hokey pokey as the smartcam swivelled toward me and facial recognition software did its thing.

"Keeps out the riffraff, eh," I remarked to the guy as the gate clicked again and swung open.

"So what? We breed our own criminals," he said, glaring back at the woman.

She waggled the cleaver at him. "Sez you, Riley."

"Gah!" Riley turned to the skinny guy. "Did you see that? Whatcha gonna do about it, Aaron, waffle as usual?"

With a sigh, I scanned the dark clouds overhead. Was a bit of comfort really worth enduring such an unhappy crowd? But I knew my solitary life wasn't mentally healthy, any more than my cheese addiction. Surely I could hang my frayed Tilley here for one night.

Besides, maybe I could help settle the dispute. I hadn't been much use to anyone lately, maybe I could use my rusty people skills to at least calm 'em down. I sucked in a breath. "I think you people are the flea's pajamas, doing what you do, way out here in the bush," I said and smiled blankly like the kindly old woman I hoped I looked like. "A bunch of nice people like you, nothing more to talk about than some chicken." My tactic worked—they all looked as sheepish as ewes at a shearing competition. I stuck my hand out toward the one named Riley. "Julie Leung, traveller extraordinaire."

"Pleased, and all that," said Riley as he gripped my fingers with a callused palm. "Come on in. We got some lentil stew with your name on it. Always glad to have a few helping hands around the farm."

"Yeah," said Laura. "We'll settle this later. I've got to get back to chopping carrots for dinner." She ran a finger along the cleaver and flicked a fleck of orange off it, grinning at me. "Betcha thought I had other plans with this beauty, huh?"

I grinned back.

Riley gestured me to follow him. "How are you at tapping maple trees?"

I regaled him with my expertise in syrup extraction skills as I followed him across the communal yard. Up on the roof of the sculpted concrete main building, a bearded guy waved, solar paint dripping from his brush. We proceeded down a ferny green trail to some tiny guest cabins. The wooden walls were streaked with the ironically pleasant blue of mountain pine beetle damage. I parked my bike in a rack made from repurposed car parts and grabbed my backpack. Dinner and bed would certainly warm the cockroaches in my heart. With the smartcam's capabilities in figuring out my real identity, I could only stay a couple of days.

∼

My aging Ikea chair and borrowed quilt had just grown comfy when the argument started up again.

About ten of us had lingered after dinner in the common room by the months-cold methane gas stove. Next to me, on an old Forest Service park bench, a woman opened her shirt and began to feed her baby, while an older guy stroked his long beard in mindful contemplation of something, and a teenager tapped away on a tablet designing a cranberry harvester. Riley sprawled in a handmade chair across the fire from me, and Aaron, the collective's leader, slouched beside him in an ancient armchair.

My twelve years bicycling throughout western Canada meant I'd seen a few hundred of these "intentional communities". By now, I could spot the reasons why they worked—or didn't—as quickly as I could gather Canada goose eggs for lunch. The way this bunch had all made a conscious effort to back down from their verbal scuffle at the gate told me Henkel's was a community of the sort I would have leaped to have joined in my thirties, or even my forties. That and the swoon-worthy food. Riley's lentil soup had been fragrant with fresh spinach, flavorful carrots, and a couple of spices I couldn't immediately recall. Coriander maybe, and cardamom. It had been accompanied by a salad of miner's lettuce, sorrel, clover, and various greens such as I might collect for myself but with a much better dressing of raspberry vinaigrette. That had been followed by a piece of excellent goat cheese made by the angry-woman-who-was-no-longer-angry and went by the name of Laura. The woman, that is, not the cheese.

Despite the appeal, would I want to join *any* collective nowadays? I'd always been an introvert and now, after over a decade of unpeopled solitude, a little peopling was all I could stand. A murmur from the baby, another beard stroke, and a tappy-tap-tap, and I edged my chair away a little bit.

Laura backed in through the kitchen swing door and began handing out cups of rosehip tea to a chorus of appreciative murmurs. She ended with Riley, thrusting the tray at him, mouth tight.

"It's just a guinea hen," Riley said, taking the last cup with both hands.

"Yeah, sure, and its eggs are just scrambled genes," she said, slapping the tray against her thigh.

"We need a decision," Riley said, gripping his mug like death heated up.

Laura nodded. "It's impairing our happiness levels."

They both turned to glare at Aaron, whose face was in shadow under the hood of a faded gray UBC hoodie. "I—I—I think that Laura had better start—"

"At least you agree on something," I interrupted brightly. Whatever he'd been about to say, telling just one of 'em what to do wouldn't resolve anything. I hadn't worked for a wildlife foundation for twenty-five years without learning something about negotiation.

"Phone home, gramma," said Laura, then looked abashed as the nursing mother raised her head and the teenager tsked. Each collective tended to develop its own slang so I wasn't sure what that meant—although I could grok the essence.

I said lightly, "Haven't owned one in years." Taking her literally might de-escalate the situation, and, besides, I hadn't. In the solar-powered communities of the New West Coast, where every kilowatt counted, one of the few advanced technologies everyone made sure to prioritize was cell coverage—generally, people agreed that a transparent society with almost all information freely available mostly worked to everyone's advantage. But no way was I going to carry a phone, even though the maps and other data would be damned handy.

When you—meaning me—are an environmental activist working for your older brother's charitable foundation and you—meaning me—become the director when he takes two years off to be a new dad, it's a big deal. And when you—yup, me again—finally have enough of whining, bickering humanity and walk out on one of the endless meetings about a federal wildlife law that affects a provincial law that affects a local bylaw that would affect the water rights of a multinational company that may or may not be leaning toward a tax-favored donation to the foundation, it's...liable to leave the foundation in the lurch. Especially after you walk out of the office building, across Bayview Avenue, and down to the Don River. Your black pleather oxfords fill up with warm algae-tinted water and you stand there and stand there until a passing mourning dove shits on you.

Meaning me. Shit on *me*.

I'd left the shoes in the mucky silt, along with my blue wool blazer, and walked unshod and unblazered for miles. And I'd never gone back despite Willi's endless phone calls and messages. I'd ditched my phone, my Toronto condo, and gone off-grid, driving north. Eventually, reading historical biographies in a rented Muskoka cottage had palled and I'd bought the bike and cart and never looked back. (Unless the cart got a flat tire. Which it occasionally did.)

I'd had a close call last month. I'd paused by a roadside hawker in Coquitlam under several streetcams. My hand had hovered indecisively over several solar-powered miniature water filters. The hawker's cell phone, close by my hand, rang and we both jumped.

"Who? Who's Julie Leung? Is this a prank?" she'd yelled into it before I'd bustled my hump along Highway 7, pumping my pedals like a well handle in a six-month Saskatchewan drought. . Twelve years later, and Willi was still needing me back. I just *knew* he was. I'd been the best damn activist my brother had ever hired. One look into his pleading black eyes and I'd return to that soul-sucking city life in a hurtbeat.

So, no phone.

Problem solved.

Maybe I could solve this problem as well. Aaron gulped down his tea, hand shaking. Laura and Riley both crossed their arms.

"Tell me, what do this collective's rules say about ownership of the bird?" I squinted, trying to see Aaron through the growing dimness.

"Ownership isn't the issue. I actually own it all," Aaron said.

"Wowsy," I said.

He leaned forward in to the light. "My mom, Helen Henkel—"

Everyone made a slow fist of respect.

"—most decent person I ever knew."

"—peace be upon her."

"—she never phoned it in."

Ah, that explained Aaron's clumsy handling of the incident at the gate. The mantle of leadership was XXL and he was an extra-small. He muttered, "Mom set this place up as a formal trust—everyone signed over their assets to her in return for lifetime rights to live here."

"And that *worked*? A dictator telling you folks what to do?" My voice squawked like the poor guinea fowl. I'd see that style of intentional community before—usually the people had a fundamentalist religious doctrine or another form of abhorrent behavior. Or a commercial agenda, like when marijuana went legal. Some of those communities made a small fortune—by starting out with a large fortune.

They were all smiling at my naiveté, or maybe I had spinach in my teeth.

Aaron spoke from the depths of his hoodie. "A benevolent dictator is actually the best form of government. *If* you can find the right person." He scrubbed his face with a hand. "Trouble is, I'm not the person Mom was."

The protesting murmurs from the other people weren't even loud enough to drown out the baby's slurps. Poor guy.

"Okay. Here's my decision." He spoke firmly, for once. Maybe I'd underestimated him. "I'm going to ask Julie to decide. It'll be impartial and it'll count as her chores, a win-win."

Yup, underestimated. He'd neatly passed the bucking bronco to me. After I hit the road tomorrow, they could collectively hate me instead of him.

I twisted in my chair. My past career meant I was pretty good at that kind of stuff, despite it not coming naturally. Plus, lack of internet meant

I'd read my way through all the classics in the past decade, from *Art of War* to *Callahan's Crosstime Saloon*. Further, my arthritic wrists hated the idea of three hours of drilling holes in big leaf maples and running sap lines tomorrow. My nimbility wasn't what it once was. I squirmed again and my hip twanged like a cheap guitar. That decided me. "Okay, deal. What's the scoop?"

They all looked blank for a minute, even the guy with the beard. Hooboy, you know you're getting old when your slang has become unintelligible. "Just tell me the problem."

"Laura says she bred the hen from two she'd paid particular attention to. Tracking software shows it eats more ticks than most and she wants to keep it for breeding. It lost its leg band and Riley says she's mistaken about which hen it is"— Riley snorted—"and it's one of several he's bred to taste better and it's now at its peak age for meat production. That about cover it?" Aaron turned to both of 'em and they nodded.

I thought it over. Whether they had a fancy genetics lab set up in one of the outbuildings or whether they were cross breeding the old-fashioned way didn't matter. Nobody relied on fancy tech solely anymore. We all wanted backups to the backups and there was no backup like a live hen strutting her stuff in the farmyard. Plus, black-legged ticks had benefited like few other critters from the long hot climate-changed summers and the dumb-ass ban on deer culling. All ticks needed were deer and humidity to spread Lyme disease, a deadly risk to us all. Out here in the wilds, they were all over humans like, well, ticks on a hound. I was picking a few of the evil beasties off myself every night. Most British Columbia collectives donated extra profits to the Lyme Research Collective in Vancouver, hoping for a cheap, reliable vaccine.

I tilted my head left and right a few times, considering both sides. Maybe a classic solution was in order. "Have the hen lay a clutch and then kill it. The eggs go to Laura and the meat goes to Riley." Solomon has nothin' on me, hooboy.

All ten of 'em erupted into arguments as to why that wouldn't work. I let 'em go on for a bit, hoping they'd settle. Sure enough they began to batten down the hatchets and discuss it more rationally. Laura spoke above the rest: "I suppose if I had a dozen eggs, I could work with those. We do need the meat for the smokehouse, or we'll be hungry come January."

"But if the hen is killed, you'd be betting on the eggs," Riley said. "And I do hate ticks with the passion of a—"

"— lipstick-covered pig," I cut in.

"Yeah, sure," he said and laughed. Laura giggled and, just like that, the tension was broken.

Laura and Riley agreed to leave the hen alive for now and work together tomorrow to construct yet another floating platform of mussel ropes. It'd have to be situated in a less convenient location than most of the existing ones, but it would help replace the protein lost by keeping the hen.

Aaron was looking at me steadily, open-mouthed. I smiled, shrugged, and sipped my cold tea.

Later, as I walked toward the cabin and its very appealing cot, Aaron took me aside. "Teach me how to do that?"

I opened my mouth, about to explain the complexities of the interpersonal techniques I'd used and the micro-expressions I'd interpreted. I opened the cabin's door. My hip twanged, this time like a whole banjo orchestra. "It's, um, complicated," I said. "G'night."

He trudged away, head down.

Hours later, I'd tossed and turned so much that the bedsheets were trussed and torn. I felt like the world's biggest meanie. The selfish kind, the kind Willi thought I was. But there was no easy way to tell Aaron how draining it was to be around people, face-to-face, aura-to-aura.

Willi had never understood that either.

∽

BY THE SECOND day at Henkel's, I'd been given a potted tomato plant and a woven hemp hat and been asked to settle four disputes. This morning's involved two new mothers and the last remaining frozen bagel. I could forgive 'em their anger, teething babies without teething rings could set anyone's teeth on edge. At least, one of the mothers had brought me a duck egg omelet, full of mushrooms and chives, still steaming from the kitchens. The mother, *and* the omelet.

I was forking in the yellow fluff of heaven when Aaron stopped by. His faded corduroy shirt hanging on his thin frame made him look a scarecrow, or maybe a scarevulture.

"Help me figure out this puzzle?" His tablet held some accounts and preliminary number-crushing. It resembled the decision-making matrices that I used to discuss with Willi.

I swallowed the last bite, washing it down with some chicory coffee. "Does the super-fiddly hand-threshing of lentils balance their higher production volume per hectare versus the ease of chick peas? Damnifino. Use some cost-benefit software, like HappyEconomics freeware."

"But it's not that simple." He sighed. "How do you know if—"

"Aaron, there's *never* enough information. You could collect it until the crows come home and still there'd be something you missed."

"I don't think I'll ever grow into this job." He blew out a long breath. I felt sorry for him—adapting to something you aren't suited for is an uphill climb, made especially tougher by putting on the wrong suit. Or an itchy blue blazer. All I could do was give him permission to make a decision. "Sometimes you just have to fish or cut loose."

He ran a hand through his hair. "I suppose. I'll figure it out, later. Come help me in the truffle orchard?"

"So they grow on trees now?" I said, determined to lighten his mood.

He only grunted and shoved the tablet in his pocket.

We stopped by the tool shed and he handed me a narrow tree planting shovel, taking an odd-looking rake for himself. I had no idea what the black plastic box affixed to the handle near the tines could be for.

The truffle orchard was down by the shore, staggered rows of hazelnuts and Garry oaks marching toward the high tide mark.

"My nose may be big but it's not all that sensitive," I said, accustomed to other collectives' use of trained dogs to sniff out the tasty underground fungi.

"We spent most of last year's discretionary funds on this baby." He patted the rake's black box proudly, then flicked a switch. The box emitted a cheery *pew pew pew* sound.

"Raygun?" I asked. I approved of the new trend of replacing the annoying *dings* and *beeps* of most electronics with music, but this concert was disconcerting.

"Texan elf owl," he answered.

After a while, we got it down to a routine. He used the fancy sniffing device like it was a metal detector wand to locate the truffles under the trees. It would go *pew pew pew* when it sensed truffle spores and he'd rake away leaves and twigs and other detritus, exposing the good dark soil. I'd dig up a handful or two of thumb-sized deliciousness, and then he'd carefully rake the duff back over.

"I'll be leaving tomorrow," I said, when I felt the moment was ripe. "Don't get to relying on me." My brother would trace me through the publicly available images the gate's smartcam had taken of my face, probably in a day or two. I could be far up island by then. I bit down on the usual wave of failure, humiliation, and regret. I'd cracked under the strain of leading his foundation and I was continually paying the price. Or pricing the pain. Or something.

"Julie." Aaron swung the rake under the next tree. "I'm…thinking of quitting, too. Collapse the community trust and give their money back. Let them run it like a democracy, with voting and everything."

"And run off?"

"Travel. Like you are."

Pew pew pew.

His raking this time was vicious, sending crisp, dry oak leaves flying in all directions.

"I've got my reasons," I said. I didn't need a home, not me, I was as self-sufficient as a…well, as a…come to think of it, *nothing* was truly self-sufficient. But this conversation wasn't about me. "Without you, Aaron, that bunch would fall apart in a week. You just need to work on a few arbitration skills," I said.

"I need *you*," he countered with a firmness that belied his shaking hands. "If you stay, I'll stay. You could give me advice behind the scenes. Just feed me what to say and I'll spout it out to them."

I dug a few cautious shovelfuls. "Like Cyrano de Bergerac? Or like Edgar Bergen?"

He frowned. "Who—"

"Never mind." I carefully eased several black lumps from the near-dry soil. "You'd really want to run things that way?" The musky funky truffles wafted their funky musk over us and we both breathed deeply.

"I'll just tell them that you've bought your way in but I won't actually charge you a single loonie."

"And one farmhand washes the other? Doesn't sound very benevolent to me."

"No one will know. Look, the night you came, I was about to kick Laura out for non-compliance to the rules."

"So you're giving yourself a choice between being Charlie McCarthy or Joe McCarthy?"

"Who are—"

"Never mind. You haven't studied history. You just know how to grow cabbage and broccoli. You're doomed to repeat."

He looked at me suspiciously. "I don't know if that was a fart joke or what, but I'm serious. I'm offering you a permanent place here."

"You don't need me, damn it." I laid the truffles in the wicker basket. "The only thing you have to fear is…spiders. How about I give you some books to read—"

"Books! That won't help, not right away. But *you* can! Please." He grabbed my cuff and I jerked away instinctively. "At least say you'll think about it."

He kept on badgering me as we filled the basket.

"Enough!" I finally said and handed him the shovel.

My pulse was racing like a racecar and I couldn't think straight. I had to get away from him. From all of them. I tore off across the orchard like a deer in flight…if deer could fly.

A few gallops and gulps later, I was out of the bright sun and in my tiny cabin. The blankets were itchy-scratchy, and the air was hot and close. Just outside the window, the rest of Henkel's bustled with people. Finally, I strode out to the back pasture and commenced pretending to ignore the one resident—a goat on a staked rope. Its face was as surly as mine must be. As the goat tore at the grass within reach, my mind raced a mile an hour…which actually seems a pretty fast speed if it's circling the same tiny topic.

What *was* I doing here?

Before my travels had started, I'd been a bit of a homebuddy and getting used to the road had been hard. My fancy would be tickled pink to settle down somewhere and not have to pitch a tent every night. I'd parked my big city pay cheques in a credit union and left it alone ever since I'd fled the city lights—maybe signing it over to Henkel's Trust would be enough to get me in legitimately? After all, good things come to those with a bird in the hand.

I licked my lips, still tasting the omelet's wild chanterelles—it really *had* been a breakfast of champignons.

Yesterday, I'd borrowed Aaron's tablet and looked up some stats. According to the Simon Fraser University Collective, more than half of the people in BC's Lower Mainland, both urban and rural, had changed to collectives. More than a third in the interior and a quarter of Alberta, too. The cognitive limit that a person could maintain interpersonal relationships, known as Dunbar's number, was about one hundred and fifty, and such small communities had proved both viable and robust—to expropriate some of my former corporate vocabulary. At that size, you always knew what your neighbor was doing so crime wasn't a problem. Basically, with Dunbar's number, the criminal element's number was up.

Henkel's Wold ranked near the top of all the collectives I'd stopped at. With good reasons (as well as good raisins). Over the last few days, I'd spent time with Laura and learned she'd been evicted from her Winnipeg apartment when her alcoholic ex-husband had destroyed her front door. Riley had been raised in Kelowna by parents who were strong on a self-sustaining lifestyle but supplemented their indifferent crops with a break-and-enter during his final year of high school. Of course, they'd been caught right away. Riley had worked at various high tech jobs around the country for years before ending up at Henkel's. Aaron's mother's up-close-and-personal government was a combination that worked for him.

The others I'd talked to here had similar stories—they'd joined due to personal beliefs, total commitment, and a work ethic that would leave a colony of ants speechless.

In the distance, Laura carried a pail of goat's milk to the cheese shed. My mouth watered while my thoughts tumbled like mismatched socks in a dryer. Opportunities like this didn't come along like streetcars.

But, maybe I couldn't see the forest for the cheese.

I'd always known that, as an introvert in a world of extroverts, I'd needed to adapt more than most folks to meet social expectations. Why would I think that Henkel's would be any different? After my soothing life in the woods, the daily interactions would rub me raw. It wouldn't smooth off my rough edges, but it would rough up my soothed edges. I should retreat back to the forest where the only aggression came from the hummingbirds when their nests got disturbed. Let someone else step up to the plane.

But, then I'd be letting down Aaron, and Riley, and Laura, and all the rest, just like I'd let down Willi and all the wildlife his foundation helped protect.

Maybe I *should* stay.

For once, I'd found a place I might fit in.

It wasn't just wistful thinking this time.

It was possible. It was possible. And, in the back of my heart, I'd always known that Willi would find me eventually.

"Hey!" While I'd been cogitating, the goat had eaten through its rope, some bamboo fencing, and most of the raspberry bushes beyond. I grabbed its collar and yanked it back into the pasture. "Well, *you* sure learned to adapt to your environment," I told it. Then I stood humming and hawing until the dinner gong rang clear as a bell.

~

PEDALING HARD, I got a ways past Nanaimo by nightfall. At first, Aaron's refurbished cellphone in my pack had weighed me down much more than its hundred grams should have but, after it didn't ring and didn't ring, I began to whistle while I pumped along past brown grasses and dull-leaved trees. Aaron wouldn't phone unless he needed to, and perhaps just being able to would mean he didn't need to. Meanwhile, I could nestle in the solitude of giant fir trees and huge ferns like the tough old woodlands creature I was.

As the sun dipped below a ridge, I pulled in by a narrow creek that chortled at my whirlpool of thoughts. I began to set up camp, a twinkle in my step. My travels were confirming that humanity, once on the path to doom, was instead becoming what both Willi and I had envisioned it could be. The new-style collectives were a success, phasering out some old-school beliefs, yet retaining the good stuff along with new tech. I glanced at the cell phone perched on a log. I was energized again. If I felt like chatting to Laura about cheese flavorings or Riley about enviro-politics, they were only a phone call away. After a bit of back-and-force, Aaron had agreed that my future advice would be presented openly to the collective, without hiding or pretense. I sat on the log and popped the last bite of Laura's truffle-smothered cheese in my mouth.

At some point, the phone would ring with an unknown call display. Willi's soft, persuasive voice would ask me to come back. I knew what I'd tell him. My sanity needed both peopling and solituding, and, like a clown on a beach ball, I'd finally managed to find my balance point.

NOTE: Originally published in Glass and Garden: Solarpunk Summers anthology in 2018.

About the Author: *Holly Schofield travels through time at the rate of one second per second, oscillating between the alternate realities of city and country life. Her stories have appeared in Analog, Lightspeed, Escape Pod, and many other publications throughout the world. She hopes to save the world through science fiction and homegrown heritage tomatoes.*

Website: http://hollyschofield.wordpress.com
Twitter: @HSchofieldFic
Facebook: @holly.schofield.33

THE HOMESTEAD AT THE BEGINNING OF THE WORLD

JANA DENARDO

Sam surveyed the glacial lake, blooming green under September's sun. Some days, he couldn't believe all of this was his. The Ojibwe had remained stubbornly rooted in their homeland when so many others had been ousted back in the original days of the European colonials and his family had owned this sizeable homestead for generations. He felt honored to be its current custodian.

A century ago, the entire world learned what the Indigenous people had felt all those centuries before: First contact. It certainly hadn't been as happy as *Star Trek* would have posited, but the fact, like Shakespeare, that show had remained in the cultural zeitgeist nearly two hundred years later said something for the show. Too bad it hadn't been accurate where first contact was concerned.

For Sam, its message of hope might even be embraced tighter now that the alien invaders were gone though no one was entirely sure why. Certainly, the human freedom fighters tried to destroy them but had been woefully outgunned. As far as anyone could tell, the aliens, the Derjviks, had destroyed themselves, and Earth had only been a hunk of rock caught between warring factions. For the last one hundred years all the planet had been nothing more than was a source of resources and its people lab rats.

Now the Derjviks were gone, and humanity was creeping forward.

Sam couldn't complain about his patch of land, some hundred acres in what northern Wisconsin had been. Now it was part of the Ojibwe Nation allied with what was left of Canada and America. He could live here without being overly bothered by either country with one big exception, what he farmed on the multiple little lakes that dotted his land. In the marshes he grew cranberries and blueberries. Some of his lakes had the wild rice and fish that had been his people's cultural foods for thousands of years but that's not what would bring the weekly visitor to his door.

Speaking of which, Dr. James was late. Maybe she was waiting at his home, but that would be unlike Linda. Leaving the lake behind, he sauntered back to the main compound. His own home was modest, and he owned several cabins along with his mother. Now that humanity had picked itself up a bit people had begun to travel. Who wouldn't want to come someplace as beautiful as this? It had been less ravaged over the last several decades than the major cities had been. The people here hadn't been herded into internment camps as slaves. There hadn't been enough humans in this area to bother with.

Still, as he wound his way along the hemlock and pine shaded pathway, evidence of the Derjvik invaders could be found pock marking the area. He skirted past a metal hunk of what had been a ship. Eventually, he'd have all the wreckage hauled off his land. There was a foundry not too far away reclaiming the metals. God knew there was enough of it to recycle into dozens of vehicles, tractors and whatever else they needed.

At the moment, most of his cabins stood empty other than the smallest of them, which housed a grandfather and his teenaged grandson who wanted to show the old man something peaceful and green. The man had spent his early life as one of the lab rats. Sam was shocked he'd hung on this long. So many died, they might never know the true number. Obsidian, one of his dogs, mostly retriever, jogged out from behind one of the cabins barking, not at him but rather at someone coming up the road. A motorcycle, old but kitted out for biofuels, sailed up the road more gracefully than Sam expected. It was as if the rider had some six sense about where the road needed grading. Dr. James knew, of course, but whoever this was, he was easily a foot taller than she was. He assumed that it was a man but who knew. The Derjviks had experimented with making humans bigger, stronger, less reliant on food and a whole host of other things. Linda and her scientist friends had said that in some areas of the world there wasn't a single purely human DNA strand to be found.

The man parked his bike and took off his helmet. Pale, nearly white hair framed his strong jaw. His skin was pale too but tinged with green. Someone in his family – maybe even him – had been spliced with chlorophyll, an aborted experiment in making them into autotrophs. Maybe the Derjvik had wanted to perfect the genetic engineering for their own people. There was a certain advantage in being able to manufacture food from light.

"Hello," Sam called, grazing his fingers over his pocket. His pistol nestled in there. He might not like weapons much but as much as he would have hoped fighting the Derjvik had brought humanity together. Overall there were still marauders and people who wanted to take anything they could.

The man swung off his bike and made Sam tense when he put a hand in his pocket. He pulled out a wallet, flipping it open to show his ID. "Dr. James broke her leg. I'm her replacement."

Sam took a step closer. Once upon a time phones would have borne a person's identification, but the information networks were still in the process of being restored. Much of human knowledge had been squirreled away and saved but the technology required to bring it back to life was still in the process of being remade. It could take years. He peered closely at the i.d., the face matched but he'd never heard the name Dr. Kjell Eriksen. "Kah-gel?"

Eriksen grinned. "It's pronounced Shell."

"Sorry."

"No worries. I'm assuming you're Sam Funmaker." His pale eyebrows rose at that as if to say he didn't have the corner on unusual names. He had no idea how unusual it was.

"That's me." He smiled. "And I'm assuming you're here to see the lakes."

Kjell nodded curtly. "How have they been doing?"

"Come see for yourself." Sam turned on heel, hiking back toward the closest lake. Kjell grabbed his kit. "Are you new to the group or just new to me?"

"Somewhere in between. I worked for the CBFD in Madison, but I wanted out of the city. Too many bad memories."

Sam glanced over in time to see Kjell's jaw tighten. He didn't elaborate, and Sam wasn't going to press a stranger on sensitive issues. "Understood. Never been to a city that big," he admitted. Madison was south of Three Lakes over two hundred miles, and he'd never had reason to make the trip. The land here held everything he needed.

"You've been here long?" Kjell studied Sam, no doubt taking in his coppery skin and raven hair. Sam's Indigenous genes were abundantly clear.

"Feel like I grew right up out of the soil. My family has been here since long before the Derjviks.

"Mine too in spite of the very Norwegian name."

"Lots of Viking types in Wisconsin," Sam agreed.

Kjell pulled himself up to his full height. Sam put it at least 6'7" and thumped his chest. "That's me, mostly Viking with a handful of mighty oak mixed in." He said it without much bitterness, surprising Sam, as he pointed to his green skin.

Sam laughed. He wondered if Kjell's skin could supply enough energy to keep him going. He'd never known anyone who'd been tampered with in this way since that sort of thing happened in the human camps in the city. Sometimes the alternation worked, and others didn't. Maybe in time he'd ask Kjell.

"What do you think of this area?"

Kjell shrugged, canting his face skyward. Sam noticed a gray wooly gathering of clouds. The winds picked up speed. A storm must be rolling in. "It's so…remote. I'm not used to there being so few people, but I'm looking forward to settling in. I've heard about the good work being done out here."

"We're proud of it. We're becoming a world leader in sustainability." Sam held up a hand, stopping Kjell in his tracks as the sounds of something crashing through the woods. Obsidian and Berry popped out onto the path all but grinning when they saw him. Makade, his enormous black cat followed the retrievers.

"Yours?" Kjell asked, a hint of nervousness in his voice.

Maybe Kjell had heard tales of the large feral packs that had formed in the Derjviks time or was he afraid of dogs. That would be sad. "Yep, apparently here to lead the parade. Obsidian is the black lab and Berry the chocolate and Makade is the cat who can't shut up and thinks he's a dog."

"Handsome bunch."

"They'll agree with you. The first lake is just over this rim."

"How many do you have?"

"Growing algae? Three. I also have one large one that produces enough wild rice to keep my town and a few others well stocked. It's almost harvesting time. I have some berry bogs as well. I make a mean cranberry wild rice pilaf. There's plenty of venison to go with it. Do you hunt at all?"

"Not a big thing in the city." Kjell grimaced, and Sam mirrored him. It was a stupid question. Weapons had been forbidden in the city under the occupation. Shot guns and rifles barely dented Derjvik armor anyhow. "The groceries are getting back to operational and the dairies outside of Madison were minimally operational under the Derjvik. Mostly we have their plants pumping out the food supplements still."

Sam nodded. Of course, the Derjviks wanted their test subjects to stay alive and that meant food production went on even if it was barely palatable.

"We have a grocery store here too, of course. But a lot of people often buy direct. I'm sure Dr. James will tell you all about it."

"She already mentioned something about a smoked fish dip you've given her." He smiled.

"She's crazy for it. I enjoy fishing. I'm happy to teach you if you'd like to learn." Sam hoped he did. Kjell's muscular frame was one Sam could picture himself wrapped around. He didn't mind green skin or manipulated DNA. Kjell could be a model for a Viking statue if he ignored the lack of beard, which if he was honest, he preferred. Green skin was fine, big scratchy Viking beards did nothing for him. He didn't mind a fuzzy chest, but faces were another story.

They crested the hill and Sam spread his arms, showing off the lake. Green flotsam might not be the prettiest of pictures, but it was biofuel gold. It kept him well off, more so than he was actually comfortable with. He sent a good fraction of his income to areas where it would help.

Kjell's blue eyes sparkled like sunlight on water. "Sweet."

"I do my best to keep it healthy. We're getting a new shot at doing life right. Respect for the land is important to me." Sam scowled. Damn, he sounded like an Indigenous stereotype, and if there was anything he loathed, it was stereotypes.

"It shows. I have tests to run. I'm sure you know the drill."

He waved a hand to the shoreline. "Have at it."

Kjell put on a mask and got gloves out of his kit. He'd be testing to see how much the engineered algae was producing. They had lost a lot of the technology to do the closed system vertical growth for the algae, which was easier to maintain than this open pond system. Sam already had an arrangement in place to host and manage some of the first restored vertical systems in the area once they could be produced.

Sam sat neat a pine, hoping it wouldn't drip sap on him. Obsidian and Berry sat with him and Makade climbed onto his shoulders as they waited while Kjell worked. As he petted various mammalian heads, Sam studied Kjell's tight backside. Kjell squatted at the water's edge pulling up samples, giving him a great view of that nice butt. The wind slid past Sam's skin, picking up speed. He spared a glance for the sky in time to see lightning jump from cloud to cloud with a faint rumble.

Setting Makade aside, Sam climbed to his feet. "Kjell, you'd better hurry it along. The weather is getting crappy."

Kjell straightened as a bigger crack of thunder sounded. "Guess I'm done now." He picked up his kit and they hustled back the way they came, not fast enough to outrun the storm.

Water whipped them as they ran. The dogs and even Makade fled faster than the their two-legged companions could. Wet jeans chafed Sam's thighs. He and Kjell slid on the wet loam as they pelted along. They finally caught up with his furry companions waiting for them under the overhang of Sam's front door. Kjell's eyebrows rose as he took in Same's odd house. The large round door and half underground left wing was straight out of his mother's beloved *The Hobbit* and the right wing blended rather clumsily with a two-story log cabin. Sam dragged the door open and his graceless companions bulled their way in before he or Kjell could get inside. Dripping on the slate flooring, Kjell stood gaping at the wood ceiling and rooms spinning off from the foyer.

"I'd heard the damn aliens never bothered too much with the out of way places like this, didn't see them as a threat but I never realized real houses were still a thing, that people lived like this."

"There was a Derjvik camp in Wausau and a little outpost in Rhinelander but here there weren't enough people to bother with. I grew up in this Hobbit house. Those old stories were Mom's only solace. Dad and his father built this and all the cabins. We lost Dad to the aliens when I was little. Grandpa is still here though." Sam stopped himself before he got maudlin. Besides, they were dripping wet, and if he was uncomfortable, he figured Kjell was too. "Let me get you a towel." Sam clomped off and a flash of civility washed over him. He returned with not only a towel but a robe he kept for the cabins for when they had guests. "If you want to follow me, you can change into this in the bathroom, and I'll toss your clothes into the dryer. You'll want to wait out the storm." He gestured at the round window where Kjell's motorcycle sat up by the road, getting drenched.

Kjell scowled. "If I had known it was going to rain, I'd have brought the company truck."

Sam had smelled the possibility of a storm in the air hours ago but held his tongue. "It won't be fun to drive in this."

"If you don't mind me staying."

"Not at all. It's quiet here. Mom is at the clinic in Eagle River. She's a self-taught nurse, works at my sister's clinic every other week just to keep a hand in it. Sis isn't like me or our brother. We're farmers and fishers. She went to the first revived medical school."

"Excellent."

"She enjoys it. I'm not cut out for dealing with the sick, I'm afraid."

"In the city, most everyone has to do their fair share of nursing the injured."

"Makes sense." Sam swept a hand toward the hall. "There's the bathroom. Maybe it'll stop raining by the time the clothes are dry."

While he left Kjell to change into the robe, Sam stripped in his room, toweled off and redressed. He tossed his soaked clothes in the dryer and put on a kettle for tea before Kjell reappeared. Sam took a cautious look at him. Not much of his chest showed, and if he had any hair it might be as whitish as the hair on his head.

He offered up his wet clothes. "Where's the dryer?"

Sam took the clothing. "Here, I'll take those. I've put a pot of tea on."

"You have actual tea?"

"They've recovered the plantations in California and South Carolina. I hear shipments from India and China will start up again soon." Sam beckoned for Kjell to follow. He tossed the clothing in the dryer before escorting his guest into the living room.

"It's still raining." Kjell sighed.

"It might be an all-day rain" Sam replied, making Kjell sigh more. "I'm surprised they didn't warn you a motorcycle isn't always your best choice in these parts."

"They're about the only mode of transport in the city. They're retrofitting some Derjvik vehicles and stripping others to make cars and trucks now, running on biofuels. Most can't afford them though."

Sam nodded. Some had predicted barter systems would prevail as humanity picked itself up off the ground. They underestimated human greed. "The roads up here are still pretty cracked and buckled. It'll make the bike challenging."

Kjell snorted. "I've noticed."

The kettle shrilled so he went to pull it off the stove. "I did put a little sassafras root in the tea."

"I have no idea what that tastes like but I'm willing to try anything once. To be honest, I've never actually had tea of any kind."

"That's the spirit. I don't put it in every time because it might be a carcinogen in large quantities. It's what originally flavored root beer because that's what I'm using, the root. The ground leaves thicken stews."

"I see I have a lot to learn." Kjell followed him back into the kitchen. He patiently waited the five minutes for the tea to brew. He scratched Berry's head as they waited. She nuzzled her nose under his hand any time he stopped, flipping his hand onto the broad dome of her skull.

"She's always so needy in case you're wondering."

"She's lovely. I've never had a pet."

"My mom always kept a dog around, guinea hens too, excellent early warning systems especially if Derjviks were around." Sam smiled. "Cats are always useful too."

"Was your mom able to kill any if they did show?"

"Sure, even I bagged a few when I was a kid, using their own weapons.

Stomping Tim – he lives fairly close – was a Derjvik Dervish, killed tons of them."

"Even I heard of that name. Heard he was crazy."

"Only a little more than the next fellow." Sam shrugged, pouring the tea.

"They didn't even allow dinner knives in the city. They watched us like hawks." Kjell shuddered cupping his tea close "Still have nightmares."

"I'm sure."

Kjell's chest heaved as he dragged in air as if about to have a nightmare while awake. Sam didn't doubt Kjell had PTSD. Most had some level of it. Kjell rolled his shoulders. He changed the subject. "So, you live up to your name."

He raised his eyebrows. "I'm not sure this has been that much fun."

"Huh? Oh, no, not that. This." He waved his hand at the rounded doorways.

Sam winced. "Linda told!"

"No, I researched you since I'd be working with you. Are you really Samwise?"

"Like I said, it's Mom's passion, old Science Fiction and Fantasy. It could have been worse. I could have been whiny Frodo."

"There would have been no hiding that name. I think it's wonderful though that your mother helped preserve those old stories. So many where I grew up…." Kjell's lips thinned. "Never mind that. I like your house."

Sam sensed the underground lake of pain inside Kjell's core, but he left it untapped. "Thanks. Where are you living?"

"I'm staying at the dorms in the lab."

Sam wrinkled his nose. "Those can't be too personable or comfortable."

"It's adequate."

"If you want a change, let me know. I have the cottages to rent."

Kjell's eyes darted about like a startled deer. "I'm not sure. It's isolated."

Sam smiled. "This whole area is. Does that bother you?"

"A little."

"I'm curious. Why are you here? To escape the city like you said or is there more?"

"Mostly the former. I needed to get out of the city. I thought my job would make it okay to stay there but, in the end, I decided a change might help."

"I understand," Sam replied not sure he did. To him, the horrors of the city were something he read about but had never seen. "If you plan on staying around, I'd be happy to help you acclimate to the place."

The dark clouds rolled away from Kjell's face. "I'd love that. I'm sure I'll be lost without some help." He cast another glance toward the window. "And those don't look like woods I'd like to be lost in."

"They're thick, and in the winter more than cold enough to kill you."

Kjell rubbed his arms as if already chilled. "I definitely need something other than the bike."

"In the Before Times, Eagle River was the Snowmobile Capital of the World. The lab has several snowmobiles biofuel retrofitted. I have one myself. I have snowshoes for that matter. It snows a lot more here than in Madison."

"That'll let me embrace my Viking heritage." Kjell grinned.

"That's one way of seeing it. Mine's more of a 'wow my balls might literally freeze off'."

Kjell laughed, and Sam was sure Kjell had checked him out at the same time. Now that could be interesting.

"You laugh but it's routinely twenty below in the winter. Another reason the Derjviks left this area…well not alone, but it wasn't a priority."

Kjell nodded then took a sip of tea. He knew well as Sam that the Derjvik preferred heat. Much of the hotter states and countries had almost no humans left. Only now were they creeping back – like his tea planation in South Carolina. The Derjvik domiciles were only semi-human compatible. They air systems that supplied the methane the Derjviks preferred had to be removed.

"This home is probably cozy when it's that cold."

Sam pointed to the woodburning stove. "That alone makes this room toasty. I have a biofuel generator and I have plenty of smoked and otherwise cured meat, canned and pickled foods. This is the place to be when the snow is up past your knees."

"I'll keep that in mind. How much do you want for a cottage per month?"

Sam waved him off. "We can arrange something if you decide you like it here and want to stay."

"Thanks. Looks like the rain is slowing."

"Eh, give it a few minutes to be sure."

Kjell did and when he left, the house – despite all the furry ones – seemed awfully empty.

∽

"When you asked me if I wanted to have a fish dinner, this isn't what I was expecting." Kjell shook the fishing rod he held. "Though it explains why you wanted me here so early for dinner."

"You said you wanted to learn about life here. I thought you might enjoy this." Sam shrugged.

Kjell considered it. After meeting Sam a few days ago, he'd pumped Linda James for information, and she sang Sam's praises. Being born inside the labor camps, Kjell had never know freedom like this, could barely dream it truly existed. Men like Sam were mythic, but he was real and hotter than he had a right to be. What did Sam make of him and his corrupted DNA? He showed no signs of prejudice, but it could be lurking That thought sparked a sudden panic. What if Sam planned to take him into the woods and do him harm? No, he was being paranoid. Sam had been nothing but sweet.

"I'm game but you'll have to help me. I barely know one end of this thing from the other."

"I'll show you, no worries."

Kjell followed Sam to another lake on his property. Two chairs perched on the bank and small boat floated, tied off on a short wooden dock. Kjell eyed the latter warily. He could see himself toppling off into the water.

"Are we staying on land?"

Sam nodded "Until you learn how to properly cast, we should stay here."

"Good. I'm not a good swimmer."

"Add that to the list of things you should learn to live around here. I can teach you, only not here. Too many lost hooks in this area."

Kjell pictured Sam shirtless and wet. It was a lovely image. "I'd like that." He'd wanted to learn to be better since he worked around water but there never seemed to be the opportunity back home.

Sam ushered Kjell toward the soft grassy edge of the lake. He listened to Sam's instructions on how to bait a hook, how to cast and how to watch the bobber. He made it sound so easy. Sam wisely stood far away when Kjell tried his own casts. Three caught tree branches and a nearly hooked Sam later, Kjell managed a halfway decent cast.

Sam cast out and sat on the chair. Kjell sat next to him, watching the orange bobber sitting almost placid on the water. It didn't take long before boredom set in. Kjell let his gaze wander along the shoreline, noting the changing leaves hanging low over the water, interspersed with evergreens. Weeds waved in the warm breeze. That wasn't any more interesting, so he watched Sam out of the corner of his eye. Sam was a hundred percent more interesting than fishing, but if he didn't try, he'd only end up disappointing Sam.

"Do you share your Mom's passion for the old books?"

"Yeah, TV too. We had pirate broadcasters here when the Derjvik were still around, turned legit now. There are problems of course with the old stuff." Sam sat forward as the bobber danced. When it didn't do more, he relaxed.

"How so?"

"Native people were always erased. We were never just a cop or a teacher on TV or the movies, our ethnicity always was the focus of whatever role we had, or we were the stoic laconic stereotype who are either angry warriors, a drunk or a mystical shaman and any of those three options are perfectly attuned to Mother Nature, who can track an ant over rock and hear a deer fart in a wind storm. Now that we're starting all over, hopefully we can do it better."

The bitterness hug in the air so thick Kjell could taste it. In the handful of days, he'd known Sam, this was the first sign of temper he'd seen.

"I can guess what you're thinking," Sam grumbled and Kjell cocked up an eyebrow. "I am connected to nature."

"You've made a scientific study of it. Different than you're good at it because of your genes. You work hard."

Sam inclined his head to Kjell. "Thanks oddly enough if it wasn't for the Derjvik I'd might never know a damn thing about living off the land. As far as we can tell, my great grandparents, and their parents were teachers, police and a casino manager. My grandfather's relatives held shamanic beliefs who helped preserve a lot of knowledge especially when books were burned, and computers destroyed. They're buried in bunkers all over the place up here over to Michigan and into Canada."

"People like them are why the universities were reestablished so quickly. I admire them. I feel comfortable in saying you are not laconic and judging by the swearing when I nearly hooked you, stoic is off the table."

Sam snorted. "I'd like to argue that, but it would be a flat out lie." He flicked the tip of his fishing pole making the bait look more alive. "Hopefully now, in this new world those stereotypes have been forgotten."

"Hopefully." His bobber dipped, and the rod jerked in his hands. "Whoa." The rod bent, and he yanked back on it like Sam had told him. He wheeled the reel frantically.

"Easier, if you go too fast the line can snap." Sam dropped his pole on the Y-shaped stick he'd shoved in the ground, one for each of them, and he helped Kjell reel in the fish.

Adrenaline shook his hands, making the rod slippery. He'd have lost it if not for Sam. He gaped when the greenish-brown fish crested the water. He'd never seen a live fish before. It was magnificent, and for a moment, he wasn't sure he could eat it. Food had always been scarce growing up, so he set aside that emotion easily enough. That said, he let Sam remove it from the hook and string it in the water, so it would stay alive until they were ready to go home.

"I...caught a fish!" Kjell rasped in disbelief. "That was so cool!"

"Glad you liked it." Sam settled back with his own rod.

"What is it?"

"Largemouth bass. They're tasty."

Kjell frowned, embarrassed by the thoughts going through his head. "You're not going to be disappointed in me if I leave the dispatching to you? I'm not sure...I've never killed anything." He glanced over at a man who'd been fighting aliens since he was a kid. Not that Kjell had had the opportunity. The labor camps were too well guarded for that.

Sam shook his head, his long braid lashing. "Not at all. I'm used to it, so I don't mind."

"I appreciate that. Oh, look!" He pointed to Sam's bobber.

As Sam reeled in another fish, Kjell cast out again. Nothing happened for what felt like forever, so he reeled in to cast in a different spot. Something hit his hook. Adrenaline surged anew, and he set the hook, beginning to drag it in.

"Oh, this feels heavy!"

"We do have big Muskie in these lakes. That would be nice, a sturgeon would be even nicer."

Kjell noticed no fight like the last time, simply a heaviness at the other end of the line. "This doesn't feel right."

Sam raised an eyebrow but said nothing. He was probably thinking how would Kjell know. "You got this?"

"Yeah."

He finally hauled the fish to the surface but what broke the brownish water wasn't a fish. He yelped seeing Derjvikian chest armor bob up. Kjell dropped the rod as if it branded him, falling off the chair as he scuttled backwards.

Sam leapt off his chair and grabbed the rod. He slapped it down into the Y-ed stick before squatting next to Kjell. Sam put a hand on his shoulder. "Are you okay?"

Kjell swallowed hard, almost unable to catch his breath. His gaze fixed past Sam's concerned face, never leaving the armor which had begun to sink again, empty of any danger. "Just startled," he lied. No one would believe him. "Derjvik couldn't breathe underwater anyhow."

Sam straightened, holding out a hand. Kjell accepted it, noticing how rough and callused it was. No judgment lurked in Sam's dark eyes. "We might not have seen the terrible action the cities did but we still have a shit ton of Derjvik junk scattered around. He let go of Kjell's hand, making him regret the loss of the comforting touch. Sam picked up Kjell's fallen rod, bringing the armor in to shore. Kjell held his breath expecting bones to come slithering out of the armor. They didn't. Sam tossed it onto the bank, out of sight behind a fallen tree.

"I'll come back for that later. Reclaimators pay a lot for that sort of stuff. We can reuse most of it."

"Good, and thanks for making me not have to look at it." Kjell sat back down trying to hide his shaking hands.

"I can't imagine what you went through with them. If you want to go back now we can."

Kjell shot him a grateful look. "Thanks, but no. I'm good. Do you think there's more junk in your lake?"

"Unfortunately. I'm always hauling up crap or digging it up." Sam shrugged. "I see it as free money."

"That's a good way to be, I suppose." Kjell cast out badly with his trembling hands. He couldn't be that blasé. He suffered daily at their hands as a child. "I hope I don't drag up more today."

"If you do, I'll handle it for you." Sam smiled. Kjell wondered if he imagined the slight flirtation in that offer. He could hope. At least Sam didn't seem to hold his fear against him.

Within an hour, they had four fish, and Sam declared that was more than enough. He took them back on a different path or, so he said. To Kjell, it looked no different than the first, nothing but trees and underbrush that he had no idea how Sam could distinguish from the other. Of course, if Sam had come to Madison, he would probably feel as lost as Kjell did now and he'd be the expert.

This path spat them out at the back of the cabins and Sam's house. A huge garden sprawled across the land. To his surprise Obsidian and Berry lounged there, two dark spots in a sea of color, greens, red and oranges.

"I thought they'd come with us today." Kjell nodded to the dogs.

"I had them on deer duty. They'll chase the deer and rabbits out of here. There's plenty for them to eat but my garden is the tastiest morsel around." Sam snorted. "While I finish with the fish, why don't you hunt up some zucchini and tomatoes?"

"Sure," Kjell said with faked confidence.

He knew what they looked like, but he'd never had to decide if one was ripe enough to be picked. Obsidian escorted him through the rows of plants. He found a few zucchinis several inches long that looked big enough to be worthwhile, so he fought them off the plant. It was tougher than expected and he nearly damaged a plant to his chagrin. The ripe tomatoes were easier, almost falling into his hands.

The earthiness of the garden excited his senses. For a moment, even he felt connected to the land. And why not? Chlorophyll coursed through his body too. He stood there, shirt used as a basket to hold his miniature harvest, studying the cabins. Maybe he should rent one. The dormitory at the lab was cramped and reminded him far too much of the rooms he'd been kept in as a kid. Maybe the freedom he sought could be found in those cabins. If nothing else, he'd be closer to Sam. He hadn't been this attracted to a man since Ryan back in school when he first realized he was gay.

Spotting Sam behind the house, he picked his way through the garden to meet up with him. He stood at a wooden work bench with a bucket next to him. Kjell grimaced at the slimy, bloody collection of guts in it. Makade watched the proceedings with great interest but made no attempt to get into the bucket. Sam looked over his shoulder at the vegetables cradled in the tent Kjell made of his shirt.

"Looks good. I was about to scale these. Want to watch?"

He wasn't sure he did, but Sam was trying to educate him, so he should at least watch it once. Kjell placed the veggies on the ground and stepped closer to the bench. Sam showed him how to use the knife to scrape the scales away. He was thankful the heads, tails and fins were already in the scrap bucket and equally relieved that Sam didn't offer him the knife to try it himself. It was a step he wasn't ready for. He liked the idea of living off the land, but he wasn't going to get there instantly.

"Does Makade ever get into the bucket?"

"Not him but the dogs will if I let them. I don't let them have the fish guts. I'll take them out into the woods and let other animals have them. I usually keep the heads for fish head soup and the bones for fish stock, but I have enough in the freezer already. I don't usually start that until next month."

"You really do use up everything."

"I try. Come on, let's get these cooking, and we can walk the guts out to dump."

"Okay."

Kjell gathered his veggies back up and followed Sam into the kitchen. He enjoyed the view of Sam's lean back and hard buttocks as they traveled. The scents wafting from the kitchen made his mouth water or was that Sam's fine form?

"I already started the meal before we left. There's a pumpkin and wild rice soup in the crock pot, and all I have to do is heat up the wild rice and chestnut pilaf."

"I've never had a chestnut!" For that matter, he'd never tasted wild rice either.

"I hope you'll like it."

"I was going to say I eat nearly anything but that's a bit insulting in a way. I'm looking forward to it."

"Good. I thought about cooking this the old way but after complaining about stereotypes, it seems ironic to whip the fish on an open fire." Sam smirked. Instead he put them in a pan with potatoes, onions and butter and popped it in the oven. "Let's go give the guts back to nature and call the hounds in so they don't sneak out and either eat or roll in them. When we get back I have spiced roasted pecans from the back forty and goat cheese from my brother's farm for snacking on until dinner's ready."

"Wow, you prepared a feast. I can't remember when I've eaten so well." For him, meals were protein drinks and bars, something to get out of the way, not to savor.

"Well is yet to be seen but I think you'll like it. Want to stay here and relax or want to come with me to toss the guts?"

Kjell wanted to spend all the time he could wring out of the day with Sam. "I'll go with."

Sam was surprisingly quiet as they walked but it didn't feel awkward in the least. Kjell didn't expect how far they'd walk before tossing the guts and other parts out, but it made sense. Things that would eat it probably weren't ones you'd want close to the house.

"Do you ever feel...I don't know, lonely or afraid out here when your mother is away?" he asked as they strolled back to the house.

"Lonely sometimes but not afraid. This is my land, and I love it. I don't feel afraid except maybe a few times when the power is out, and I'm relying on a generator and wood to keep warm in intense cold. All of us feel a little nervous then." Sam gazed at him. "You're a little nervous, aren't you?"

He scowled, hating to admit it. "I am. I tried to pay attention to where we walked but if you weren't here I'm not sure I could get back."

"If it helps, I'm not likely to abandon you here. You'll get the hang of it, just like learning a highway."

"That makes sense."

Kjell made an effort to remember the path, but all the trees looked alike to him. Relief washed over him when he recognized the back of house. He waited while Sam hosed the bucket out and put it on his bench. The house smelled even better now as the richness of the fish and potatoes.

It suddenly hit him that Sam hadn't used the vegetables he'd sent Kjell after. "Hey, what are you using the zucchini and tomatoes for?"

"Today nothing. Maybe you'll come back for fried zucchini and marinara tomorrow." Sam beamed.

Kjell returned the high-wattage smile. "I think that I might do that. Do you always cook so much?"

"Depends on if I'm alone or if Mom is here. Grandpa stays in one of the cabins half the time and with my brother, Aragon, the rest of the time. I'm a pretty good cook. Go wash up, and I'll get the snacks."

Kjell washed his hands and was on the couch with Makade by the time Sam arrived with a tray of nuts, cheese and crackers. He sat them on the table and plopped on the couch on the other side of his large cat. Kjell slathered a cracker with the goat cheese, eager to taste it. The strong flavors of the soft white cheese flooded his mouth.

"This is so good! I've never had anything like it." Kjell grimaced. "I keep saying that, don't I? I never."

Sam bobbed his head. "You'd definitely win that drinking game."

Kjell cocked his head, reaching for the nuts. "Game?"

"I never, it's a game where someone says I never, and if you've done it, you have to drink."

"So, if I say I've never gone fishing, you have to take a drink."

"Exactly."

"You'd die of alcohol poisoning playing against me." Kjell laughed. He popped the nuts into his mouth.

"Seriously."

"Outside of your family, you don't share this land with anyone?" It was a dangerous question, but he had to ask.

Sam's eyes hooded. "No, I haven't found the guy I'd like to share it with yet."

Kjell's spirit soared. He didn't want Sam to be lonely but knowing he was gay gave him hope. "It's difficult, isn't it?"

"Up here where there's more deer than men, damn hard. I suppose if I play a few rounds of I never with city boys, I'll find someone who might do unspeakable things to me." Sam grinned, his cheeks pinking up.

"I think I'd prefer you sober when I do those unspeakable things to you." Kjell cupped a hand over his mouth, turning his peculiar shade of green-tinged red, like a Christmas tree of decades past. "That came out wrong. I'm not usually so forward."

"I kinda like it." Sam leaned over Makade who watched him with feline curiosity. Before Sam could kiss Kjell the kitchen buzzer sounded. "Damn."

"A timer with lousy timing."

Sam laughed and unfolded from the couch. Kjell brought the snack tray back into the kitchen in case Makade or the dogs decided to help themselves. He poured water for them as Sam plated the fish and wild rice pilaf. He served the soup alongside of it with bread for dipping. They didn't talk much as they ate, Kjell completely invested in savoring every bite.

"I'm sure this is the best meal I've ever eaten," he proclaimed as they cleaned up.

"Thank you. I'm glad you enjoyed it. I'm not good at making desserts. That's more mom's specialty so I have nothing to offer but some home brewed wine. It's on the sweet side because Concords are what grows best on my property."

"It's a full-time job running this property."

"Definitely. Of course, maintaining the algae lakes for you guys takes precedence but I do my best to not only keep the rest of it going but to write papers on how I'm doing it. They want me to teach at the new branch campus the University of Wisconsin put in Rhinelander. It mostly does agriculture and health care. It's too much to keep this running and teach too."

"I can't imagine and yes, I'd like to try the wine."

"Sure thing. As soon as we wash up."

Sam washed and Kjell dried before Sam poured the wine. They

retreated to the coziness of the living room. Kjell sipped the red wine, sweet as honey.

"I'm going to hate myself for saying this, but I shouldn't have flirted so openly. It's not that I'm uninterested because I sure as hell am but I want to find my feet before jumping into a relationship." Kjell studied Sam's face, praying he wouldn't see pain there.

Sam simply shrugged. "Makes sense. I'm not one for rushing into things either. I prefer sleeping with friends but you're well on your way to that."

"Good. Before I went and made things a little awkward, I wanted to ask you something."

"Go ahead. And it's only awkward if we let it be."

Kjell smiled softly. "Good. I wanted to talk to you about the cabins. The dorm isn't working for me. It's too much like what I'd left behind, what I want to get away from. How much would it cost to rent one?"

"Let's go have a look. The wine will wait on us. Let's find you one you like. They're not all the same."

"Sounds good."

Out of the six cabins, the largest was his grandfather's. Two were small, bigger than his dorm room but not what he wanted. The one closet to the gardens had a stone fireplace and a loft bedroom.

"I like this one. It's close to the house, which makes me a little less nervous."

"Fair enough. We can discuss cost, and I'm always willing to knock a little off in trade for help around the homestead."

"Okay, sounds great." Kjell noticed the sun was already further down in the sky than he expected. They bartered the price as they strolled back to the house. In the end, they settled on a price Kjell assumed was too low, but he didn't protest too much. He could use a break.

By the time they got back inside, Obsidian and Berry had claimed the couch, only reluctantly leaving it when Sam told them to get down.

"Do you have any of that pirated TV you mentioned? I'd like to see that."

"I do and that is a new smart device from the west coast, not old tech cobbled together like when I was a kid." Sam jutted his chin toward the screen on the far wall.

"Do you mind if I stay awhile for that?" Kjell couldn't contain a little bounce of excitement at getting to see TV.

"I'd be delighted. If you want to get the snack tray back out of the fridge, I'll set it up."

Kjell happily settled in with Sam. The shows, like so many other things were new to him, in spite of being so old, before the invasion, in a time that seemed almost mythical. By the time they finally stopped for a pee break, the view out the window was inky, tinged red at the horizon. He hadn't realized it was so late. To his surprise, some of the trees glowed in the dark. "The trees."

"They're spliced with bioluminescent jellyfish. It cuts down on the need for electricity, but you have to wonder if that's one of the things we should have messed with."

Kjell glanced at his own greenish skin. "Yeah, I know. It's gotten pretty late." Before he could take his leave, a cry ripped the night air. Kjell leapt off the couch, backing away from the window. Sam stared at him, startled.

"What the hell was that?" He thrust a shaking hand at the pane of glass.

"The Hodag." Sam deadpanned.

Kjell glared. "What nonsense is that?"

"Surely you've heard of the Hodag." A smirk played in the corner of Sam's mouth.

"Never."

"It has an elephantine face, the body of a dinosaur, huge claws and a long tail full of spikes." Sam stood. "I have one around here somewhere. Hodags have been seen since the 1830s."

Kjell sat back down as Sam searched his book shelves. "We both know there is no such thing."

"No, it was faked, of course, but we had the Derjviks convinced for years the Hodag was real. Hodag hunts were legendary and let us sneak a lot of shit past them." He plucked a statue off a shelf and presented it to Kjell.

"Good." He studied the green quadruped monster. As he handed it back, the cry sounded again seeming even closer to the house. He widened his eyes at Sam. Why didn't the dogs seem upset by this? Makade was in the window, staring out.

"It's a bobcat, nothing to worry about. They're shy but they're also why I don't usually let the beasts out at night. We have coyote too."

"We had them in the city. I know what they sound like."

"Good, then that won't startled you."

"Watch it echo weirdly here or something. I should get on the road. It's late"

"You can stay in a guest room. I don't have a cabin ready but the rooms here all have fresh bedding."

Kjell thought for a moment. Would that be weird given how attracted they were to each other? They were also adults who could control themselves. He wasn't keen on riding his cycle over the rough road in the dark. "You know, that would be safer. Thanks. I'll call the lab, and let them know I won't be returning, in case someone worries."

"Sure. I'll get a spare toothbrush out for you. We have plenty."

"Thanks."

"And that way we can watch so more TV. This is fun getting to share it with someone who hasn't seen it all a thousand times."

Kjell smiled. "Sounds perfect."

∾

Sam glanced over his shoulder, trying to judge Kjell's expression, to see if he still had that bemused look he'd been sporting since he moved into one of the cottages. Having Kjell close tempted Sam but they hadn't dropped into bed. By mutual consensus, they gave it time to strengthen the relationship. Surely knowing each other two weeks was time enough, or at least one impatient part of him insisted. It wasn't happy that Sam rarely let it make any decisions.

Kjell stopped eyeing the cabin tucked into the woods behind a high fence. Sam doubted that was what made Kjell skitter from side to side a bit, as if ready to run. The Derjvik armor and bones adorning the fence probably was the root of his nervousness. Sam supposed a skull dotting every fence post could be unnerving.

"Where are you taking me?"

"Stomping Tim's." Sam patted the container he carried. "Going to trade him smoked fish for eggs and see if his kids want to help bring in the cranberry harvest."

"Really? Stomping Tim?" Kjell shook himself. "I half didn't believe you knew him, that he even actually existed."

"He does exist. He's a bit…eccentric. His wife, Hope, is a sweetheart. Just don't take any meat from him," Sam replied, hoping he wasn't going to scare Kjell off for good.

"Do I want to know why?"

"All these Derjviks you see hanging here?" Sam gestured to the fence. "He probably ate them all."

Kjell clapped a hand to Sam's shoulder. He trembled slightly. "Tell me you're joking."

"Wish I could. I'm sure after so many years the jerked, frozen and preserved stuff is gone. I usually say no to most meats. He doesn't offer me anymore."

"That is so…disturbing." Kjell shuddered.

"Swore their fat was the best."

Kjell gagged. "I'm not sure I needed to know that."

"I want you to have a full picture," Sam said knowing that meeting Tim could be hard for Kjell who struggled to understand the survivors in this area who were so different than the city folk.

"Congrats, now I'm picturing him naked slathered in alien oils, and I sort of want to puke."

"Mission accomplished. Sorry." He sure as hell didn't sound it. It wasn't that he was teasing Kjell, not really. Tim simply took getting used to.

He pushed the button to alert the household someone was at the gate, and he peered into the camera to let Tim see who was there. Quickly the front door banged open, and Tim made his way to the gate, demonstrating how he got his name. If anything, he was taller than Kjell and broad as a barn. His gray hair ringed his head except on the top, which gleamed in the sun. Tim often lamented not being able to transplant his thick chest length beard to the top of his head, and then he'd be 'properly handsome.' Sam would argue that he'd be the perfect thug on any ancient crime show but Tim had a good, if a bit flinty, heart.

"Hey, fuzzy feet, you brought the Green Man with you."

Next to him, Kjell stiffened. "This is Dr. Kjell Eriksen. He took over for Linda, and he's renting a cottage from Mom."

"Nice to meet you, Doc. Don't worry. I ain't got a problem with hybrids. Figure you got more reason to hate those fucking aliens than anyone. 'Sides, the Green Men were protectors of the earth and sounds like you're doing that if you're doing biofuel work."

"Thank you, sir."

Tim chuckled. "Fuck the sir shit. I'm just Tim."

"I know. Everyone knows your story or more likely the legend. However true or embellished it is," Kjell babbled.

Tim beamed, thumping his chest. "I need no embellishment."

Sam swore Kjell paled a little at that. To be fair, Tim's legend was terrifying. "I've brought fish dip and some of Aragon's goat cheese."

"Thanks. Hope's set aside some eggs in the kitchen."

They followed him into the house. Kjell's head swiveled around taking it all in as if amazed that instead of trophies of dead Derjviks, Hope chose to decorate her home with dozens of teapots and baskets, many of them woven by Sam's Ojibwa cousins. While Tim bellowed for his wife, Sam leaned into Kjell and whispered, "All the other trophies are in his garage."

Kjell shuddered.

"Will you stop screaming, you crazy old man. I'm not deaf." Hope stalked into the kitchen giving her husband a playful swat. Bearing six kids had stamped that love into the curves of her body. Hope may carry some extra pounds, but she also had strong hard hands and a heart big as the northern sky. Sam was incredibly fond of her.

"Hello, Sam, Sweetie." Her gaze slipped over to Kjell. "And who have you brought us."

"Dr. Kjell Eriksen. He's taking Linda's place for the time being. He's fresh up from Madison."

Both Tim and Hope eyed Kjell with some respect for simply having survived the atrocities of the city.

"Fresh from hell you mean," Tim muttered.

"I hope you're liking it here, Dr. Eriksen. Nice to meet you." Hope stuck out a hand.

"Please, call me Kjell." He shook her hand. "I'm still trying to fit in. This is the most remote place I've ever seen." Kjell shivered a bit. He pointed to Sam. "This one keeps laughing under his breath at me every time something new startles me."

"Oh, no, I laugh right at you some of the time." Sam protested, grinning. "Like when you were afraid of the tree frog on the window."

Kjell glared.

"I'm sure this would be very...different compared to the housing blocks down there. Would you like some pie?" Hope asked.

"We're meeting Mom and Granddad soon to get in the first of the rice harvests so we're a bit pressed for time," Same replied.

"Shame because pie is my favorite." Kjell smiled at her. "Whenever I'd get enough coin saved, I'd skip the food and go for a slice."

"You're having pie." Hope declared, pulling one out of the fridge and putting the whole thing in a travel container.

"Oh, I couldn't take all that!" Kjell waved his hands.

"Nonsense. Consider it a welcome gift." Hope insisted, nudging her husband.

Tim blinked, catching her meaning. "I have a welcome gift in the freezer. Prime meat."

Sam couldn't help himself. He belly laughed at Kjell's panicked expression. He never thought Tim would make that offer.

"Samwise Funmaker! What have you been telling people about my husband?" Hope swatted him too.

"It's squirrel." Tim glared at Sam. "Ass."

"I..." Kjell sputtered then settled on "Thanks."

Had Kjell ever had squirrel before? Mostly he seemed to still subsist on protein supplements that the Derjvik had made them eat. He supposed there wasn't a lot of making your own food in the city, at least not yet. Farms were being reestablished to a point where they could sustain their town and a few adjacent ones but soon they'd be able to do more.

"You're welcome."

"And, Hope, I wanted to see if we could borrow some child labor to get in all the cranberries," Sam said.

She snorted. "I'm ready to drown a few children in the cranberry bog. Sign me up too as a helper, sweetie. All I ask is a few buckets of berries as payment."

"And easy access to drowning mediums." Sam smirked.

"Exactly."

"Consider it done. Well, I have to meet Mom at the lake soon and break Kjell in as a poler," Sam said.

Hope appraised Kjell. "Bet he does nice pole."

Tim snorted, and Kjell went bright green and red like an old-fashioned Christmas. "Dirty old woman," Tim said.

She pinched Tim's butt. "Just like you like it."

"I'll remind you that's how you got so many damn kids, woman." Tim chuckled, wrapping his arms around his wife.

"I'll take that as our cue to leave," Sam said.

"It was nice meeting you," Kjell sputtered.

They left loaded with multicolored eggs and a few frozen squirrels.

"You met Stomping Tim and lived to tell the tale," Sam said as they got back in the truck.

Kjell snorted. "I may survive country life yet."

∼

KJELL QUICKLY REVISED his opinions on his survivability. How in the hell was Sam's granddad poling the canoe so easily? He had come to like both Douglas and Jessica quickly after moving into his cozy cottage. Sam's mother was delightful and talkative but seemed to know instinctively when to give her son space. She'd give Sam sly looks and subtle nods to Kjell before she'd disappear, which was about as much of matchmaker as she played. Kjell appreciated that. Douglas was quieter, more serious but still friendly.

Right now, the old man poled his canoe through the grassy lake almost effortless, standing at the back of his and Jessica's canoe. Sam had Kjell remain seated to paddle their canoe, figuring he could do less damage that way. Kjell knew how to handle a canoe but to move along this slowly made his shoulders ache.

As they pushed along near the shoreline both Sam and his mother worked two sticks that resembled shortened pool sticks that they called knockers. They'd capture the spikelets of the wild rice grass with one knocker and use the other to gently tap the grass. The rice fell into the tarp-lined canoe bottoms. As tired as Kjell's arms were, Sam and Jessica's had to be worse, but they worked without complaint.

Kjell wished he had the balance to stand like Douglas because it wasn't just rice that fell into the bottom of the boat. Caterpillars and spiders creeped about. Spiders might be good for an ecosystem, but they made Kjell want to scream like a kid. He tried to ignore them but was grateful that when he took his shirt off to enjoy the sunlight and ramp up his chlorophyll energy stores that he had chosen to sit on it. He still might not want to put it on until he did a complete spider search.

His skin gleamed with sweat, getting greener by the minute. He caught Sam eyeballing him more than once, stalks of grass sliding by unmolested by a knocker. What if Sam's relatives noticed? That thought made him oddly shy. For his part, he got a great view of Sam's broad back as he worked the knockers. His shirt stuck to him a bit as he sweated.

Kjell enjoyed the view. It was time to do more than look. He liked Sam a lot. This connection they shared grew more daily. He might fit in here after all. It might be too soon to be sure, but it was time to move forward. He swatted away a beetle that flew from the grass right at his face. Okay, maybe not quite the time. His arms would be too tired to do much, and no doubt by the end of this his back would be tight and sore. It wouldn't be a good first time. That was okay, he could wait a few more days.

"How are you hanging in there?" Sam asked.

"This is not how I expected this to go."

"How so? Sam quirked up his eyebrows.

"I don't know." Kjell pushed against the pole inching them forward. "I guess I never thought much about food."

"Not surprising," Doulas said, propelling his canoe on a parallel track through the water grass. "You grew up on protein supplements." His dark eyes swept over Kjell. "And sunlight in your case. To you, food is a powder you add water to and shake."

"Don't forget chewy yet somehow tasteless – no matter what flavor they claim it is – bars of soy and other proteins." Kjell shuddered, nearly knocking them off course. "I didn't realize how much *work* this all is."

"Arm wearing out?" Sam poked Kjell's chest with a knocker.

"A little. Don't worry I'm hanging in there, but I'm impressed,

Douglas, by how effortless you make this seem. With my luck, someone is going to have to spoon feed me by dinnertime."

Sam chortled, nearly whacking himself in the knee, laughing at Kjell.

Douglas smiled easily. "Been at this since I was far younger than you."

"Don't praise him too much. His head won't fit through the doorway if you do," Jessica added.

"Do you have work tomorrow, or can I drag you out to the cranberry bogs?" Sam asked.

"Work, thank you! Nice easy work," Kjell said, meaning every word of it. Maybe he could carve out of a life here, but he was a scientist not a farmer. He wasn't sure he was cut out for it.

Sam simply laughed harder. It took another hour before they finally tied the boats up and started home with the tarps. Kjell and Sam sat in the bed of the trucks making sure the tarps stayed tight and they didn't lose any of the rice. Just what Kjell wanted to do: risk his skull in an open bed while sitting on a spider-ridden tarp. By the time they rolled into the Funmaker complex thick dark clouds had formed in the sky. Sam scowled up at them.

"We won't be able to lay this out to dry," Sam said.

"We'll put them under the lean to," Jessica replied.

To Kjell, the lean to looked more like the bus terminals back home, only wooden. They stretched the rice out on the tarps with the hopes not too much would wash away. The forecast had said nothing about rain when they had left for the lake. Their skill in prediction hadn't gotten any better in the new age.

Jessica and Sam cooked some chicken from Sam's brother's farm for dinner. Kjell didn't know chicken could taste so good. The end of the night he'd been too exhausted to invite Sam to his cabin. All he'd be able to treat Sam to tonight would be him yawning and their snoring. Maybe tomorrow Kjell thought as he tumbled into sleep.

～

SAM DIDN'T KNOW what woke him first, the lightning or the screams Makade stood on the dresser looking out the window, his tail twitching. More lightning and more screams echoed in the night.

Sam rolled out of bed, jamming his feet into rubber-soled slippers before grabbing his gun from the nightstand. The screams were coming from the direction of Kjell's cabin. Sam grabbed the master key from the key rack near the door and raced across the grass nearly slipping from the rain. He pounded on the door as lightning illuminated it. Sideways rain whipped him. The screams didn't stop, and no one came to the door. Sam opened it with the master key and thundered up the stairs to the loft. Kjell did battle with his sheets obviously lost in some hell.

"Kjell," he shouted, not getting within striking distance. He knew better from Hope's stories about Tim's PTSD. Kjell didn't respond. "Kjell, wake up!"

Suddenly Kjell lurched upright, spilling off the mattress. He ran the moment his toes touched the wooden floor, launching himself at Sam. Unprepared from the depth of the night terror, Sam went down under Kjell. His head hit the spruce boards, causing lightning inside his head to match the storm raging outside. Kjell's fist to Sam's face increased the fireworks. Damn but he could hit hard.

Kjell struck him twice more before Sam could even gather his wits. He didn't want to hurt Kjell, but he had to protect himself. He'd be lucky to escape a concussion as is. Sam kidney punched Kjell, unrewarded as Kjell pounded him harder. Giving up on the niceties, Sam kneed Kjell in the groin, clumsily since he was on his back and only managed to get mostly thigh. It proved enough.

Kjell grunted, rearing back, eyes wide as if finally awake. "Oh, god! Sam!" He scuttled backwards off Sam and didn't stop until he slammed into the bed. "What have I done?"

"It's okay. I'm fine." That might be a lie. Sam tasted blood. He rolled to his knees. At least the room didn't spin much, concussion hopefully averted. "You're okay, Kjell. You're safe. It was just a dream."

Kjell uttered a broken noise, staring down at his shaking hands barely visible in the darkness. Sam got up and stumbled to the light switch. He hissed once the lamp cast Kjell into sharp relief. His face was colorless, his eyes wild as a trapped animal. In his dreams, he probably had been. Sam sat next to him, but Kjell shied away.

"I am so sorry," he whispered.

Sam shook his head. "It's not your fault. You don't have to tell me what the dream was about. I'm guessing it was about the Derjviks."

Kjell's head sagged like a sunflower in the dark.

"I hate them for what they did to you." Sam stroked Kjell's shoulders. "To this world."

"It's the storm. It sounds so much…bigger here. It reminds me the noise from their factories where…that's where they took the troublemakers and you never saw them again." Kjell shook all over.

Sam tugged him close, putting his arm round him.

"I don't know if I can live here, Sam. God, it's so different, so foreign. I haven't had a nightmare like that in years."

"You're unsettled. Give it time." Sam told himself that wasn't an entirely selfish request. Kjell was unsettled, and things did take time. "You're not alone here."

"I was dreaming…." He shook his head. "You have to understand, they would take me away as a kid. Experimented." Kjell's voice fractured, his throat convulsing.

Reading the sick expression, Sam scrambled to his feet and quickly found the only thing handy, a small plastic garbage can next to the nightstand. He got it in front of Kjell in time. Kjell grabbed it from him, vomiting hard. Helpless, Sam let the sickness run its course before taking the bin back and heading downstairs to dispose of it. By the time he came back from the outside bin – where he'd met up with his mother also coming armed to check on the screams and he sent her back to bed - Kjell was holed up in the bathroom. Sam poured a glass of water for him. He turned on the TV. He rummaged in the recordings he'd left for Kjell to enjoy coming up with something old, from a world that no longer existed. The new stuff was coming out in drips and drabs since so much more work needed to be done to simply keep on living that entertainment took a backseat.

Kjell staggered out of the bathroom. He stopped dead. "Your poor face!" He covered his mouth with a hand. "What did I do to your beautiful face?"

Sam touched his cheek, feeling how swollen it was. "Don't worry about it. I wasn't exactly beautiful to start with."

"Disagree."

Sam wished he wasn't blushing because the uprush of blood made the throbbing bruises hurt worse. "Thanks. I thought you might want to unwind a little, so I planned for us to sit on the couch and watch something. But thinking on it further, maybe not. Most of my stuff is action adventure with some violence."

Kjell waved him off, sitting on the couch. "It's fine on screen."

"If you're sure." Sam handed him the glass of water before sitting next to him.

"Thanks, and I am." Kjell took a drink, leaning against Sam. "I'm sorry I hit you. I'd get you something frozen to put on your face but there's nothing in the freezer."

"It'll be fine." He'd probably look like Quasimodo come morning, but he'd worry about it then.

"It's not fine."

"You're not the first person I've met with PTDS, Kjell. I'm not blaming you, and I'm not going to make you talk about it." Sam put his hand on Kjell's knee. "But if you want to talk about it, I'm willing to listen."

Kjell's jaw tightened, and he closed his eyes. "Thanks," he whispered. "Not tonight. It's too fresh. How can I live here, Sam, if everything frightens me? What if being here keeps kicking me into worse and worse dreams?"

"We're often scared of change, and you're a city boy. You're definitely not the first to come out and look at all this open land and panic a bit." Sam squeezed Kjell's knee. "But give it time. You've only been here a month give or take. Give it a season and see how you feel. If you think it's not for you, you can go back down to the city." Sam couldn't hide how sad that would make him.

Kjell frowned. "I'd miss you."

"And I'd be sorry to see you go but if it was what your health and sanity needed, I'd let you go."

He mouthed another 'thank you,' and took a long drink of water. "It seems almost strange that small places like this were the ones that preserved all of our culture, the books, movies music and the rest."

"We went more or less unnoticed while they destroyed the cities. We had time to stockpile everything." Sam smiled faintly. "In another few decades scholars will be writing books entitled how Podunk Saved Humanity."

"I believe you're right." He nodded to the tv. "You can start it, if you want. It seems like you're staying."

"I'll go if you want me to."

Kjell shook his head. "Not on your life."

"Good."

Sam turned the show on, settling in shoulder to shoulder with Kjell. This wasn't the romantic setting he'd imagined for couch cuddling but it was far more meaningful. He could almost feel Kjell soaking comfort out of him like a sponge. His presence made a difference. What more could he ask for?

∼

Kjell hadn't gone into work after all, calling in sick after a night that rough. He almost hadn't followed Sam off to the cranberry bogs once he saw how bruised Sam's face was. Sam merely pulled back his hair and tugged on a cap without a word about how he looked like a topographical map with big purple-blue lakes. Kjell had been too sick to his stomach over it to eat much more than a few bites of toast. He slipped his egg to the dogs when Sam wasn't looking.

If Sam was tired, Kjell couldn't tell. They had already picked two of the bogs. He hadn't realized that a bog could end up dry, and they could harvest by hand. Sam said they were working on building a machine from old specs that could do it more efficiently. These would be the best berries. He said there was a third bog that had been flooded, and they would be wading in to get those ones too. Those berries tended to be bruised by the process and ended up as juice down the road.

Kjell had been sidelined as too inexperienced to help, and Sam had told him that he knew Kjell was exhausted from last night. To be fair he was, and so was Sam who didn't show it with how hard the man worked. All Kjell could do was rest on the big blanket they'd brought, covering the ground. Obsidian, Berry and Makade lounged with him, supervising the goings-on. He removed his shirt, letting the sun soak into him.

He didn't know if he could work this hard. Of course, he probably didn't have to. He was a scientist, not a farmer or hunter. Kjell shut his eyes, resting back on the blanket, lazy and vaguely embarrassed by lounging like this. Sam had insisted but Kjell had been inclined to argue until Hope chimed in with her best mom voice ordering him to relax. It must have been blatant how exhausted and emotionally drained he was.

He tuned out the chatter of Hope's brood as the kids helped with the berry picking. Kjell wanted to fit in here badly. He didn't think he could go back to Madison and the harsh life inside the city. Too many memories haunted him there. Back home he saw the Derjvik around every corner. He remembered the feel of their hands on him. He remembered the lab.

Hell, Kjell was shocked he even wanted to be a scientist. He had an aptitude for it that refused to be ignored. At least the human labs felt different, probably because they weren't torturing children like the Derjvik had done to him.

Prying his eyes open, Kjell studied Sam as he worked. Could he tell Sam the whole truth? Could he detail all the pain and horrible things he had suffered growing up? Would putting it into words exorcise his demons? Would it make it worse? Could Sam look at him the same if he learned the full truth? Kjell wished he had answers for that, but it wasn't something anyone could predict. He would have to put all his trust in Sam. Was he ready to do that?

Kjell didn't know. He merely felt certain that remaining in Madison would end him, probably by his own hand. But could he stay here? This way of life was so alien Kjell didn't know where to begin. Outside of his job, he was utterly unsettled. He was used to a regimented life. Up and out of bed early, protein shake for breakfast, go to work and then home again, protein and soy supplements for lunch and dinner, then take some time to read before going to bed early. He might as well have been an android.

Sam's life flowed and ebb with the weather, with the various harvests he had to drag in, or at least it did in the autumn. Spring probably looked a lot different. Winter too. The whole idea of real food, good nourishment, was foreign to Kjell. He enjoyed that much at least. With so much open space and so few people, Kjell found the isolation eerie. That was probably the trigger for last night's PTSD episode, that and the storm. He needed to get a handle on it. He'd have to ask Sam's mother the nurse if she worked with anyone remotely trained in psychiatry or psychology.

Maybe talking to someone would help him adjust. He didn't want that burden on Sam. He could be Kjell's lover or his therapist, but he couldn't be both.

Kjell probably needed both, but he knew which he preferred for Sam. Tonight would be no better than last night for moving on to lover status. He couldn't look into that battered face and feel the least bit romantic, knowing he had done that however unintentionally. The thought of it made his stomach roil. Yes, he'd better ask about finding a therapist.

Kjell rolled onto his side, letting those chlorophyll sacs get their due. He needed this time to relax and recharge, quite literally. Sam had been right about that. He watched Sam, Hope and the kids tackling the berry laden vines.

How could Sam possibly look so happy doing back-breaking labor like that? Even Hope seemed placid and at peace. Maybe Kjell could learn to be like them. If not, maybe it didn't matter because he was here for a different sort of job, one he loved. Being able to bring cheap and renewable, not to mention clean, energy to the people as the world collectively picked itself up and dusted itself off was a true honor. Kjell was proud to play his part. However, there seemed to be something perfect about a man named Samwise being content with farming life down on the shire.

Eventually, Kjell settled on his belly so he could sun his back and promptly fell asleep. He didn't wake until something icy slithered down his back. He startled awake to find Sam running a cold bottle of water down his spine. Sam grinned at him.

"Wakey, wakey sleeping beauty."

Kjell grunted rolling up into the sitting position. "Prince Charming is supposed to wake her with a kiss."

"I would but Hope would explode into hearts and flowers and pester us the rest of the afternoon with her matchmaking."

"I would," she assured him unpacking a picnic basket.

"Did you get a nice nap?" Sam asked.

"Yeah." Kjell rubbed his eyes.

"Man, you are so *green*!" one of Hope's kids exclaimed. "That's so weird."

"Dylan! That's rude. Apologize," Hope snapped, and Dylan mumbled a halfhearted 'sorry.'

Kjell glanced at his torso. He was pretty damned verdant at this point. "I suppose it is a bit strange."

"Did one of those damn devil Derjviks do that to you?" Dylan asked, ignoring his mother's 'language' comment.

Kjell nodded. "When I was a baby. I don't remember it. I've always been sort of the color of grass." He offered the boy a wan smile.

"If they were still around, my dad would kick their butts for you." Dylan punched the air for emphasis.

"I have no doubt of that."

"Here, have a sandwich. It's chicken salad," Hope said, and when Kjell eyed it suspiciously she sighed heavily. "It's really chicken. Dammit, Samwise, quit telling people Tim eats aliens. We haven't done that in years."

Kjell didn't comment that statement obviously meant alien truly had been on the menu. He took a tentative bite, treated to something mustardy and creamy at the same time. "This is delicious."

"Thank you. I try." Hope beamed. "It only has a little bit of powdered Derjvik bone in it."

Kjell stopped chewing.

"He went even greener!" Dylan crowed.

"She's joking." Sam chuckled.

"You people are so damn strange," he replied drily. "But you make a mean chicken salad sandwich. I've never had food so good."

"I'm not sure you ever had food until now."

"No, not really." Kjell helped himself to a pear. The sweetness filled his mouth. Which of them grew it, Sam or Hope? He glanced out at the mostly picked over bog. . "Part of me thinks I should be in there helping you. The other part of me thinks thank god I'm not because it looks hard." Kjell set his sandwich down on its wrapper, keeping a hand over it as Obsidian took notice. "And that makes me wonder, do I belong here?"

"Not everyone here lives off the land, sweetie. We have medical staff, teachers, grocers, police just like anywhere else," Hope replied.

"Not to mention a huge lab filled with scientists like you. Don't minimize what you contribute, Kjell. It's equally as important." Sam nudged Kjell's shoulder. "It's bothering you, isn't it?"

"Like I said last night, I wanted to come here, but I don't know if I belong, if this is the right choice. It would be one thing if I'm wasting my own time. I don't want to be wasting yours as well. I don't want broken hearts all around if I can't cut life in the wilds." Kjell sighed. He hadn't meant to dump all that out everywhere, especially with an audience there. On the other hand, he owed Sam the truth.

Sam looped an arm around Kjell's shoulders. "Let me ask you this, why did you come here? Was it for the job or was it to escape the city?"

"Both," he replied without hesitation. "I felt trapped. The dreams were getting worse. I hoped this would be better but last night..."

"You don't get better overnight, sweetie." Hope reached over and patted his knee. "My Tim still screams in the night sometimes. So, do I because I did my own share of fighting the Derjviks."

Kjell didn't reply for a few long moments. The silence was broken by Hope's kids bickering good naturedly. Kjell paid them no mind as he gathered his thoughts. "I know but...maybe it's unrealistic how fast I think I can change. I'm not ready to throw in the towel yet. I wish I knew if I've made a good choice in coming here."

"That's the sort of thing that is rarely ever clear," she replied.

"The Ojibwe have this concept of Bimaadiziwin. It's a way of looking at life, a way of keeping in harmony and the circular aspect of life. It's a holistic way of living. Honestly my grandfather could explain it better than I. I don't have his spirituality." Sam scowled. "I should learn more of the old stories while I have the chance. So much was lost, and I'd hate to lose this too."

Kjell took a deep breath in. "Think he would tell me more about this bim...." He trailed off at the unfamiliar word.

"Bimaadiziwin, and he would be happy to. Grandfather loves talking about the manitou, the mysteries."

"I think I'd like that. I'm trying to find my way. That way might not be mine but hearing it certainly can't hurt. I suppose I could trade stories from the Eddas, sort of the tales of my people." He sighed. "I guess my struggle is, how do I know if I made a big mistake? Maybe in this situation I can't, not until it plays out. I mean, sometimes you can look at something and think 'that'll never work' or 'any idiot can see that's stupid.' But there's nothing inherently foolish or wrong about coming here. It's all on me and the chaos in my head."

"And I wish I could help with that, and I'm willing to do whatever is needed. Give it time, and yes, I have an ulterior motive for saying that." Sam grinned.

"He wants to kiss ya!" Dylan crowed, making Sam blush.

Kjell's own face heated up. "I am aware and have literally no objections."

"No adult kissing!" Melissa, Hope's daughter, cried.

"That goes for me and Tim too, just so you know." Hope chuckled. "I have no objections personally."

Kjell's blush intensified. "I'm shy about stuff like that."

"We'll save it for later to spare poor Melissa," Sam said.

"Thanks, Sam!"

"And Kjell, if you want to pitch in with the harvest you can. I didn't exclude you because I thought you'd be bad at it. I wasn't sure you felt up to it after such a rough night."

"I'd like to try. If I'm not up to it, I'll stop. Show me how and what to pick."

Sam's brown eyes brightened. "I can do that."

Kjell eyed the bog. What the hell did he agree to?

∼

Sam wiped the sweat from his brow. It was a shockingly warm autumnal equinox, a day which had been appointed Liberation Day. Around the equinox several years back they learned that the Derjvik were truly gone. The holiday was celebrated worldwide. The parties in towns like Sam's were small in comparison to the cities but he thought they were more companionable. This one was certainly downright colorful.

The fairgrounds were ripe with the scent of barbequing meat. Tables overflowed with dishes full of any number of casseroles, veggies and desserts. Kjell's eyes had bugged out when he first saw it, so used to the food replacements still so prevalent in the cities. Sam's tribe was everywhere, many of them like him, currently in their dance outfits.

The tonnage of glass beads on his outfit, black cloth with the brightly colored floral patterns favored by the Ojibwe, weighed down his shoulders. The bell anklets on his feet jangled more than his sister's jingle dress.

Under the feather headdress and tail feathers his hair and backside sweated. Sam wasn't sure if the distance Kjell kept between them was respect or if he simply smelled.

"Did you like the dance?" Sam sucked water out of the thermos Kjell had handed him after the dance was over for the evening. It had been the third session of the celebration, and his feet and legs ached.

"I've never seen a pow wow before. I am amazed at how much of your culture your people retained in spite of the occupation. It was beautiful."

Sam snorted. "We didn't lose our traditions entirely to the European invaders, and we sure as hell weren't about to let some damn aliens steal it away."

"I'm glad of that. This would be a shame to lose. But I do have one question. Aren't you hot?"

"I'm boiled," Sam chuckled.

"Well it was worth it. It was lovely to see all the dancers. Did you make your outfit?"

"Mom and Arwen did all the bead work. I did everything else."

"It's so intricate. You all did fantastic work." Kjell glanced around. "What happens now?"

"Food, drink, music." Sam grinned. "All night long but I need to get out of this stuff." He tapped his beaded chest. "I might sneak away for a shower."

Kjell scowled, a nervous expression coming over his face. "I don't think I'm ready to be here alone. I know your family is here and so are Hope and Tim but…"

"Come back to the house with me. I won't be long. Don't worry, there's plenty of food for when we get back."

"Okay."

Sam took off the feather bustle and head dress, putting them carefully in the storage container in the bed of his truck. He and Kjell climbed into the vehicle and headed back for his place. He was looking forward to showering the sweat off of him. He'd set the rest of his outfit to hang in the laundry room until he had time to hand wash it.

Once showered, he found Kjell waiting on him in the living room, stretched on the couch with a big grin on his face. "So how long will the food be there?"

"Hours, all night." Sam grinned back. "Have something in mind?"

Kjell levered himself up off the couch, sauntering over. He tugged Sam into a kiss hot enough to steam up the room. Sam's knees went a little weak.

When Kjell let him go, Sam said, "We definitely have time for that."

~

Kjell lounged at the picnic table, well fed and well loved. True to Sam's word, there had been plenty of food left after they had finally dragged back out of bed and showered. He almost wished they had stayed there. But the food and the company were worth taking a break. They could easily pick up where they left off later. He was looking forward to it, though after all he and Sam packed away at the buffet, he might not be able to move for hours.

Sam tapped Kjell's shoulder, beckoning him to follow. He'd gotten a blanket and a basket from somewhere. Kjell followed him into an open field. At the far end was a stage with some chairs on it. Sam put the blanket on the ground near the tree line.

"What's going on?" Kjell asked.

"Local school bands play tonight. It's sort of the capper of the day. It's usually pretty nice." Sam sat down patting the blanket.

Kjell sat with him and accepted a bottle from the basket. The beer was still cool. "This is not what I expected. I love how everyone comes together here. Oh, I'm sure there were squabbles I missed but I enjoyed this day. Your dancing, the food, the games the kids were playing. We had parties in the city of course, but none of them felt this...real. I think for the first time I really have hope we can shake off what the Derjvik had done to us, that this world can heal."

Sam looped an arm around Kjell pulling him closer. "I'm so happy to hear that. I know you've been uneasy about this move."

"You have made it better." Kjell swung an arm out. "All this has helped. I'm looking forward to the bands."

Sam smiled and clinked his bottle to Kjell's. "Here's to liberation."

"I'll drink to that."

The bands started taking the stage and the fairgrounds filled with the townspeople. Kjell barely noticed them, content in his little bubble of space on the blanket with Sam. The bands weren't bad, but he eventually found his attention wandering from the stage to the sky. Above the sky was cloudless, stars sparkling bright. It seemed impossible that a century of pain and heartache had come from them. Staring at them now he could only pray that nothing as dangerous as the Derjvik would ever come from them again.

"You look lost," Sam whispered, resting his head on Kjell's shoulder.

"I'm enjoying it all. You're right about how beautiful it is here." Kjell licked his lips. "I'm staying. I can live here. In this moment, I can't imagine living anywhere else."

Sam kissed him. "I can't even tell you how happy that makes me. I'm glad you're finally home."

Kjell smiled, his eyes welling up. "Home," he whispered, staring back up at the stars. "Yes, I finally am."

At that a sense of peace settled on him. Kjell couldn't imagine himself anywhere else. He was home.

About the Author: *Jana is Queen of the Geeks (her students voted her in) and her home and office are shrines to any number of comic book and manga heroes along with SF shows and movies too numerous to count. There is no coincidence the love of all things geeky has made its way into many of her stories. To this day, she's still disappointed she hasn't found a wardrobe to another realm, a superhero to take her flying among the clouds or a roguish star ship captain to run off to the stars with her.*

Website: https://www.janadenardo.com
Twitter: @JanaDenardo
Facebook: @jana.denardo

ABOUT OTHER WORLDS INK

Other Worlds Ink (OWI) is the brainchild of author J. Scott Coatsworth and his husband Mark D. Guzman. It's part publisher, part blog tour company, and part author support organization.

We publish the annual Queer Sci Fi flash fiction anthologies, many of Scott's books, and we're now branching out to other things, including this anthology.

We are dedicated to making the world better, now and in the future.

OTHER BOOKS FROM OWI

Queer Sci Fi Flash Fiction Anthologies
Impact | Migration | Innovation

J. Scott Coatsworth's Works:

Oberon Cycle:
Skythane | Lander (Nov 2020) | Ithani (Dec 2020)

Liminal Sky:
The Stark Divide | The Rising Tide | The Shoreless Sea

Other Sci Fi/Fantasy:
The Autumn Lands | Cailleadhama | The Great North | Homecoming | The Last Run | Spells & Stardust Anthology | Wonderland (rereleasing Dec 2020)

Contemporary/Magical Realism:
Between the Lines (rereleasing soon) | I Only Want to Be With You | Flames (rereleasing June 2021) | The River City Chronicles | Slow Thaw

99¢ Shorts:
A New Year (double edition) | Avalon | Chinatown | Eventide | Morgan | Gargoyle | Re-Life | Repetition | The Bear at the Bar | Tight | Translation

CPSIA information can be obtained
at www.ICGtesting.com
Printed in the USA
LVHW081906280321
682719LV00024B/531